The Chupacabra and The Bat Rastard

Drink in the adventure

Mark D Trollinger

Cover: Abir Hasan

Copyright © 2016 Pensive Opossum Productions, LLC

Fifth printing

All rights reserved.

ISBN-10: 1546721959

ISBN-13: 978-1546721956

DEDICATION

To my lovely wife Susana, her kids, and her mom for listening to me talk about the chupacabra for years. To my mother for always being a role model and showing me to always pursue your dreams. To my college and high school friends who have written books and made me wonder why not me? And to World of Beer (Tempe, AZ) and JP Watts for expanding my world...of beer. Thanks to James Clark for the WhaleSlayer™ and Charles Verner for the Old Bat Rastard.

Thank you. Without your support and patience, I would have never achieved this.

CONTENTS

	Acknowledgments	i
	Prologue	1
1	The Ranch	3
2	Giddy Up	19
3	Man in the Mirror	29
4	Ace of Base (or I saw the Sign)	35
5	Are You Ready for Some Football?	39
6	Some Assembly Required	41
7	Second Thoughts	59
8	Cuppa Joe	62
9	waelzbro	66
10	Town Hall	90
11	Interview Process	104
12	Basecamp	129
13	Nighttime Investigation	142
14	Flutters in the Basement	157
15	Tracking the Beast	179
16	Exploring the Evidence	193
17	Last Drop	213
	Beer List	218
	About the Author	221

ACKNOWLEDGMENTS

I started the idea for this story back in 2012. I was just getting into drinking craft beer and enjoyed learning more about it. Sitting in my apartment at the time I remembered that my ex-wife used to love to read mysteries. She liked Aaron Elkins and the Gideon Oliver series where he was a forensic anthropologist and his stories incorporated actual forensic science into solving the crimes. There was also Carolyn Hart and the Death on Demand series with Annie Laurance who owned the Death on Demand bookstore and the mysteries incorporated mystery books and authors into the plot. Lilian Jackson Braun and the Cat Who series that incorporated a cat as a lead character in solving the crimes. Then I thought why not apply that concept to things I like? I like craft beer and it is, after all, growing at an explosive rate across the country currently. I also like cryptozoology and the paranormal. At least on television. I liked MTV's Fear, Ghost Hunters, Chip Coffey, Destination Truth, Fact or Faked, and my current favorites Ghost Adventures, Dead Files, Mountain Monsters and Ghost Brothers.

I love to see those shows on TV, but the few instances of real life unexplained situations that have happened to me - like growing up in a house where I always heard faint music and once someone whispered my name, to an odd night at the Stanley Hotel, the time a friend and I saw a boy's face in the window of the school house at Bodega Bay only to realize years later on a television show no one lives there, an unexplained face I had appear on a photo taken during a behind the scenes tour of The Winchester Mystery House, to being downstairs at Sun Devil Liquor in Tempe, AZ and feeling a hand on my shoulder – so much so I thought it was my friend coming up from behind so I stepped aside…only to see him just coming down the stairs – the real life unexplained events have left me uneasy, unlike the countless hours of shows I watch on television. Still, all of those shows I enjoy are some of the more popular on television. Last year I wrote an idea for a television show that a TV executive was interested in, but the television channels said they had a full slate of paranormal shows already, so it didn't get off the ground.

Why not combine two areas that are both seeing expansion growth – craft beer and cryptozoology? And with that the idea for Carson Quinn was born – a cryptozoologist who enjoyed a beer, but only the traditional beer he was used to drinking. His story was similar to some of my friends who only enjoyed the beers from the big companies. My Dad loved beer and drank a lot of it, but that was before craft beer. He drank Red, White, and Blue, Weiddeman, and Hamm's mostly. My first beers were in college when I purchased some Keystone and Keystone Light off a friend on my floor. From there it was mostly Jack Daniels and Flaming Dr. Peppers, but when I drank a beer it was a Natural Light. We both liked beer, but only once did we have a drink together, like I envision a lot of father & sons doing – at my cousin's wedding, and that was a Bud Light. I was still mostly drinking Natural Light and Miller Lite until 2012, when I discovered Stone's Russian Imperial Stout. I remember thinking "$6 for a beer?!" But it was so good I returned multiple days and had one or two. A few weeks later World of Beer (WOB) in Tempe, AZ opened. I liked them on Facebook before they opened and before I even knew what it was, but the people were friendly and I enjoyed the beer. The staff there, especially JP Watts, really helped expand my beer knowledge.

Sadly, the Arizona WOBs closed, but during its time I spent countless hours there racking up loyalty points (which thanks to awful laws in Arizona do not allow customers to receive rewards like in other states) and I even managed to work on my dissertation along the way in the bank vault. Thinking of the world of beer and the world of cryptozoology I envisioned a ten book series where the crew of Carson, Tyson, Tegan, and Kareem traveled the country, explored the local monsters, and drank the local beers.

So with that, I set out to write the tale of a group of adventures who not only get to the bottom of cryptozoology mysteries, but get to the bottom of local pint glasses. I have spent several years writing research papers for my master degrees and my currently on hold Ph.D., but getting back to creative writing has been a challenging work in progress. I did try to incorporate research into my story. When I started it was present time, but by the time I finished it was more than a year later. I used a calendar and I tracked the date in the story so that it would properly flow with the storyline and real life events. I used Google maps to zoom into the exact locations so I could see what was actually around the area. I used Yelp to access businesses and pull up their menu so it would match what a person could really order there. When I named a bar or brewery I used Untappd and slowly scrolled back through sometimes hundreds of user activity to see what was actually on tap that exact day the story was taking place. The same occurred with local events such as baseball games, basketball games, and concerts. I tried to make it as realistic as possible, yet ultimately it was a story based in fantasy. Near the end I found myself challenged with how far to drift from reality into fantasy, and yet still make the story enjoyable. As I write more, including future adventures with these main characters, my hope is to improve my creative writing and tell even more interesting stories. I hope you come along with me for the journey.

So here we begin a tale weaving together some of the things I like – urban legends, craft beer, and a sprinkling of pop culture. Hopefully it comes out okay.

A special thank you to Abir Hasan who designed the book's cover. I appreciate your work!

PROLOGUE

Monday, June 8, 2015

The night air was thick with humidity in the small southeastern San Antonio community of Elmendorf. Just after 3 a.m the last quarter moon rested high overhead, providing a peaceful illumination over the farms below while chickens roosted in their coops and cows laid across the hilly landscape in a calm state of sleep. A lone grazing goat wandered about in the stilly night, making its way toward a small pond while walking between the slumbering cattle.

A snap of a branch in the distant brush and bramble near the edge of the farm broke the silence of the night. The goat instantly halted grazing and raised its head toward the woods in the distance. The goat continued to pause with ears raised. It looked around attentively sniffing the early morning air. Uncertain what lurked nearby it changed direction and bounded off through the lower pasture and to the safety of the old wooden barn.

From the shadows of the woods a dark figure emerged. It lowered itself into a crouch and crept slowly forward. Even though the moon provided a soft illumination the figure moved stealthfully in shadow toward the unsuspecting animals. The only visible feature was a pair of red eyes that appeared to glow in the darkness of night. An unfamiliar scent in the night wind caused some of the light sleeping cattle to stir; their senses alerted to the strange invader. An old bull stood an faced the woods with a lowered head and arched back. He let out a series of snorts while he vigorously pawed the ground with his front feet. The bull's alerts fully awakened the rest of the herd. The combined sounds of moos and bellows filled the air as the animals stirred hurriedly in a chaotic yet cohesive group.

The mysterious creature remained unseen, but the cattle knew something dangerous was near. The increased fear motivated the cattle to move, but in the commotion, some of the younger calves fell behind as the lead steer began to lead the herd quickly toward the barn. The small gap was all the stalking creature needed to charge the lagging animals.

Once within range of a young calf, the dark creature used its paw to slap the rear of the animal at its legs to knock it off balance before it dragged it down to the dusty ground. A high-pitched bawl alerted the mother and others that the calf was separated and in distress, but the herd continued to move. Claws dug into the calf's hide and moonlight shone on sharp teeth from drooling, rabid jaws. A powerful bite to the neck quickly killed the animal and ended its cries for help.

1 THE RANCH

Wednesday, June 10, 2015

A storm neared. Despite the best effort from the comfortable King-sized foam mattress purchased just three months ago from Billy Bob's Beds, Fred Dalton laid awake plagued by uhtceare. Two days ago a young calf from his neighbor's herd was found dead and the culprit remained unknown. Although Fred hoped it would be an isolated issue, he empathized. Rising feed and machinery costs made life on the farm more difficult, and a loss of livestock would severely affect an already strained paycheck. A strain that Fred knew all too well. A similar loss on his ranch would put his family in a tough financial position. The recent attack was not far from his ranch and since then Fred's herd appeared to be on high alert. The impending storm would inevitably push them over the edge.

Fred was still tired from the night before. A sleepless night worrying about his herd and the unpaid bills only added to his exhaustion. He briefly fantasized about catching a few more minutes of sleep, but it was 3:25 a.m. and he knew it was time to get up. He also knew he had to check on the herd and start the morning chores despite the rain. Maybe he could steal just a few minutes? Five short minutes later the alarm clock came to life and fittingly Clint Black began to sing *Killin' Time*. Fred blindly slapped the alarm clock's snooze button and silently begged for a few minutes more.

Too soon the clock sounded again as Garth Brooks' *Unanswered Prayers* ended and San Antonio's 92.5 K-BUC transitioned to George Strait's *Amarillo by Morning*. "Fine!" Fred sighed as he turned the clock off and slowly sat upright on the edge of the bed. He lowered his head, ran his fingers slowly through his short, brown hair, and tried to grasp the idea of another day. He paused for a moment, then wearily reached for the well-worn jeans on the floor beside the bed. Getting up in the morning had become an increasingly slower, more difficult process than he expected at his age. Naturally working on the ranch was hard work, but he often wondered if all thirty-four-year-olds felt like this each morning. He looked over at his wife Jess who lay motionless, still sound asleep. "Must be nice," he quietly uttered.

His face responded with a slight wince as Fred lifted his aching legs and purposefully placed his right leg into the jeans and slowly stood. After stepping into the left pant leg he arched his back and gave a slight stretch before he slipped each foot into his worn brown Cattleman's boots. He maneuvered into the dark room through piles of "clean" clothes on the bedroom floor, made his way to the bathroom for a quick stop, then into the small walk-in closet. He pulled a long sleeve plaid shirt from a hanger and grabbed his brown leather cowboy hat from atop the shelf. He put on the hat first, then slowly put his aching arms into the shirt and slowly buttoned it as he shuffled toward the dark kitchen.

Fred always started the morning with a cup of black coffee before heading out to tend to the herd and start the day's chores. Despite many technological advances, Fred continued to use his trusty percolator. It had been his father's and he had strong memories of his dad brewing coffee before the two of them went out for the day. The sound of coffee made as it splashed against the clear top reminded him of the sound of waves crashing on the beach, and the coffee coming from the percolator still made the best coffee Fred had ever tasted. His current brew was a blend of Trader Joe's Ultra Dark French Roast and Trader Joe's Ultra Dark Sumatra. The combination provided enough of a kickstart to slowly awaken him from his sleepy-state. The coffee's aroma always made him forget how painful it was to be awake; at least temporarily.

The recent events were particularly troublesome, not just because a neighbor lost a valuable calf, but Fred realized the financial hardship it would cause the family. He thought of himself in a similar position and knew it would be difficult. Additionally, the herd felt the tension. San Antonio typically did not experience much annual rain, except during the rainy months of May and June. Normally the storm would be a welcomed sight. This storm was blowing hard – a real gully washer. The rainfall would help the drought-stricken area, particularly the hayfield Fred grew for the cattle to supplement the time when the pasture grass was scarce. But this time it was different because of the attack. During the monsoon seasons the rains in Texas blow up fast with sheets of hard rain, strong winds, and lightning. The cattle already had their ears back and had a heightened awareness of their surroundings.

Fred finished his coffee and sat the empty blue tin cup in the sink. As he made his way to the dimly lit entry room he heard the sound as the wooden screen door banged against the doorframe; a signal the increased wind outside. Through the front window Fred saw the driving rain and the front yard trees as they swayed in the breeze. Fred removed his Carhartt overcoat from the coatrack and took his grandfather's old Winchester from beside the doorway before he headed into the elements to check on the cattle.

Fred walked through the newly-formed puddles gathering in the dirt driveway, his size twelve boots leaving new indentations as he briskly walked to the old wooden tractor barn. He removed the blue tarp covering the Kioti 4x4 UTV and loaded two plastic buckets filled with corn kernels in the back. He was only five-nine and average build, but he was country strong. The rain battered down on the barn's tin roof while Fred gathered tools he needed to use to repair any damage to the fence around the ranch.

   The dirt driveway stretched from the house, between the tractor barn and hay barn, down a small hill, and across a cattle guard. It wound into a half-mile lane that ran through the center of the sixty-two-acre ranch. The pasture rotation fenced all of the cows and chickens into the back twenty acres. The path rose over a slight hill which cut off the view of the heard until Fred reached the hill's crest.

   As Fred reached the top of the hill, the cattle came into view. Some were up at the bale feeder, some at the feed bunk, and others busily grazed in the pasture even as the rain fell. Others stood under small sheds and others still held under a grove of trees on the east end of the field. As he passed the mobile chicken houses some hens ran to greet the 4x4 thinking more food was coming.

   Fred stepped off the utility vehicle and grabbed one of the buckets filled with recently ground corn. As he walked through the gathering crowd of hungry chickens he plunged his hand into the bucket and broadcast the grain across the wet ground. The chickens hurriedly pecked the strewn kernels. Even though a small group of chickens came out to greet Fred, the majority stayed back. Fred knew chickens to be good watch dogs – intelligent and aware of their surroundings. The demeanor and noises coming from the flock indicated there was a problem or recently something unwanted in the area. The longer Fred stayed, the more a few individual hens nervously approached. Fred generously blanketed the immediate area with corn and walked through the rows of mobile chicken houses liberally broadcasting food for its residents.

   Fred returned to the 4x4 and continued down the dirt road. Just past the mobile chicken houses the first of the herd appeared. The rain lightened slightly as Fred drove closer. The rain and colder weather found several cattle lying down on the muddy earth. Others looked at the incoming Kioti but offered little interest in inspecting the vehicle.

The next group of cattle Fred encountered stood with their tails tucked slightly between their legs, an indication of either being cold or scared. Further back in the pasture near a large pond and bank of trees Fred noticed the herd with tails raised, showing they were alert and exploring possible threats.

Fred dismounted the vehicle and walked toward the alarmed cattle. A young bull dashed to the top point of the dirt bank around the pond. He lowered his head, shook it from side to side, and arched his back as Fred approached. Fred stood his ground and kept his eye on the bull. He knew never to turn his back on an aggressive animal.

Closer cattle reacted to the approaching human by observing his movements and then turning away to escape. Turning away indicated Fred entered the flight zone; the space around a cow where she felt safe and represented how close a person could get before the animal ran away. As Fred continued to walk toward the pond, the cattle galloped away once he got within two meters. The bull no longer showed aggression but maintained a watchful eye on the intruding man.

Nearing the bank of the pond Fred stopped. He felt his heart sink as he saw the motionless lumps of not one, but two bodies. Both were in the mud along the dirt bank with their head partially in the water. The dead cows were both Charolais yearlings not yet ready for market, but the future financial loss would still be challenging to overcome.

Fred hurriedly returned to his vehicle and retrieved his cell phone from the glove compartment. He called the Bexar County sheriff's department to report the incident and request an officer investigate. The dispatcher took down the information and said the sheriff would drive out to the ranch to take a look. But Fred knew without an incident in progress there would be little the sheriff could do except file a report.

Half-past nine the sheriff arrived and was greeted by Fred. Sheriff Barnes was a plump man in his mid-fifties with straight gray hair and a scruffy mustache. His uniform shirt tucked snuggly into his pants as his belly hung over the hidden belt. He slowly walked with Fred as both men scanned the pasture's landscape. Fred told Sheriff Barnes all the cattle were fed between noon and 1 p.m. the previous day and they heard nothing unusual that evening. The animals appeared to be fine when he and Jess headed to bed around nine-thirty. Fred desperately wanted to know who, or what killed his and his neighbor's cattle. A killer at large could be devastating for the economy of the local community.

As Sheriff Barnes explored the scene of the incident, he paused and scratched his head. One of the most puzzling things about the remains was the lack of blood. Both bodies were drained entirely, and there were no visible signs of scattered body parts – just three small puncture wounds in the neck. In fifteen years as a farmer, Fred had never seen anything like this before, and the sheriff in all of his years of experience was equally unfamiliar.

The first suspect in Fred and Sheriff Barnes' minds was a large canine; a carnivore, probably a coyote or wolf. That would not be uncommon on a large ranch, but predators don't usually leave a carcass intact or drink nearly eleven gallons of blood. There were also mountain lions, but they stayed in the montane regions and were rarely seen on the ranches.

Another known eater of cattle in North America was the grizzly bear, although nearly all of them lived in Montana and Wyoming. Reports had recently surfaced indicating an increased number of black bears in Texas, but their diet mainly consisted of plants, fruits, nuts, insects, and small mammals – nothing the size of even a yearling calf. There were rumors of a black panther spotted in the Hill County a couple of years ago, but that creature was never caught or identified, although it was thought by many to be a jaguarondi.

With a shake his head, the sheriff turned toward Fred with a puzzled look, "I don't know, Boss…aliens?" The two exchanged a welcomed chuckle as they continued to search the ground for clues. Footprints formed in the soggy ground as the two traipsed around, but any prints from the night before were likely washed away with the heavy rain. After another twenty minutes, Sheriff Barnes concluded they found just about everything there was to find – which was nothing.

"Best thing you can do, Son, is to buy a couple of them trail cameras," suggested the sheriff. "I've seen them used on those Bigfoot shows on Animal Planet. You might just get lucky enough to catch something on film – hopefully before he does any more damage to your herd! Sorry I couldn't be of more help, but I will file this report and we'll go from there."

Sheriff Barnes gave Fred's hand a hardy handshake, wished him well, and returned to the dry interior of his white Ford Explorer. Fred turned and gave another long distance scan over the pasture before slowly returning to the 4x4. As he drove back up the road to the barn, the cattle casually returned to eating grass as they were before the rancher interrupted.

Hours later it was afternoon, but Fred didn't feel like working. He entered the mudroom of the house, removed his soggy boots, overcoat, and hat before joining Jess at the kitchen table. She saw his tired, worried look and asked what was wrong. When he explained, she shared his fears regarding not only the immediate impact on their financial situation, but potential long-term implications if the killer could not be caught. What would happen then?

Knowing her husband hadn't eaten all day she offered him a B.L.T., but he declined, instead satisfied to occasionally steal a Lay's lightly salted potato chip from her plate. As he sat quietly pondering his next move, he remembered the sheriff's suggestion and walked over to the sideboard to get the laptop. He returned to the table and searched online websites for reviews on the best trail cameras. He initially narrowed his choices down to Moultrie, Bushnell, and Browning, but then chuckled when he saw the Primos Truth was highly rated and cheaper priced. He told Jess the truth is what he wanted to find, so it sounded like that's the one he should purchase. He could order it on Amazon but didn't want to wait the 5-10 business days for it to arrive. "When are they going to start using those drones to ship products in a couple of hours?" he asked rhetorically. Instead, he decided to visit All Seasons Feeders later that afternoon. He called his friend and fellow local rancher Eric Vega to see if he wanted to run into town with him. He figured they could pick up some cameras and talk about the events over a couple of beers. Fred agreed to pick up Eric around 5:00 p.m.

Eric was a young rancher – a tall, lanky, Puerto Rican man in his mid-twenties who recently married and moved into the area last year. He and Fred liked to talk about ranching over a couple of beers. Respecting Fred's ranching experience, Eric looked at him as an informal mentor and was eager to learn more about the insights of the industry.

Arriving at the Vega Ranch, Fred gave a quick two-honk signal, which Eric soon acknowledged with a wave as he emerged onto the front porch. He adjusted the position of his hat as he walked to the truck. K-BUC played faintly in the background as Fred drove down Stuart Road toward Highway 87 East. After twelve miles, they arrived at All Seasons Feeders. Walking around the store Fred did not immediately see the trail cameras, but according to the website, they were in stock. He reluctantly asked a store associate and after some searching in all the wrong places, the clerk located two cameras in stock and on sale for just under $60. Fred decided to purchase both of them. He glanced over at Eric. "Ready for a beer?" Eric nodded in agreement.

Not far from All Seasons, Longbranch Saloon in Adkins was a family-owned business that was known for good food and some of the coldest beer in town. It was a nice local spot where everyone seems to know everyone else - a little country/cowboy spot with darts, pools, and a large stage area for musical acts. Sitting at a wobbly wooden table in the corner, the duo ordered a bucket of beer and a large pizza. Ten minutes later the server brought a Miller Lite bucket filled to the top with ice and five Bud Light bottles inserted up to the base of the necks. There wasn't a band that night, but the beer was cold, the pizza hot, and the karaoke bad.

Each man grabbed a bottle, twisted the cap off, and took a couple of long drinks from their bottles, nearly bringing it down to the halfway point. Eric said, "Brewed the hard way!" and they both laughed. Still, it was refreshing on a humid June evening. By the second bottle and third poorly sung karaoke-version of a Hank Williams, Jr. song, Fred suggested a game of pool. As they removed and caulked the sticks, Fred began to tell Eric about the day's events.

Being a new rancher Eric was concerned with the news. If an experienced rancher like Fred had not experienced anything like that before and was uncertain who or what the culprit was, Eric knew he couldn't possibly handle the situation if a similar event happened with his herd. Just starting out his ranch was in even worse financial position due to startup costs and not having many calves sold. A loss of one or two heads and it could signal an end to his ranch. He hated it happened to his friend, but Fred was in a position to absorb the loss a little more than a newbie like Eric. He hoped it would be a limited incident and the trail cameras would help to identify the thing behind the killing. He wanted to help in any way he could to end this situation quickly without further incidents.

Eric took the final Bud Light and signaled the server for another bucket. "So what's next?" he asked Fred as he place the triangle rack on the pool table and set up all fifteen balls within the triangle in random order.

"I don't know…hang the trail cameras and see what turns up?"

With that, Fred broke the balls and a stripe fell in the corner pocket. Eric hit three solids in a row, and a couple of turns later called the eight ball for a quick victory. Grabbing the newly delivered bucket and beers, they returned to the table to each have another slice of the now room-temperature pizza. The simplicity of a pepperoni and cheese pizza always hit the spot for Fred and ranking the past few pizzas he enjoyed, this one was near the top. As they finished the final bites of the pizza pie, a patron attempted a drunken version of Billy Currington's *I'm Pretty Good at Drinking Beer*. From the sound of it, he was an expert at drinking beer. After listening in wonder for a few seconds, it was an excellent opportunity to down the remaining beer and head for the truck. Eric offered to stop by in the morning and help Fred install the cameras and whatever else was needed. Fred agreed, dropped a five on the table for the tip, and both men exited to the parking lot.

Early the next morning, Eric pulled into Fred's ranch in his 1979 Chevy Scottsdale truck. The truck had seen it had seen better days, but it previously belonged to Eric's late uncle. Plus, the upkeep and maintenance of the old vehicle was much simpler than today's trucks with their complex computer systems. Fred heard the sound of Eric's tires against the few sparsely covered areas of gravel on the driveway and walked out to greet him. Fred had read the trail camera manual after returning home the night before and was ready to install them. He already determined the locations to set up the cameras in hopes of identifying the unknown assailant.

Walking to the tractor barn, Fred and Eric each grabbed a couple of plastic buckets to put in the back of the 4x4 and nervously made the drive to the back pasture hoping not to see a repeat of the day before. Fortunately, there were no new developments. The friends exchanged a sigh of relief and exited the vehicle.

Fred decided to place one camera on a tree close to a fence that overlooked the pond where the bodies were discovered yesterday. He wanted to save the second camera to mount on the back side of the hay barn. It was closer toward the house, but it overlooked the pasture and might give a long-range view of the ranch and woods past the edge of the property. After quickly installing both cameras, the men returned to the utility vehicle, "Not much else to do now, but wait," said Fred. He invited Eric in to watch the game and have a beer, but he declined. Fred thanked him for the help and Eric headed back to his ranch to complete work on his own ranch and look over his herd. Fred grabbed a bottle of Budweiser, the half-empty bag of chips, located a comfortable spot on the sofa, and turned on the San Antonio Silver Stars vs. Atlanta Dream basketball game.

He dragged the ottoman closer and prepared for some deep-couch sitting. His favorite player on the Silver Stars was Danielle Adams, a product from the 2011 Texas A&M National Championship team. She reminded him of Charles Barkley with her ability to run the court, block, rebound, plus she could hit the three. Another of his favorite WNBA players, Shoni Schimmel, was playing for the home team Atlanta. Fred felt she was an incredible athlete – one of the best ball-handlers in the league with an ability to make a highlight reel pass at any time in the game. She reminded Fred of Steve Nash in his prime. It amazed him that other men did not watch or attend the WNBA games as much as he did. The women played hard on every play, the games were exciting, and in person, always had an electric atmosphere. Plus, there wasn't the constant flopping that comes from the men in the NBA games. That was one aspect of the NBA that Fred absolutely hated.

After the game, Fred walked to the window and looked out toward the barns. He wondered what was out there in the woods. Not much to do now as eventide approached, but wait. Soon it would be nightfall and the unfolding mystery would be to wonder what morning would bring? Nothing he could do about it now. He returned to the living room and Jess joined her husband on the couch. She grabbed the remote and turned the television over to *Property Brothers* on HGTV. She leaned against him, put her head on his shoulder as her long dirty blonde hair draped down his back. Watching the show she began to get drowsy, but managed to comment favorably on the open-concept of the proposed remodeling design. The couple fell asleep on the couch following the third episode.

A couple of hours passed before Fred awoke. Jess was sleeping on his arm and *House Hunters International* played on the television. He thought maybe they should be like the couple in the episode and move to Puerto Peñasco to get away from this ranching life and its financial troubles. Besides, the beach looked wonderful. A couple of margaritas, a cigar, and the ocean might just be the ticket. He allowed himself the fantasy for a few seconds before he skooched forward, put his hand under Jess' head, and slowly lowered her to the couch. At only five-one she could sleep comfortably on the couch. Besides Fred's curiosity was getting the better of him and he wanted to go out to check on the cattle.

Grabbing his small flashlight, Fred snatched his hat in passing the coatrack and walked out the front door. It was 12:15 a.m. and completely dark. He recalled that the according to the movie *Midnight in the Garden of Good and Evil*, he was not only right in the middle of dead time, but the half hour after midnight was for evil. It was something evil he was looking for and he wondered if this might be approaching the time to find it.

He slowly walked from the driveway toward the barn. Two things amazed him about living well outside the city: how silent it was at night and how bright the stars were. He took a few pronounced footsteps toward the barn while he soaked up the moment and looked up at the night sky. As he got closer, he heard a noise coming from the tractor barn and quickly shined his light in the direction where it appeared to originate. His light illuminated a couple of stacked bales of hay, a small pile of hay on the barn's dirt floor due to a busted bale, a knocked over tin watering can, and 50 lb. bag of yellow corn. As he nervously walked at an increased pace toward the noise, he discovered its source was a couple of guinea hens that were in the barn. Relieved, he walked on. The rest of his walk around the two barns and dirt road proved to be quiet and uneventful. He walked up the dirt road toward the pond where the deadly incident took place a couple of days prior.

The light from the flashlight ebbed and flowed across the pasture as Fred's arms swayed while walking. As he reached the top of the small hill, he was startled to see an animal walking along the dirt wall around the pond. The creature was dark and mostly hidden in the shadows, but he could see it was hunched low with its head down and slowly walking in the manner that a cat stalks a bird. It was unlike anything Fred had ever seen before. It looked like a medium-sized dog, but it didn't appear to be a canine. It seemed to have no hair or possibly short light brown hair that made it look hairless. As the light shone upon the strange creature, its eyes glowed red in the darkness. It had a hunched back and appeared to have a concentration of bluish-gray spikey fur covering the spine. The creature stopped, raised its head to look at Fred, and Fred back at it. It stared for a moment with large pointed ears, then turned and ran back toward the woods.

Fred froze momentarily but decided, perhaps unwisely, to give chase even though being on foot there was no way he could keep up with the creature. Fred quickly realized his cardio days were well behind him and pulled up out of breath, bent over with his hands on his knees and his eyes steady on the horizon where the creature was last seen. Who would believe him? Hopefully, the trail camera picked up some shots of the animal. One thing was certain, if he had not been there at that moment be would have awoken to at least one more missing cow.

Fred walked over to the fencepost overlooking the pond where the first trail camera was mounted. He opened the unit, removed the 8 GB SD card, and walked back toward the barns to inspect the other camera. After Fred removed both SD cards he went back to the house. Too excited to sleep, he inserted the cards into the laptop and downloaded the photos.

The camera from near the barn didn't turn up much except some guineas and a distant cow that wandered into view from the barn. As Fred looked at the captured images, he realized the location was too far to pick up anything long distance in the woods. Unless the animal was close to the camera it wouldn't snap the photo.

The second camera had many more pictures, but most were of cattle. But then he found it – actually *them*. Three images of the unknown beast he encountered near the pond. The only issue was the quality of the photos. They were a little overexposed, somewhat blurry, and lacked sharpness on the animal. Still, it was captured on film. Fred was excited to show Eric his proof and hopefully solve the mystery of what type of animal was stalking his herd.

Early Thursday morning Fred and Eric met for breakfast at Baldy's Classic American Diner. Fred ordered the "Big Nasty", a fried chicken breast stuffed between a home-baked biscuit and topped with sausage gravy served in a skillet with fried potato hash browns with onions and green peppers, and all on top of two eggs over-easy. Eric went with an enchilada omelet topped with sour cream and avocado. He ordered a side of bacon and toast, and both men ordered coffee.

"I saw it last night, Eric! I saw the creature killing the area cattle!"

"Really? What was it?" asked Eric.

"I don't know – I have never seen anything like it in my life. But I did get these from the trail camera," he said as he removed the photos from inside his jacket.

Eric stared at the somewhat blurry, somewhat dark photos of the animal. "Maybe a coyote?" he said with uncertainty.

"No, definitely not a coyote," responded Fred. "This animal was appeared hairless with a hunched back and some patches of fur along the spine!"

Eric studied the photos but wasn't able to determine what he was seeing. "What the hell is it? A wolf? A mountain lion? I can't tell if it is canine or something else!"

"I don't know. I have never seen a wild dog attack and completely drain a cow like that," revealed Fred.

"Yeah, me neither...and I don't know that the sheriff will be much help either." Eric paused and continued to look at the photo. "You know...I heard about a guy a few years ago, but I haven't heard anything from him since." Eric took a bite of his omelet and a swig of lukewarm coffee. "This guy was up in Austin, I believe. He was said to be an expert in cryptozoology." Fred looked puzzled at his friend.

"What the hell is cryptozoology?"

"You know, hidden animals....bigfoot and shit." Fred looked at his friend skeptically.

"C'mon, Eric, those things don't exist. If there was a Bigfoot don't you think we would have discovered one by now? At least a body or a pile of shit or something"

"Well, I don't know buddy...but you and I have never seen

anything like the animal in those photos, but there he is."

Fred looked at his friend with an awkward pause, but he couldn't deny Eric's words. He had never seen an animal like that until the night before, and see it he did – and not just in some blurry photos – he came face-to-face with it. "You're right – I may have to look for alternative experts to help track this monster. Do you know who this guy is?" Eric picked up his cellphone and started looking through the contacts.

"It's Carter I think. I met him once at a dive bar before a Texas Longhorns football game. He was working at a middle school, I think as a teacher, but somehow we started talking about mythical creatures." As Eric continued to scroll through his phone, he stopped. "Carson – that's it. Carson Quinn. I have his number here if you want it." He asked the server for a pen and scribbled the number on a napkin.

Fred looked down with a stare of uncertainty at the number, then up at Eric. "Yeah, I guess…What the hell can it hurt? I'll give him a call and see if we can get him down here."

2 GIDDY UP

Friday, June 12, 2015

A lush field of bluebonnets overlooked a crowded cracked and weathered blacktop driveway of a South Austin classic, Giddy Ups Saloon; a piece of old Austin that's still in business – a little divey and a lot of honky tonk. It had a small stage inside with live music every night, darts, shuffleboard, a small dance floor, a great patio in the back, and was often busy. Since the remodeling and re-grand opening last November, which also brought a new liquor license that allowed for a full bar, the saloon had been packed nearly every night.

Past the jukebox blaring eighties and nineties country music, the pool tables with worn green felt covering, glowing neon beer signs, and dense clouds of cigarette smoke sat a wooden corner table. At that table sat a gloomy, lonely man with a slightly scruffy beard and tired brown eyes that made him look older than his actual mid-forties age. The man had been in that same spot since early afternoon, which was not an uncommon occurrence. He was one of the many regulars who frequented the saloon and usually greeted strangers with what some described as the "small town gaze". The past couple of years had been difficult times for the man, a once upbeat and optimistic man, now quiet and dejected. As he finished the end of his Lone Star beer, he pushed the empty bottle into the center of the table with four others and motioned to the server for another. Lone Star, an American adjunct lager, was a staple of Texas and a prominent feature in one of the man's favorite movies, *Urban Cowboy*. He felt like a cowboy when he drank it, even though he did find it somewhat odd considering Pabst Brewing Company owned it and the label showed "brewed in Los Angeles."

The man pulled the brim of his dark brown straw cowboy hat down and wondered how much time had to pass before he could no longer consider himself "between jobs". It was March 2011 when the Round Rock Independent School District principals met with employees to talk about job cuts after a $60 million budget shortfall. The announcement affected two hundred eighty employees, two hundred thirty-four of them probationary classroom teachers like Carson Quinn. The most substantial cuts to campuses was the elimination of more than fifty positions at district middle schools. Carson was part of that demographic as well. In the months following the cuts, the district was able to find new placements for about a hundred other employees whose jobs had been eliminated. All displaced teachers had to reapply and interview for the new opportunities, but Carson was not one of the fortunate ones.

Occasionally Carson did talk to the bartenders and at times even some of the other patrons, though he found most of them to be ultracrepidarians. Still, sometimes it was nice to have someone to talk to even if they didn't really know what they were talking about. Tonight he didn't talk. He sat slightly hunched over at the table, lost in between memory and pensively pondering the future while he drank his Lone Star, and listened to the sounds of the Sam Bentley Band on the stage.

The band's drums, two guitars, and the lonesome cry of the steel guitar provided the perfect slow downbeat honky tonk music of heartbreak. As the band played *Excuse Me (I Think I've Got a Heartache)*, Carson realized he was feeling the same emotion, but it wasn't due to a woman, but the turn of life events he experienced over the past few years. After the teaching job he tried his hand at a couple of entry-level jobs in customer service and retail in an attempt to keep up with the mountain of student loan payments and regular monthly bills, but none of those jobs interested him enough to display the type of work ethic managers were interested in retaining. Other than teaching the only other "job" he ever enjoyed was more of a hobby and one that others often considered unusual and even a bit weird: cryptozoologist.

He liked enjoyed being outdoors and he loved animals, but most of his time in the woods wasn't spent hunting deer or looking for wild turkeys, but the more legendary creatures. Animals that many called urban legends and ignored by modern scientists, but Carson felt - no he *knew* existed. He had been a middle school science at Walsh Middle School and he considered his hobby to be science as well, even if it could at best be considered fringe science. To him, he used the same scientific methodologies in the field that he did in the classroom – being objective, being open-minded, using comparative analysis, and collecting data. And there was a lot of data and evidence to support the existence of these "mythical" creatures. He used to enjoy his time searching for and attempting to prove these animals existed, even if when talking about them others tended to view him like the crazy-haired guy from *Ancient Aliens*.

As Sam Bently sang a cover of *Amarillo by Morning*, Carson drifted away into nostalgia not only of his days as a "monster hunter", but to growing up and hearing that song on the radio in 1986 while riding through Knoxville on vacation with his grandparents. Young and the whole world before him then, how did he get to where he was today? More importantly, could he get back? He deeply sighed as he sunk his head down and stared distantly at the can in front of him.

In his daydream-state he was momentarily oblivious to the other people in the bar. As if the universe reached out to intervene, a man walked past, stopped, and returned to stand in front of the table. He paused, squinting his brown eyes to look at the more than slightly inebriated man in the brown straw hat.

"Carson?" inquired an African-American athletic man in his early forties. Carson slowly raised his head and tried to make out the figure in front of him, slightly wincing as the lights from the bar shone behind the man's head, concealing his identity.

"Carson Quinn, is that you? If it is, you look like shit" replied the man. Carson recognized the voice. A ghost from his past, Tyson Carr worked in the IT Department and taught an occasional computer science class at the University of Texas. They were roommates long ago in college and remained in contact for a few years afterward, but then time got away and they hadn't spoken in probably five years. Carson and Tyson were good friends back then and used to go out together to search for those legendary animals that Carson was just reminiscing. With Carson's science background and Tyson's technological background, they were an impressive team.

Carson reluctantly invited his old friend to sit with him. Tyson turned and looked over his shoulder.

"I can sit for a few – I am here with some coworkers for happy hour. This isn't normally my place – they don't serve much of the type of beer I usually drink." He looked at the island of bottles in front of Carson. "I see you are still drinking that swill," Tyson badgered.

Carson scooted over and allowed his friend to sit down. "It's been a few years, Ty – how the hell have you been? And what the hell are you drinking?" Carson asked with a slow and slightly slurred diction as he looked at the unfamiliar label on the bottle in his friend's hand.

Tyson laughed, "It's a brewery called Austin Beerworks from right here in Austin. I like to support the local guys when I can. They are small, independent companies providing jobs and supporting the local community. I also like the variety. Those Lone Stars you are drinking are the same every time and it is mass produced for a wide audience. Craft beer is brewed in smaller batches usually using traditional brewing ingredients. But what's cool is the brewer can also try innovative brewing methods or different ingredients to alter the recipe. With each batch you see the creativity and passion of its maker and the complexity of its ingredients." He sat his empty bottle on the table and raised his glass. "This one is called Peacemaker and it's a light session pale ale."

Carson looked at his friend with a puzzled expression. "What is a *session beer*, or a *pale ale* for that matter?" he asked, his head swimming with unfamiliar words. Tyson defined a session beer as having a relatively low alcohol content, usually under five percent alcohol by volume to allow a beer drinker to have multiple beers, within a reasonable time or session, without reaching inappropriate levels of intoxication.

"That Lone Star's just over four and a half percent, so *technically* you're drinking one now." He added, "One difference between a pale ale and the lager you are drinking is ale is brewed with top-fermenting yeast, while lagers use bottom-fermenting yeast."

"If I had to choose, I think I would rather be the top," Carson said inappropriately. Ty stared at his friend as if he were still a teenager.

"Yeah...well another difference is the temperature at which fermentation is conducted. You're a scientist. You know about the importance of temperature because chemical reactions happen more slowly at lower temperatures." Carson sat up a little taller in his seat. The science behind Ty's answer piqued Carson's interest, but he still quietly looked befuddled.

"Tell you what, I see you're empty. I'm gonna buy you a beer."

"Uh...I don't know. I'm not much on trying new things," hesitated Carson. Ty motioned for the server to come over to the table. Dot Ross was working Carson's section, which was also a regular occurrence. Dot, a short, young college girl with jet-black hair and a tattoo sleeve on both arms was Carson's favorite. Maybe it was the tight sleeveless tank top, the short denim cutoff jean shorts, or the thick Appalachian accent from her native West Virginia. He thought it was probably a little of all of those things, plus the fact he thought she looked like a SuicideGirls model, but whatever it was, she was his favorite and he always made an effort to sit in her section.

She hurriedly arrived at the table, glancing around to see if anyone else was in immediate need of a drink.

"Hey, boys," she said with a flirtatious smile.

"Hey, can you bring my friend a Guns & Oil Maverick Lager?" asked Ty. "This one's on me," he said to Dot. He turned back toward Carson, "This beer is going to be comparable to what you are drinking now, and similar in alcohol content at four point six percent." Dot opened the bottle and poured it in a pint glass before handing it to Carson.

He stared at the glass uncertain about this unknown beer but decided beer was beer - especially after the number he already consumed. How bad could it be? He cautiously took a sip.

"Tastes the same, except maybe a little lighter." Carson said. "And..," he said as he looked over the menu on his table, scanning the beer section, "it looks to be a couple of dollars more than the Lone Star...I think I will stick with the Lone Star...And what's with the fancy glass?" questioned Carson.

"The glass alters the aroma, appearance, and even the taste of the beer," reassured Tyson. "If you want some more science, scientific studies show that the shape of glassware will impact head development and retention – and that directly impacts the volatile compounds that evaporate from beer to create its aroma. Things like hop oils, all kinds of yeast fermentation byproducts like alcohol, fusels and fruity esters, spices or other additions." He paused while Carson drank more of the Maverick.

"I mean, it's fine, but it's more expensive and tastes the same as what I already got," said Carson. Ty looked at his closed-minded friend sardonically.

"Here, let's try something a little different. Move your scale a bit," he suggested. When Dot returned to check on the table Tyson ordered a Pearl Snap, another beer from Austin Beerworks. When it arrived Dot brought a different glass – this one tall and thinner.

As she poured the beer Ty spoke as he could sense the confusion in his friend's face even without looking at him. "That's a pilsner glass. The tall, slender shape helps to showcase color, clarity, and carbonation. It also promotes head retention and enhances the volatiles I mentioned earlier. What you had before was a lager – an American adjunct lager specifically. A pilsner is also a lager, but specific to the Pilsener region of Germany."

"There are two main types of beer," Ty explained, "ales and lagers. Lagers come from all over and have various colors and flavors. Pilsner beer is simply a lager from that area of Germany. You'll notice this one is also light, but you will get a bright hop character. It's about five percent, clear straw color, and has a head that dissipates quickly. You should smell just a little maltiness and some grassy, slightly citrus hops scents. That's a classic pilsner, and the refreshing taste makes it a great drink for our hot summer days. I think that's one of the better beers produced in Austin."

Carson cautiously took a sip but this time Ty could instantly see a light in his friend's eyes as if a door somewhere deep in his mind slowly began to disengage from its locked casing. Carson seemed surprised at saying it was good. "It has a pleasant bitterness that I kinda dig," he said.

"That's the hops," added Ty. "It's a good gateway beer into other craft brews and a good lawnmower beer after being out in the hot sun."

Ty looked at his watch and stood up. "Well hey, I better get back to my coworkers," he said as he jerked a thumb toward the area behind him where his other friends were sitting. "It was great running into you. We should get together again and kick back."

Carson agreed and said with sincerity and a little more clarity, "I enjoyed seeing you again, and I appreciate the lesson. It's been a rough few years - I need to get back into the world again... Hey, maybe you could introduce me to some more of your fancy beers sometime?" Carson said openly.

"For sure – I'd enjoy that! Catch ya on the back side, Brother," Ty said with a firm handshake. The two men exchanged numbers and Ty disappeared into the crowd of people.

Dot returned to check on Carson and collect the various empty bottles and glasses from the table. "Who's yer frien'? Typically yer alone," she inquired.

"Yeah - that's my old college roommate and we just happened to bump into each other tonight after several years. Crazy! It was fun – brought back a lot of memories."

"Y'unt some wings? Maybe 'nother beer?" asked Dot. Carson paused and looked around the room assessing the situation. The band was on an intermission break, but he figured he would stick around a little longer.

"Yeah, let me get a dozen hot wings," he ordered. "And, uh…what other local beers do you have, Dot?" She gave a dimpled smile and returned with another Austin beer, Austin Amber from Independence Brewing Company.

He looked at the glass. This beer was a darker beer, causing him to give the glass another suspicious glare. At least the ones Ty had him try were similar to what he was familiar with, but this?

Dot encouraged, "'t'aint gonna bite! – ya fixin' ta juss look at it or ya gonna drink it!"

"I don't know about dark beers, Dot. I've never had one before."

Dot chuckled as she replied, "I figured, but that I'den dark beer. It's amber – they's much darker beers." Carson stared at the glass and noted the color and the thin white head. Dot suggested he smell it first saying that the sense of smell creates anticipation of taste.

"Normally you just drink beer," he said. "I don't ever stop and smell the Lone Star, but whatever. I guess I'm learning somethin' new."

He slowly raised the glass and inhaled cautiously. His eyes contracted slightly, he looked puzzled but intrigued. It smelled slightly of yeast, or was that bread? Maybe biscuits? He also thought it smelled kind of malty, butterscotch, or caramel – maybe even creamed corn? "Hmm, that's interesting." He pulled back and looked at the glass curiously and again focused on the color and appearance.

He noticed the modest level of carbonation.

He looked at Dot, raised the glass in a toast. "Welp, bottoms up I guess." He took a slow sip and was impressed that the taste followed what he smelled – malt up front then hints of sweet crackers, and then just a little bitter finish. He remembered Ty saying those were hops. He imagined hazelnuts, maybe leather, and it was a bit sweet, like brown sugar. The whole sensory appeal of using his nose and eyes before tasting it allowed him to enjoy the drink on a different level than he had experienced before. He could see what Ty was talking about when he mentioned not only the appeal of the beer and the volatiles but also the creativity of the brewer. From working in the science classes he knew that even slight adjustments to the recipe created drastically different results, and that was interesting to him. Another smile crossed his face as Dot placed the order of wings in front of him and the smell of the seasoning hit him.

"How did you learn all those things about beer? I mean, I know you work in a bar, but Ty said it's not the type of beer y'all typically sell," inquired Carson. He began to guttle the wings, distracting Dot a little as she told him about a group of friends who also worked in various bars around town. They usually got together on their days off and drank beer. With the increased number of breweries, not only around Texas but also just in Austin, the friends liked to try new beers and support the local beer culture scene.

"There is a beer culture scene?" interrupted Carson.

"Yessir!" she exclaimed. "An if aye had my druthers, I'd stick ta craft. Tastes better ona count'a tha brewers focusin' on tha quality ratheran focusin' on marketin' an' stock prices. Plus they's more alcohol in 'em. Two er three beers packs a wallop like five or six a'yurs, that and ya ain't fixin' ta go ta tha bathroom alla tha time. Ya don't bull moose or shotgun 'em – ya slowly drink 'em and enjoy the 'sperience. Some say craft beer's got more health benefits an' more nutrients than red wine."

"Yeah, but those beers are more expensive than the beer I'm used to," replied Carson.

"Ya had what, six Lone Stars? That's $4 each - $24 fer a six pack and it ain't got no flavor. Same beers'll prolly be two'er three good craft beers - and even if they's five'er six dollars, comes out cheaper. Folks'll sell growlers for five bucks on some days."

"What the hell is a growler?" asked Carson.

"It's a vessel for carryin' beer. Some'a tha breweries dudden have bottles or cans – only beer on tap, and ya caint take it home 'less ya got a growler. Ya can sometimes geta 64oz fer that $5, and that's more than five beers fer five bucks. Even yer Lone Star cain't beat that!"

Carson finished the final wing and licked his fingers clean before reaching for the napkin. "Well, between you and Ty, I am interested in learning more. I guess I'll have to expand my horizons and get out there more. Maybe that will help snap me out of my funk?"

Dot smiled, "Might could! Ya can meet nice folks drinkin' craft beer or go out fer some beer with friends 'n family 'n make it a point that everyone hasta try a new beer. Get everyone talkin' about tha beer. Smell, taste, whatcha like, and that sorta stuff. Plus ya can meet tha brewers. They's festivals and stuff where ya can try samples 'n learn more. It will get ya outta the house fer sure!"

With that, Carson stood up, dropped cash down on the table to cover the bill and tip. He hugged Dot and thanked her spending some time explaining the Austin beer scene. As the band played the final number of the night, Carson waited outside for his Uber to show up and take him home for the evening – for the first time in a long time, he had an enjoyable evening.

3 MAN IN THE MIRROR

Friday, June 12, 2015

The Uber ride home was quiet. The driver attempted to talk, but Carson was too not interested in conversing. He was tired from the drinking, the eating bar food, and all of that talk from Ty about different kinds of beers. It was kind of nice to see a familiar face for a while, but it was good that he was gone now. Carson didn't like people seeing him like this, especially people that knew him before. He remembered earlier in the evening when Ty approached he wasn't even confident it was his old friend, and he commented if it was he looked like shit. Ty wasn't wrong. Carson not only looked like but also felt like shit.

How many days in a row had he been to Giddy Up's now? He couldn't recall. Probably enough to make a person wonder how a man without a regular job could afford to drink beer and eat wings so frequently. It was quite easy, if you skipped a few payments on the credit card, paid the electric bill a few days late, and always fought with the cell phone company to turn the service back on. Then the money that was supposed to go to paying those bills could be used to forget those problems as well as others that maybe had not yet presented themselves.

He was home now. He didn't have to worry about being on the roads, and it was late. Might as well pour a little bourbon nightcap and see what was on the television. It wasn't like he had to be anywhere in the morning. His hands were a slightly shaking as he picked up the glass and stumbled into the living room. He was aware of his poor motor skills as he made his way through the cluttered living room and plopped in the overstuffed recliner. The room was dark, which is how he liked it and usually kept it. The only light was coming from the kitchen, which he didn't turn off when he left the room. "Hmm, maybe a zombie movie?" he thought as he thought about his limited ability to walk at this time. He scrolled through the channels. Nothing good. He wondered how is it we have all of these channels today and still nothing on television. At least it wasn't like when he was a kid of the television channels signed off. He could watch infomercials or a shopping network if he got desperate enough.

His mind drifted to earlier in the night and he wondered why did he have to run into Ty? The conversation was kinda interesting, but life was comfortable now. A bit shitty, but comfortable. He had his routine, as depressing as it was, and here comes Tyson Carr like a blast from the past attempting to ruin it and make things uncertain again. He took a sip from the glass and thought about their past experiences. Undoubtedly there was something about Ty he didn't like, right? They probably had some fight back in college, or maybe it was after college when they stopped talking? Why did they stop talking? He couldn't remember. Perhaps another sip would bring it back. Jog his memory about the events of the past. Then he remembered – he had an old photo album in the nightstand across the room. It had a door on it and he hadn't opened it in years from what he could recall. "Time to walk down memory lane," he said as he wobbled to stand up. As he stumbled, he placed a hand on the arm of the chair to right himself.

Looking down at his glass, he noticed it was already empty. "Better fill 'er up before I look at those photos. Strolling might conjure up a powerful thirst. He ran his fingers through his hair and took a deep breath and sigh as he prepared to pour another drink. He poured it, four fingers width this time and started to head back to the chair. "I gotta whiz first," he said crudely, talking aloud to himself and he slowly walked to the bathroom, using his hand against the wall for balance.

In the bathroom he noticed the scale on the floor. "Might as well check out and see how the old bod' is doing," he said looking down at the gray metal device. He gingerly stepped on and attempted to maintain his balance. The red numbers displayed a rotating line while calculating, then finally stopped.

He gasped at the large red number staring back at him. "Jesus!" It was obvious his days of drinking and consuming bar food as his only source of nutrients was having a negative effect on his health. "Who asked you anyway?" he said in an irritated tone back at the still object as he kicked at it with his right foot causing him to stumble. "Damn thing must be broken," he decided as he turned toward the sink and quickly bent over uncertain if he were going to puke up the evening's beverages.

He braced himself with both arms, bent over, and waited. His hair fell in front of his face, but nothing happened. He took a couple of deep breaths, then rose his head. Still bracing the counter with one arm, he used his other to brush his hair back. He took a long glimpse in the mirror and didn't recognize the face looking back at him. He was a scruffy man, appeared to be older than him, and definitely disheveled. Who the hell was in his house and looking back at him? "That thing must be fucked up too," he decided as he returned to the living room barely lifting his feet and moving more in a shuffle.

He made it to the opposite end of the living room and opened the door to the nightstand. He had to get down on one knee to see in inside, but there it was, a green photo album just like he remembered.

"See, the old noodle still works like a charm," he said as he put his hand on top of the nightstand and slowly stood by pushing his weight down until he was standing. At least somewhat standing. He stared at the chair, which now appeared to be an impossible distance away. He grabbed the glass of bourbon from the top of the nightstand and made his way back to the chair. Dropping into the chair quickly some bourbon splashed on his shirt. "Damn it! That's expensive shit too!" he growled.

He placed the photo album on his lap, and the drink on the floor where he could still grab it. "Now, let's see what we have here. Let's see what the hell ol' Tyson Carr did back in the day," he said somewhat eagerly. The binder of the album creaked as he slowly opened it. It was the first time in probably more than five years it had moved. The pages were stuck together with static cling as he pryed the first page from the adjoined second page. He looked at the images on the pages as if he were looking back at someone else's life. He stared at each photo and tried to recall the day the photo was taken. Images of track meets, parties with friends, sporting events, and pictures of him and Ty back in the dorm. He was much younger then, and judging from the man he just saw in the mirror, maybe a little more time had passed than he recalled. In all of the photos Carson was smiling. A fresh, clean-shaved face, shorter hair and well-groomed. He smiled briefly as the images and some memories came flooding back to him. Then the moment passed quickly.

He continued to stare at the book and slowly turn page after page looking on at happier days. Days when he was enjoying the college life with friends, especially Ty. There were a couple of photos of them going out on one of their expeditions. Who took that? Maybe an old girlfriend? Yes, that's it. What was her name? He thought about it, but couldn't recall right now. It was on the tip of his tongue. That seemed to happen more and more lately. He didn't find anything that would appear he and Ty were nothing but the best of friends. So why would he come into life now and disrupt a good thing? Well, a mediocre thing, or was it even that? He stared distantly straight ahead, sighed loudly, and closed the book. "Forget this thing," he said as he put in on the floor, exchanging it for his drink. He talked into the glass as he prepared for another drink, "they said glory days will pass you by." He finished the drink. "Quicker than a wink from a young girl's eye..."

He staggered back down the hall and into his bedroom. It was already dark in there - and fresh, thanks to the air conditioner. He hadn't made the bed in days, so it was easy to fall into it and pull the covers over. He usually didn't bother to make the bed because he was going to sleep again the next evening and mess it up, so why take the time to make it? He crashed onto the mattress then rolled over onto his back looking up at the ceiling fan.

He was exhausted, as he was most nights. He didn't understand how he could always be so tired, yet also have incredible insomnia. His body was begging for sleep, but his mind would not grant it. Images ran through his mind, constantly ran through his mind – bills, work – or lack thereof, his appearance, his healthy, he was tired from always thinking about being tired; it never seemed to end. And he was tired – tired of dealing with it and all of the aches and pains his body was feeling.

He thought about the happy young man in the photo album, the crabby townie man in the dark corners of Giddy Ups, and the weary old man in the bathroom mirror. Those were all the same guy? How could that be? Impossible. It had to end, some way, somehow. But how? That was the question. He couldn't even wrap his mind around the problem and the needed steps to correct the descent into darkness. That made him chuckle. He used to be a problem solver. People used to bring their problems to him to solve because they trusted him and he had a logical, analytical mind that relied on the scientific method to explain issues others couldn't grasp. Now he was the one who could not understand. But it was nice seeing Ty...no, no that's too much to deal with, he thought as he pulled the blankets closer to his head. Too many new things and he couldn't possibly do that because every time he tried before to change he failed. No matter what, all roads let to failure, and he was tired of trying.

He definitely could not sleep now with all of these images races through his mind. So rapidly, like a blur. A blurry movie of his past life, a life that he barely recognized now. Then the images began slowing down as they crept more into more recent events, then they stopped at just one visual: the medicine cabinet. He remembered the medicine cabinet – behind the mirror where the old man stared at him. They said mirrors are gateways into other dimensions. Maybe this dimension had the answers to his problems? Yes, he did have a bottle of Valium in there his doctor prescribed for anxiety. A few of those and another bourbon or two would do the trick. It would be so easy. So peaceful. Who would notice? Probably no one, he thought as he contemplated the walk into the bathroom. He wouldn't have to worry after that. Everything would be gone – the pain, the depression, the loneliness. A calmness fell over him and a peaceful smile graced his face. Yes, that's what he would do.

But he didn't move. He just laid there thinking about it, smiling, and feeling a warm glow, too tired and too drunk to stand up. With his mind in a calmer state his body took over claiming what it desperately needed until finally, he slept.

4 ACE OF BASE (OR I SAW THE SIGN)

Saturday, June 13, 2015

It was early afternoon when Carson finally awoke on Saturday. His head rang with an all too familiar hangover. The old morning after was getting increasingly more difficult to handle. Waking up in the afternoon usually depressed him even more because he felt as if he had wasted the day. A day that he never had anything to do in the first place, but he thought there was always the possibility this day would be different. But it never was.

But what if it were? Maybe today he would get out of the house, take in some fresh air, and do something. He thought about the prior evening's events. It was a day that was the same as every other day in recent weeks, yet it was different. An unexpected anomaly occurred – a long-lost friend resurfaces. He wasn't looking for him, but there he was, and that chance event did bring a few moments of happiness or at least nostalgia, and that was something he hadn't often contemplated. But was it a chance event? There was a time when he didn't believe in chance. Everything happened for a reason and things like good luck, chance, or accident did not exist. He struggled to recall distant knowledge that once was very present in his daily life. He thought back to physics and its general principles, "There are no uncaused effects." There is no such thing as chance - chance is not an entity which causes things to happen. Nothing happens by accident. Causality is the *Law of Identity* applied over time. The *Law of Identity* is one of those elementary ideas that is so universal it's difficult to describe it in words. It is merely the fact that whatever exists, exists in a particular way. Everything that exists has an identity.

He recalled the book *The Celestine Prophecy* which follows an enormous shift in consciousness for the main character as he comes to understand nothing happens by coincidence. Even small things that seem to be innocent accidents, such as running into Ty at a place Carson regularly visited, were not without meaning. No one is here by accident. Everyone who crosses our path has a message for us. Otherwise, they would have taken another way, or left earlier or later. The fact that these people are here means that they are in our lives for some reason.

That was the message of the book, and now Carson pondered how it applied to him. What was the purpose of running into Ty and what was the message he brought? As he drove through the streets of South Austin he pondered that incident. He remembered daydreaming about life and how simple it was growing up. He remembered thinking about things he enjoyed in life, and his time in college was one of those. Fun times with his roommate talking science, hunting for creatures most people did not believe in, and a youthful determination to prove them wrong.

That roommate during those good times was Ty, and even though he was unaware of his surroundings at that moment, it is as if the universe heard him and sent Ty – out of nowhere – into his life. Maybe Ty is a spirit guide? Or a spirit guide took the place of his old roommate Ty? He tried to process the problem as he continued to drive. In research we have assumptions, and if we assume Ty is a spirit guide, what is the message he wanted Carson to receive? "He said I look like shit, which the bathroom mirror later confirmed," he thought. "He told me craft beer is better than the stuff I have been drinking. But more than that, he spoke about socializing and having fun – things which Dot also substantiated," he continued as his analytical mind struggled to resurrect itself. "So what does it all mean?"

He had zoned out while driving and paid little attention where he was going. Almost as if the universe had him on auto-pilot. He stopped along the side of the road – he didn't know why or even realize that he did in his disconnected state. When he looked up he was parked across the street from an Austin brewery – South Austin Brewery to be exact. He had driven down St. Elmo road many times and never realized there was a brewery here. But here it was, and here he was, and he was stopped on the street right in front of it.

Undoubtedly this was another sign from the universe? First Ty and now this. A nervous feeling ran down his body. This is it – Ty talked about craft beer and how different it was. The few beers he tried last night while Ty introduced them seemed to be enjoyable. He was slightly interested in the topic yesterday and briefly allowed himself the fantasy of a life where he was social with friends and hanging out having fun, but later he realized that was a crazy pipe dream. But was it? He was here – all he would have to do is walk inside. But what would happen then? He wouldn't know his pale ale from his saison and whatever other crazy words Ty used to talk about things that to Carson were just "beer" earlier in the day.

He remained in his car staring at the gray aluminum siding building, on the precipice of opening the door and walking inside. He imagined inside there were cool vibes, a river of beer flowing with ecstasy, and cool, interesting people who would embrace him and welcome him into their niche community.

The longer he sat in the car and thought about those things, the more nervous he became. Sure, yesterday it was all fun discussion with Ty and Dot, but here he would be on his own, and those people would not embrace him, but realize him for a fool. They would laugh at him and it would be embarrassing. He didn't want to be embarrassed. His life was already in enough disarray. He couldn't handle another failure. The universe must be wrong with its messages of athletic African-American men and shiny aluminum beer houses. He wouldn't succumb and be made a fool. He was too smart for that.

    He looked in the rear-view mirror. Besides, his hair was a mess. He looked down at his outfit, a gray t-shirt with black letters reading, Sorry I'm late I didn't want to come." That shirt perfectly summarized his mood, and he realized he didn't want to come here, and it was time to leave. The universe would have to do without him in whatever part of the puzzle it was trying to place him. Feeling a need for comfort and familiarity he put the car in drive and proceeded to head to Giddy Ups. At least there, people knew him and welcomed him. He has a regular table and a regular waitress that accepted him and whatever flaws he had. That is where he belonged, and that was where he would return and spend the rest of the evening.

5 ARE YOU READY FOR SOME FOOTBALL?

Sunday, June 14, 2015

The morning after this time was much smoother than previous nights. Carson had not spent the entire day and night drinking at Giddy Ups. Instead, he had a couple of beers and returned home sober. Perhaps it was because he was thinking about Ty and the universe's message, but likely it was because Dot was not working and he didn't find Brad the bartender to be nearly as exciting. Either way, he was able to drive home on his own and didn't spend much money – not to mention, he was able to get to bed and enjoy a good night's sleep for the first time this week - maybe even this month.

Things were looking up today. He didn't have a hangover – not even the slightest sign of a headache. Like Ice Cube said, *I don't know but today seems kinda odd...* He found himself at home and thinking about the coming months. He realized that soon football training camps would start and it would quickly be summer camp for the NFL and back to school time for college. He did enjoy football, both collegiately and professionally. He thought about the upcoming seasons and contemplated taking in some games with Ty. It would be an excellent way to catch up, and if memory served him, Ty also liked football. Of course he did, what guy didn't like football? Yes, he would call him and ask him if he wanted to catch a game. Ty wrote his number down for him and they were old friends, even though it had been years since they hung out, surely he would say yes.

Right? Or would he? Maybe he wouldn't want to hang out? The talk the other day was probably one of those gestures people do when they run into someone – speak with good intentions, but not meaning to follow through. They hadn't seen each other in about five years, what would be the chances that either of them would call and attempt to reconnect? Yes, the other night was just a safe conversation.

The more Carson thought about it he realized Ty was just being polite. He saw Carson and obviously couldn't just ignore him, even though Carson didn't see Ty, there was the chance he would notice, and surely Ty didn't want to come off as a dick, so why not say hello and be polite? That must be what it was. It was a moment that was nice when it happened but was now gone.

He realized if he did call Ty it would be awkward as Ty would be in an uncomfortable position of having to say no when he had no expectations of hearing from Carson again. If he called, he would take being polite and move it into a weird space. He always did that - move things into awkward places. He should learn from his past mistakes. He knew better than to do that and instead this time he would let it be. It is what it is – it is an unexpected happy moment that was fleeting and has since passed. Maybe understanding that and enjoying those small moments of happiness was ere the key to turning around this mood and shaking the funk?

6 SOME ASSEMBLY REQUIRED

Monday, June 15, 2015

Carson reflected on the events and the ups and downs of the past few days. Despite the difficulties in attempting to alter his mindset, he did have an overall positive feeling about his encounter with Ty at Giddy Up's and getting a brief introduction to craft beer. He still liked his Lone Star, but was a distant curiosity about trying new beers in the craft world. He was equally interested in the social aspect that Dot described. Maybe getting out and trying some of these new beers would be the thing he needed to break out of his funk.

As he reflected on the weekend, his phone rang. It was Ty following up after their reconnection.

"Hey, man! It was nice seeing you the other night. Whatcha got going on tonight?" inquired Ty.

"Hey, buddy!" Carson said in a surprisingly optimistic tone. "I had a great time catchin' up too. I don't think anything. Probably was just hangin' around the house maybe watching the Astros on television," replied Carson.

"Man, forget that! They play like six months out of the year. You can watch them another time. Come with me instead." Carson sounded intrigued.

"Well, I guess that's true...what'd you got going on?"

"Some friends and I usually get together every Monday evening and try a new brewery. Want to join us?" invited Ty.

There was a long, silent pause as Carson didn't say anything for a moment. Then he thought about the movie *Yes, Man* where Jim Carrey played a recluse who didn't have fun or hang out with people until he stumbled upon a motivational speaker who challenged him to say "yes" to every presented opportunity. It was one of Carson's favorite movies.

"Are you still there, Carson?" Ty asked, breaking the silence.

"Uh…Yeah – Yes, I'm here…sounds good. Where and when?" Carson asked cautiously.

"We are going to meet about 7:00 p.m. at Black Star Co-op on Easy Wind Drive here in Austin," replied Ty. "I have two other friends coming tonight, so it will be good for you to meet them. Kareem and Tegan will be showing up and I think you will like them. They both are cool people and they love trying new beers too." Carson paused again until he heard the voice of John Michael Higgins in his head – "Yes, man! Yes, man! Yes, man!"

"Um-Yes, I can make that," Carson said cautiously.

He had said yes but was fighting the urge of not showing. It had been years since he hung out with Ty, except for the few moments a few days ago. Surely he would get over the small disappointment if Carson failed to show up. He doubted it was that important, especially since he said he had other friends coming with him. But as he continued to think about it and his new, odd fascination with the "universe" he decided to take the chance. "What the hell could it hurt?" he pondered. His brief stop in front of South Austin Brewery was a solo mission and he wasn't prepared. This time there would be at least one person he knew, and who knows, maybe meeting Ty's friends would be entertaining.

He changed into a fresh pair of jeans, a Spawn t-shirt, and an Astros baseball cap. Thirty-seven minutes later, Carson pulled into a large parking lot behind the bar's patio area. The weather was a little humid, but the temperature was not too excessive. A man, two women, and two dogs relaxed on the back patio enjoying a round of drinks – beer for the humans, water for the dogs. Not seeing his friend, Carson made his way inside. An audible "wow!" escaped his lips as he walked inside. He was used to dark, loud bars overcrowded with people who had been there for a large part of the afternoon, jukeboxes, and shenanigans that looked like a prelude to something seen on the reality show *Cops*. But this place was different. For starters, the exterior was a large blue building with clean lines. Not an old barn-like structure with faded red paint from twenty-five years ago or old white concrete like another one of his local hangouts.

As he opened the large wooden door, he cautiously looked around in wonderment. A large wooden bar separated the patrons from the staff and behind them, a red wall with an aluminum backsplash containing more than twenty tap handles. Above it, a chalkboard spanned the length of the taps and announced the available list of beers. Brightly colored walls of orange and green surrounded tables in an open room. The front window allowed full light into the bar during the day but gave a beautiful view at night. The other wall contained a glass wall that separated the main room from brewing tanks. Carson was amazed looking at the tanks and the colorful walls. While looking around in amazement, his jaw gaping, he heard Ty call out to him. He snapped back to reality and noticed his friend and two others sitting at the end of one of the tables.

Carson made his way to the table and Ty stood to greet him. Extending his hand to his reacquired friend, Ty introduced Tegan Stone, a Caucasian woman in her early thirties with a bright smile and deep red hair just little past shoulder length that fell across her face, slightly covering one of her green eyes. She was seated, but her feet were barely reaching the bottom of the barstool revealed she was somewhat short. She looked like she worked out frequently, and by the tone of her arms; Carson suspected CrossFit. Carson was immediately drawn in by her smile. A warm smile that brought a sparkle to her eyes and dimples in her cheeks. Ty said she was a psychologist who specialized in behavioral and cognitive psychology. Carson assumed she was very successful at her job because her smile alone immediately connected with him. It was so genuine that he instantly felt comfortable and a feeling of trust in her.

The other man at the table was Kareem Ortiz, an athletic Hispanic man in his early to mid-forties with a tight haircut that revealed a slight salt-n-pepper tint. He had the build of a long distance runner and Carson was somewhat surprised looking at him that he wasn't purely a water drinker. Carson was acutely aware of his recent display of the stereotypical beer belly most people assume signifies a beer drinker, but Kareem was solidly built. Carson looked him over and smiled with an almost jealous admiration, wishing himself to have a similar physique. Kareem returned a confident, bright-eyed smile that reflected a man happy and energized on life and its opportunities. Working as a physical therapist, Carson could tell Kareem was supportive and compassionate, knowledgeable, positive, yet realistic and humble.

"Guys, this is my old college friend, Carson," introduced Ty. Tegan smiled and Kareem gave a solid handshake that made Carson realize he did more in the gym that just ran on the treadmill. Carson nervously pulled up a stool next to Kareem and across from Tegan.

"Hey, guys," he said quietly as he sat down to join them. "Thanks for the invite, Ty." He was worried Ty's other friends would not accept him. He didn't have a nice job or a fancy title to go with this introduction, what if they wrote him off as a loser?

His thoughts were put at ease and they brought him into the conversation.

"So what do you like to drink?" inquired Tegan in a silvery voice.

"I am trying to wean him off the Lone Star," interrupted Ty.

"Yes, guilty as charged!" said Carson raising his right hand. "I drink the popular, big label beers. I am a craft beer virgin…well, near virgin thanks to Ty the other night!" shared Carson.

"Just the tip, buddy. Just the tip," Ty added sarcastically as the table erupted with laughter.

"Hey, don't let Ty give you a hard time," added Kareem as he gently tapped his right hand on top of Carson's left hand resting on the table, then retracted it. "We all started there, and there is nothing wrong with the popular beer brands. Even now sometimes – not often, but sometimes, I still have one. Some are quite nice, but what I like is craft beer is something different, yet still familiar. Look around. The appearance of the bar, the large tanks, and with Black Star there is an added feature of it being a member-owned co-op. It shows the care that the brewmaster puts into making each batch and the value he places in member feedback. This place has tasting panels and member-owner beer-design meetings that give the brewers input into what customers want to drink, and they brew beer to meet those wants." Carson was immediately put at ease with Kareem's acceptance and showing his support for Carson against Ty's rantings.

Ty spoke up, "You don't see Bud Light asking people what they want and changing their recipe or product line based on that information." Carson picked up a menu from the table and looked confusingly at it and the wide selection of beers on the page.

"I don't know...there are so many choices and Ty showed me some more at Giddy Ups. There are a lot to choose from – more than just Bud, Miller, Coors, and Lone Star!" realized Carson.

"Yes, there are a lot of choices. That's one of the cool things about microbreweries," said Tegan. "There are more than three thousand active microbreweries in the United States, each making sometimes dozens of different beers per year – and that number, both breweries and the number of beers – is rapidly increasing each year," she added.

"I heard there are festivals where you can meet cool people and even the brewers," spoke Carson.

"Oh man! We have to get him to a festival!" said an excited Kareem.

"Not to mention a Jester King release event!" added Tegan.

A young lady entered the room, her hips swayed as she approached the table. "Have you decided what you all want?" asked Hannah, a tall, blonde that resembled a professional football cheerleader.

Ty ordered first, "Do you still have the El Vulcano cask?" he asked. Hannah affirmatively nodded her head. "Let me start with a pint of that," said Ty. Kareem ordered next while Tegan and Carson reviewed the menu.

"Let me have the Conceit." He looked at Carson and added, "Sour beers are so hot right now." Carson looked at him, then over to Tegan.

"You better go next. I am still confused!" Tegan ordered the Waterloo.

"Easily one of my favorite styles of beer – a nice Berliner Weisse."

"I don't even know what you guys have said! Is that English? I am going to need the Rosetta Stone to order beer from now on!" quipped Carson.

Hannah suggested a flight so that he could sample a variety of styles and beers. "A flight?" asked Carson. "Another new term for me. Oh man!" Hannah smiled.

"A flight is a sample. You get four 4-ounce tasters so you can try a few different kinds and decide what you like better. Sometimes people just come in for the flights and a burger," she added. Carson looked up.

"Okay, here goes! Waterloo, Moebius, Epsilon, and I guess...um... Brimstone Barrel-Aged Crotchety Dockhand – just the name sounds cool on that one!"

Hannah clarified, "that last one is $2 more because it is a special barrel-aged beer from 2013. Is that okay?"

"Yeah, sure. What the hell - let's go for it!" said Carson.

"How about some food?" suggested Hannah.

"Not just yet. Let's have some drinks first, then we will order food," spoke Ty. "This place does have some excellent food!" he added in a softer tone.

Hannah brought out the pints for Kareem, Tegan, and Ty. She sat the wooden paddle down in from of Carson.

"What the heck? Am I in the fraternity again?" joked Carson.

Hannah explained, "Think of a flight of steps as a series between levels. A flight of beer is the same thing. The beer is arranged on the paddle in a particular order. We typically start with the lighter brews instead of the bolder, darker brews. Drinking the beer this way ensures that you'll be able to enjoy each brew's distinct flavors and nuances without being overwhelmed by the previous sample. So from left to right, we have Waterloo, Moebius, Epsilon, and finally the Dockhand."

Carson chimed in, "Dot said the other day there were darker brews. Looks like I just found three of them!"

"Looks great to me!" reacted Ty. Carson looked at the samples and did feel excitement to try them. He wasn't sure what the terms meant, but he was open to taking the road less traveled, at least for him.

"Tegan, we both have the Waterloo. You mentioned it was your favorite style of beer. I forget what you called it…can you tell me more about it?" requested Carson.

"Oh man, it is so refreshing! Especially on hot summer days," she said. "It is sour, tart, and typically low in alcohol. Something interesting about it is that it is only brewed in Berlin and dates back to the Middle Ages," explained Tegan.

"Wow! That old? And why just Berlin?" asked Carson.

"It is protected by law, an appellation d'origine contrôllée, if you will. Like Trappist beers in Belgium or how French wine Bordeaux only comes from that region, or true champagne comes from that particular region? You get the idea," said Tegan.

Ty spoke up, "Carson is a science geek." He added, "it ferments with both yeast and lactic-acid bacteria. The bacterial strain used in Berliner Weisse is called Lactobacillus delbrückii, so-named after Max Delbrück, a noted biochemist and 1969 Nobel Laureate in medicine.

And it's named after him because he isolated this lactobacillus bacterium while he was head of the Institut für Gärungsgewebe in Berlin during the 1930's," said Ty.

"Those foreign phrases are more captivating when Tegan says them," Carson said to Ty. Tegan smiled and the guys chuckled. "So Ty said you guys all hang out every Monday?" asked Carson, "How'd you all meet?"

"Hmm, that's a good one," reflected Ty.

"I think for us it was back last year, wasn't it?" asked Kareem. "I think at the release of Kentucky Streetwalker at Naughty Brewing."

"Yeah, that's right!" Ty remembered fondly. "We were both there waiting in line and started talking," he said.

"That was a damn good beer too," recalled Kareem.

"I think I still have a bottle in the cellar," said Ty.

"And that I Think She Hung the Moon with the Belgian candy sugar, the Mexican piloncillo sugar cones, sweet pecan smoke, and the hibiscus was a great beer as well," said Kareem.

"For me and Ty it was a little longer. I first met him at the 2013 Austin Specialty Beer Festival when some friends I was with also knew him. But later we met up again when one of those same friends had a bottle share," said Tegan.

"2013? Wow, it has been a couple of years, hasn't it?" replied Ty.

As they shared their stories and enjoyed the memories, Tegan and Ty also shared laughs, her personality and smile shining through and Carson understood why the guys liked hanging around her. When she laughed a small crinkle appeared at the top of her nose, she smiled with her dimpled grin as she chortled in amusement. Carson watched the others and joined in laughing in more of a nervous titter at the inside jokes he didn't grasp.

Kareem enjoyed the discussion as well and laughed with Ty and Tegan, but his laugh was more of a measured and restrained chuckle. Looking at Tegan, in his mind her smile returned her to the innocent smile and laughter a small child but holding a beer.

Kareem took a sip from the Conceit. "This is an English pale ale, but it is also sour," said Kareem. "It's tart and fruity, a soured mash and single-hopped with Amarillo hops. It's a nice sour, but not overly tart or sweet." Carson looked puzzled for an instant, and then Ty explained the mash is what is created by combining crushed malts with hot water. It's a step in the brewing process to convert complex starches into simple sugars so they can be more easily fermented, and a sour mash involves using Lactobacillus delbrueckii bacteria.

"This beer is locally made here in Austin, but it is a collaboration with another brewer in London – Beavertown Brewing."

Taking his first taste of a sour beer, Carson slightly drew his head back and furrowed his brow, but not in a negative manner. More like surprised. It was tart, maybe a hint of peach – or was that apricot? No doubt it was a refreshing drink with a little pucker, but not like Warhead sour.

"Wow! I could see drinking a couple of these on a hot summer day," stated Carson.

"See? That's what I said!" replied Tegan. "It is so smooth and light. I could drink these all day – and just 3.8% you could have a few."

Carson called over to Ty – "how's your Volcano or whatever you called it?"

"That's El Vulcano, but technically you are correct. This is a rye beer, so that means that some malted rye is used instead of some portion of barley malt. And cask is the vessel it comes in. You are familiar with a keg - When beer is first put into the keg at the brewery, it has just completed fermentation and possibly some aging. For some beers, a filtering process will be used to extract most of the yeast and protein particles, making for a nice, clear beer. Once the beer is inside of the keg, CO_2 is pumped in and all of the air is pumped out. Because of pressurization, the CO_2 will slowly mix with the beer itself, creating carbonation. Once a keg is tapped, more CO_2 is pumped into the already pressurized container so that beer will pump through the line into the glass. CO_2 not only carbonates the beer, but it also keeps the beer's shelf life nice and long. Just like food, beer can spoil if put in contact with oxygen for a prolonged period...follow me?"

"That's pretty intense, but yeah, it makes sense to me," Carson responded favorably.

Ty continued, "Casking is much older than using a keg. 2500 years ago casks were often made of clay or even wood. Today it is usually steel or aluminum. But when beer fills these containers, it is neither filtered nor pasteurized, which is the way beer has been served since its creation. By not filtering the beer, even though it may look completely clear, yeast remains floating in suspension, and this is where the difference begins. Yeast works by eating simple sugars such as maltose, glucose, and fructose, and their byproducts are alcohol and CO_2. With yeast still in the solution, more sugars can be added with the beer to the cask giving the yeast something to eat. Once the cask is closed off, the yeast does their thing. When the CO_2 is created, it has nowhere to go since it is in an enclosed area, forcing it into the beer creating natural carbonation. Once the beer is ready to be served, it can either be poured directly from the cask or pumped from a beer engine. The carbonation level of the beer is going to be much less than that of a kegged beer, which makes the beer itself much smoother and easier to drink. Because air is pumped inside of the cask instead of CO_2, the shelf life of an opened cask is only about three days, and the serving temperature is typically warmer than a kegged beer, but the characters the beer can pick up from its location make for a truly remarkable drink."

After the lengthy explanation Carson waited for a second. "So, how's it taste?" Ty smelled the glass and took a small sip.

"It smells fragrant,"....thinking about the initial taste he said, "I think the rye masks the hops a little. But still some hops, and a smooth finish. It's a good variation of the regular Vulcan, which is a good beer itself. I like it."

"Okay, I am moving on to beer number two!" Carson said with optimism. "Lighter to darker like Hannah said, so that makes this one the Moebius." He paused and asked the group "Isn't that a vampire or something from Marvel Comics?"

Kareem quickly replied, "No, that's Morbius. But it is 10.1%, so it does pack a bite!" he said with a laugh.

Ty added, "The guys who created this bar are math fans. Hence the beers are classified as rational and irrational. In this instance, it could be named for the Möbius strip or the Möbius function…but likely just named after German mathematician and astronomer August Ferdinand Möbius who was responsible for both things."

Hannah dropped by again to check in with the group. Seeing where Carson was with the flight she said, "Mobius is one of the most time-intensive beers we make and most complex in ingredients and flavors we produce. It is aged for six weeks in Balcones Brimstone whiskey barrels."

"That's the same barrels used in the Dockhand?" asked Carson.

"Yes, but instead of six weeks that Dockhand is aged in the barrels much longer. That version is 2013."

Carson noticed the beer had a smooth mouthfeel and he detected bourbon, but also a hint of coffee, maybe dark roasted malts, dark Belgian candy sugar, and possibly even a little like licorice sticks. He was surprised that he liked it also. "Who's ready to order some food?" asked Carson. Like elementary children, eager hands shot up making it unanimous. "So do you guys go somewhere every week?" inquired Carson. Tegan answered saying their weekly meetings were still somewhat new, but the goal was to try somewhere new each week.

"So I take it this is your first time here?" asked Kareem

"Yes, I typically only go one place and drink the same beer, so this is all new to me – the beer and the brewery concept," Carson replied.

"And we are kind of crazy – crazy in general, but also crazy about the beer," said Tegan. "Hopefully we don't come off as weird. I know you and Ty were friends before and sometimes that can be awkward meeting other friends you don't know," she said.

"No. No, it's cool. It's actually kind of nice really. I have been down for a while – a lack of interest in doing things, distancing myself from the few friends I did have, poor eating and sleeping habits, and just kind of being a loner. It kind of sucks because I used to be pretty fun," said Carson.

"You *think* you were fun," added Ty.

"No, I am fairly certain I was. I was looking at an old photo album recently. Back from when we were in college, and I looked fun. You were in the photos too and you didn't seem to mind hanging around me," Carson said with a smile.

"How did you feel looking at the album?" asked Tegan.

"Truthfully, I felt sad. The night I ran into Ty at Giddy Ups I heard a song playing and was daydreaming about growing up when things were easier…and happier. Not really and stress then. No bills to worry about, no concerns about a job, about health issues, and everything we worry about today. I didn't even notice Ty walk up. If he hadn't noticed me, and looking like I did I am surprised he did, I would likely still be there in the dark corner pondering life. But it was nice reconnecting and I thought maybe this is a second chance," said Carson honestly.

"It is important to take those chances. As Ty said, I am a behavioral and cognitive psychologist, so I work with people struggling with the same thing. It is scary to take chances, but there is also reward. Do you write in a journal?" she asked.

"No, I haven't done much writing lately. At least since college," he said.

"I recommend it. You can write about things that are happening and I suggest including things that were positive things that happened – no matter how small. Like you made the bed, you ate a healthy breakfast, maybe took a walk, reconnected with Ty, or made new friends like you are doing now. Many times we see small things and take them for granted, but when you look back over the journal and you see win after win after win, which builds confidence. Plus you are learning new beers and breweries. It would be a good place to record them so you know later what you liked and didn't," she suggested.

"That sounds like something I could do," he said positively.

"Whenever I get down I just go back and read my eBay feedback. 'Great buyer', 'fast shipper', 'highly recommended'. 'Would use again'. Perks me up every time," said Ty. After a chuckle from everyone at the time Ty continued. "Just kidding, but you are a scientist. You know the importance of documentation and building supporting evidence," reminded Ty.

"I would suggest you also give that photo album a second look. You just said you were happy and smiling in the photos. Look at it for the positives rather than dwelling on the negative aspects or thinking that those days are over. You can get back to those feelings," she said.

"I certainly hope so," Carson replied.

"Can I ask you something else?" asked Tegan.

"Sure."

"Have you ever had thoughts about hurting yourself?" she asked. Carson just looked at her, then down at his beer. "Well…to tell you the truth, yes. Just the other day actually, but I know that's not the thing to do, and I didn't attempt anything," he said.

"I will give you my number and if you ever feel like that again, please call me. I am glad to talk to you and listen," she said.

"Me too," said Kareem. "Plus, now that you met us, I am sure you instantly love us and will want to do things together all of the time. There will be no time for those thoughts," he said.

Hannah returned once more, ready to take the food order. It was a nice break from the heavy conversation. Kareem said, "I am all over this Doughnut Double!" He read the ingredients to the group, "two 44 Farms ground brisket patties, several slices of American cheese, sautéed onions, and aioli on a jalapeño glazed doughnut!" Carson looked on in shocked silence as he remembered his initial impression of Kareem and how healthy he looked. Kareem looked up, "I will burn it off at the gym tomorrow, but tonight I am relaxing."

"Put me down for a burger, too," said Tegan as she tossed the menu on the table in front of her. "I will have the Root Beer Burger;

Root beer caramelized onions, pickled jalapeño, gruyere & cheddar cheese, bacon, and beer mustard. Just sounds good!" Ty was the third to choose a burger as he ordered the rainbow chard kimchi burger topped with a fried egg, cheddar cheese, and sriracha aioli.

"I am not going to be the one to disrupt the burger trend. Make it a Chili Pequin Burger for me," said Carson as he ordered the 44 Farms ground beef brisket burger, topped with chili pequin dust, avocado, jalapeño, LTO, and chili pequin aioli.

Ty spoke, "Another cool thing about this place is not only the beer, but the food is local. All of those burgers use beef from 44 Farms – all locally sourced beef. That keeps ingredients fresh, nearly farm to table, and helps the local farmers."

While Hannah was still at the table Tegan, Ty, and Kareem took the opportunity to order another drink. All three ordered an Elba – a four percent pale wheat ale garnished with a cucumber. Carson moved on to the twelve percent Epsilon, a peated Scotch ale aged in Balcones Brimstone whiskey barrels.

"Man, they love these Brimstone barrels. That's three of my four beers in them!" But this one really caught Carson's attention. It was dark, but twenty and a half IBU – not as bitter as the more than sixty-six IBUs on the Moebius. Earlier he learned from Kareem that IBU stood for International Bittering Units and the higher the number, the more apparent hop bitterness in the beer, contributed by the alpha acid from hops. He told Carson it was chemistry measuring how much isohumulonic acid was in a finished product. Isohumulones is an acid in hops that is bitter. Different hops contain different amounts. It is not flavor, just bitterness. Flavor comes from other aspects of hops. The isohumolone is all the same except for concentration, so dilution also affects how bitter a beer is.

Epsilon had a smooth but unexpected somewhat thick mouthfeel and a sweet and nutty taste. He could taste the peat heavy with minimal bourbon. It was well aged like a nice cognac, and Carson understood what both Ty and Dot mentioned the other day about these beers being sipped and enjoyed. Definitely no shotgunning this bad boy! There was a hint of grape musk or perhaps prunes, but not overwhelming – just enough to make it interesting and a little mysterious. The combination of flavors was extremely complex and Carson noticed that since it had been sitting and warming a little longer the bourbon notes increased. This was one that he could really enjoy.

The final beer was the Brimstone Barrel-Aged Crotchety Dockhand, a stout. Ty told Carson that Dockhand was a popular beer with a lot of variations. In addition to the Crotchety Dockhand there was a Recalcitrant Dockhand, a Rebellious Dockhand, a Cantankerous Dockhand, and an Insubordinate Dockhand listed on the brewery's website. The menu described this version as being inspired by the old, grouch of a man that enjoys roasted coffee with his morning oatmeal. Carson thought that somewhat sounded like him, at least before meeting back up with Ty the other day, and now his other friends seemed really cool. He was surprised that it was another fun evening and now it was about to get even better as Hannah approached with the burgers!

"How are you, hun?" asked Hannah with a wink.

"Doing great – and loving these beers!"

"Can I get you another one?" she asked.

"You know what? I really loved that Epsilon. Can I get a full sized one of those? It can warm up while I finish this Dockhand."

"That's how you do it," she said. "You learn fast!" The words of encouragement made Carson feel happy, and a smile crossed his face.

Hannah walked away but quickly returned with a short glass of beer - a beautiful reddish amber, light tan head that lingered. "Is this beer rational or irrational?" asked Carson.

"It is actually in the Infinite Series subset of the Irrational Series," responded Hannah. He returned to the Dockhand to finish it up. That had less alcohol, but a higher IBU, making it have more of a dark and roasty taste with the added morning flavors of coffee, oats, and molasses. Looking at the empty flight paddle Carson was impressed with the beer – their taste and the complex characteristics.

They were all good, but that Epsilon was his favorite, followed by the Moebius, the Dockhand, and finally the Waterloo. It was good too, but he really enjoyed the darker beers more than he expected. He looked eagerly at the Epsilon, then turned hungrily toward the burger. Great beer, great food, and great friends – all surprising discoveries.

Carson grabbed the burger with two hands and took a huge bite. With a full mouth he mumbled, "Sweet mother of Jesus, that's good!"

As he chewed Tegan said, "you're right – so fresh!' Carson looked around at the table, the brewery, and other patrons enjoying beer and food at their tables, and back at his new friends. He took it all in and was enjoying his night.

"Can this night get any better?" he asked internally.

He squirmed a little as he felt the cellphone in his pocket vibrate. He was having such a good time he momentarily forgot about the phone. Usually it was always in his hands and he was surfing the internet, but he hadn't looked at it once since arriving at the brewery. He looked at the unknown number and attempted to recall if he knew the number.

"What's up?" asked Ty.

"Hmm, I don't think I know this number. Someone in San Antonio," responded Carson.

After another ring Ty said, "Either answer the damn thing or turn that ringer off. What is that, Justin Bieber?"

"No, smartass! It's Tom Petty!" sassed Carson. He clicked the answer button and the unknown voice on the other end spoke.

"Hello? Carson? This is Fred Dalton down in Elmendorf. I got your number from Eric Vega."

"Eric Vega?" Carson searched his mind and concluded, "I don't think I know an Eric Vega. Are you sure you have the right number?"

"This is the number he gave me. He said he met you a couple of years ago in a bar before a Longhorns game. Said you were a science teacher."

Carson said, "well I *was* a science teacher."

Fred continued, "He also said you were into mysterious animals and things maybe not everyone believes in." Carson listened quietly. "Thing is," added Fred, "I am in need of someone with your expertise down here. Something killed a couple of my cattle, and others in the area have been found as well." Carson paused for a moment and reflected on his past adventures, but that seemed like a long time ago.

"Yeah, well I don't really do that anymore either," a dejected Carson replied.

Fred reassured, "Well, I don't know anyone who does, so you are kind of my only hope."

"I don't know…," pondered Carson.

"I can pay. Not much, but some. Finances are tight now, but if I don't stop this creature I will be out of business," confessed Fred.

Intrigued Carson asked "Creature? How do you know it's a creature?"

"I seen him! And I got some photos on my trail camera!" Fred said excitedly. "Can you get down here closer toward this weekend and have a look? The local sheriff has been out, but it isn't something that really fits his skill set, but you – you have experience with this sort of thing." That *Yes, man*! voice returned to Carson's head. He did have a good time researching in the past, and he did need money – even if it was a one time, small paycheck.

"Let me check my calendar and get back to you. What's a good number?" He asked Tegan for a pen and transcribed Fred's number on the back of a Black Star napkin.

As he pressed the *End Call* button, Ty asked if everything was okay. Carson had a distant, uncertain look on his face, but filled in his friends in on the details of the call.

"What type of creature?" asked Ty.

"I don't know. He didn't say. He just said it was a mystery and something law enforcement couldn't help with."

"Hey, that sounds like our old times, buddy!" reflected Ty.

As the two looked across the table at each other Kareem interrupted, "Road trip! Let's all go down and take a look. We will see what this creature is all about– then hit up some local San Antonio beers!"

"Are you guys sure?" asked Carson.

Ty nodded his head, Kareem smiled, and Tegan said "hell yeah – I'm in! Make the call!"

Carson hit redial. He told Fred he and some friends could be down Thursday morning. Fred acknowledged and provided the details.

"Thanks, Carson. See you guys Thursday," and hung up the phone.

7 SECOND THOUGHTS

Tuesday, June 16, 2015

Carson awoke about 9:00 a.m. and suddenly realized what he agreed to last night. He thought about the call from Fred and wondered what he was thinking. Maybe those beers were much stronger than he was expecting and he wasn't in his right mind. He just stared at the ceiling while the thoughts ran through his mind. It was crazy enough to agree to meet new people and try new beers, but to agree to drive down to San Antonio and look into some insane story about a creature running around killing livestock?

Not only that but to drag those new people into the situation with him? What was he thinking? It had been several years since he went searching for any animal, and even then it was a jackalope – not like it would kill anyone if it were out there. Besides, he never did find one. Is it they didn't exist, or he just wasn't good at looking for them? Even if he failed then no one would care, but that was then.

This time a town was feeling threatened and some of the ranchers could seriously lose their life savings, their house, their farm, and whatever else. These people depended on answers, and if the truth turned out he was not good at searching for these type of creatures, it would be a colossal failure. Tegan and Kareem seemed nice, but that's now when they are just meeting him. What if he took them all the way to San Antonio only to look like an idiot? What would they think then? And how would that look on Ty? He would definitely be pissed and regret running into Carson that night at Giddy Ups.

He thought more about it and decided the only thing to do was to call Fred back and call the whole thing off. This was something much too big for him. Sure, Ty could help, but it had been many years since he was out in the woods searching for hidden animals. At least Carson assumed it had been. And Tegan and Kareem had no experience. He figured they were viewing this just as a road trip with some potential for adventure, but how would they hold up if they were in the woods? The woods can be scary during the day, but at night it takes on a whole different persona. What if they freak out then? And what if – just by chance – they happen to actually find this creature? The shit might hit the fan once things go down. Not only for Tegan and Kareem but likely him too. It had been a long time since he felt that adrenaline rush. How would he react? Yes, best to call it off and save everyone the trouble.

He continued to look at the ceiling and work through the problem. But what if they were able to help? How cool would that be – to help multiple people in a small community. People were asking for help, and if they were to receive that help they would be grateful. And talk about win – if they could pull this off it would be a huge confidence boost. He thought about his assembled team – his science background, Ty's technology skills, Tegan brought psychology, and Kareem was strong and compassionate. Carson could tell he was patient and humble. He was likely cool under pressure. They seemed to complement each other's skills well and might actually help increase the chance of success.

It would also be a good distraction. As Tegan told him yesterday, specific ways of thinking can trigger particular health problems, such as depression. Taking on this project is a whole different realm than he had been operating in lately, so it might be a good distraction. It would certainly take his mind off his fears and worries. Plus the journal was a good idea. Documentation in a journal could be useful not only to alter his thinking and help remind him of the little victories and positive experiences each day, but say there was an unknown creature in the woods of Elmendorf…the journal would be scientific evidence of their discovery. That could lead to huge opportunities to maybe get back into work. Not just a job but meaningful work that he truly enjoyed. At least he knew he used to enjoy it, and he thought he could enjoy it again – being outdoors, searching for clues, proving those who had doubted him wrong – those were things he was interested in doing. Maybe he could do it after all?

He decided not to call Fred and cancel.

Not just yet at least.

8 CUPPA JOE

Wednesday, June 17, 2015

Early Wednesday morning Carson found himself awake at 7 a.m. without the aid of an alarm clock. Just the chirping of birds outside. As he awoke, he opened only one eye, wincing with the other as a ray of sunshine broke through the slightly opened blind, and it fell across his face. Instead of being irritated, he felt rested. He immediately got up and instead of sitting on the edge of the bed dreading the day, he started making the bed. It crossed his mind during the activity that he couldn't recall the last time he had made his bed.

Afterward, he stood in his room and looked around. He walked over to the blinds and opened them to let in some sun. That was a nice change from the darkness that usually lived in the room, but now he could see that the room was a mess. Without thinking he immediately began tidying things up and soon turned to his phone for some added music to aid in the cleanup. It didn't take long to transform the dingy and cluttered room into something presentable. Now for the other rooms in the house. It was more than an hour of work but the house looked and smelled wonderful, and Carson was proud of his work. "Hmm. Write that down in the journal," he thought to himself. Not that he had a journal yet but he was planning on taking Tegan's suggestion to heart. He looked at his phone and was impressed it was still early. Typically, he wasn't even out of bed yet, but today he already accomplished more in just about an hour than he productively did all yesterday, or the day before, or any day for that matter.

Full of energy he decided to put on his shoes and go for a walk. It was less than one mile to the Coffee Cup Cove. The exercise and fresh air might do him good, he thought. Plus then he could hang out and people watch. That used to be fun. He left the house and began walking to the coffee shop.

He looked around almost astonished at the surrounding neighborhood. The trees were bright and full of leaves that swayed in the gentle morning breeze. The sky was a beautiful blue, and he noticed that the clouds were different colors. Everything was more vibrant than he remembered, and he smiled. A squirrel scampered up a nearby tree as he walked a little too close, neighborhood dogs barked as he passed by their houses, and the birds chirped as if they were happy to see him. He wondered if this is how Snow White felt when she opened the window in the morning?

About twenty minutes later he arrived at the coffee shop. A nice leisurely stroll that made him feel relaxed. He walked up to the window and placed an order for a medium hot breve, then found a table outside near the sidewalk. How nice to just relax outside and watch the world pass by. It sounded pleasant and peaceful to him. Moments later his name was called by the young man in the window. He smiled and signaled an acknowledgement to the man, picked up his drink, and returned to the table to enjoy it.

As he sipped the hot coffee he thought again about San Antonio. That trip was supposed to be tomorrow. Yesterday he was ready to call it off, but today, not so much. Now it sounded like something exciting – a gateway into a new life of adventure. That's probably why people sleep on big decisions he thought. His mind was made up – they were going to go and check out this creature.

Just then his phone rang. He looked down and was surprised to see it was Tegan. He wondered if she misdialed.

"Hello?" he answered cautiously.

"Hey, Carson. It's Tegan – from the brewery yesterday?"

"Uh, yeah. I remember. How are you?" he asked.

"Oh, I'm good. I was just calling to check in on you, see how you were doing. Are you ready for tomorrow?" she asked.

"Yes, I am ready. I was just thinking about it. I got up this morning and went for a walk. Now I am at a coffee house enjoying the nice weather. It has been a long time since I was up and outside enjoying things," he admitted.

"Well good. I am glad you are out. It is good to get sun and fresh air, plus a little morning caffeine never hurt anyone, am I right?" she laughed again with that laugh that made Carson smile.

"I think the trip will be great. It will be nice to get to know you and Kareem a little more and see what all this fuss is about some creature down there," he said.

"Yep – who knows what we will find?" said Tegan. "I am excited as well to see what's going on down there. Well, hey – I will let you get back to that coffee. But hit me up any time you want to talk or need someone to listen."

"Thanks, I really appreciate that," he said.

"Yeah, and take another look at that photo album like I suggested as you get out and take an interest in the world around you I bet you see those photos in a different light," she said.

Carson enjoyed the walk home as much as he did the walk to the coffee shop. Occasionally he passed people in the front yard or getting in their car to head to work, and they smiled and waved at him. He returned the gesture and smiled. He returned home and to his familiar chair, but this time with the curtains open and the windows ajar to let some of the fresh air into the house.

The photo album was still sitting on the floor next to the chair. He picked it up and thumbed through the pages. They weren't stuck together as much as they were the other day. The images staring back at him were the same as the night after Giddy Ups, but he could see them for what they were – glimpses of happy moments in his life. He understood then that time was fleeting and even in the most comfortable times, it would eventually pass.

He took pictures to remind himself of those happy times and to capture what he considered a full life. Yes, these were not memorials to past events that were to be forgotten, but instead reminders of what happiness looked like: hanging out with friends, taking on new adventures into the unknown, and celebrating little achievements in life. These photos were a roadmap on happiness and he could use it to follow the route and get back there. Hanging out with friends and taking on new adventures happened in the past, yes – but they also were happening in the future – tomorrow, and he couldn't wait to begin the journey.

9 WAELZBRO

Thursday, June 18, 2015

Carson woke up early in anticipation of his new friends' arrival. It wasn't typical for him to wake up at 5 a.m., although there were times in the past when he had drug himself home not long before that time. But today was different. He walked into the bathroom, sat his phone on the counter, and hit play on his music library. He reached into the shower, turned on the water, and stepped out of his shorts as *Hey, Soul Sister* began to play. He squirted an ample amount of body wash that smelled of cedarwood onto a blue mesh body sponge. The friction between the sponge and his wet body caused the lather to build and the aroma of the cedarwood to reach his nostrils.

He took a deep breath and smiled. Surprisingly his toes began to tap in the sudsy water and he started to sing along with members of Train. He turned his back to the shower head, letting the water fall over his head, then stepped forward and applied shampoo. He massaged it into his hair, then turned around grabbing the wooden handle of an exfoliating loofah back scrubber that he discovered adequately doubled as a microphone as the phone's media player moved to Bon Jovi's *Living on a Prayer*.

Stepping out of the shower, he dried off with a towel and continued to sing and dance with the radio – a feeling he had not experienced in a long time. Wrapping the towel around his waist, he turned on the water in the sink and removed a can of shaving cream from the underneath cabinet. He took the razor from a drawer in the cabinet, wet his face, and applied the shaving cream to the areas of his face he wanted to shave. He still kept his beard and mustache, but both were in need to some maintenance. The mint from the shaving cream caused his face to tingle causing him to feel alive and inspired like the old Zestfully clean commercials from the early 1980s.

After his shave he returned to his bedroom to get dressed, grabbed a comfortable pair of jeans, and a blue Nirvana t-shirt. He sat down on his bed, put on his socks, then stood to step into the jeans. He looked down at his watch and slipped a foot into his brown loafer as he heard a car pull up in the driveway.

At 6:45 a.m. Tegan Stone's 2015 white diamond Buick Verano pulled into the driveway of Carson Quinn's 1973 avocado green single-family home on Deadwood Drive. Two quick honks of the horn signed their arrival. Carson headed out of the house with a grin, actually eager to begin the adventure. He locked up and slightly jogged to the car.

Tyson Carr sat up front in the passenger seat and Kareem Ortiz was in the back ready for the drive down to San Antonio. As Carson opened the rear driver side door Tyson held up a medium-sized white bag. "Sausage Egg & Cheese McMuffin or McGriddle?" asked Ty.

Wiping the sleep from his eyes Carson muttered, "McGriddle".

Tyson added, "We picked up some Dazzle Coffee on the way. We have a Zebra Mocha, a Caramel Macchiato, or a Snickers Mocha. Tegan already laid claim to the coconut latte." Carson selected the Snickers. With breakfast served the quartet began the ninety-minute drive down I-35 to Elmendorf.

Carson was surprised and impressed to discover Tegan's car had Wi-Fi. Now he could use Hotels.com to book a hotel for the weekend. Searching the local area he found a Red Roof Inn off 10 east for a low price of $46. "Free breakfast, free parking, and free Wi-Fi? What more do we need?"

Tegan suggested, "Carson, if you and Ty don't mind sharing a bed we could just get one room."

Ty spoke up, quoting Phil from the *Hangover* "Guys, we are not sharing beds. What are we, twelve years old?"

The passengers laughed at the line, and Carson changed the search to include two rooms. He and Ty could share one room and Kareem and Tegan in the other. With a couple of clicks on the mobile app, the trip was booked.

Carson asked Ty, "Are we going right to Fred's place first?"

"We might as well. He's a rancher, so 8:15 – 8:30 isn't too early for him...but it is too early to start drinking!" quipped Ty.

Kareem added, "Hopefully we will have some time for that! There are a few craft beer spots in San Antonio I have wanted to check out!"

Carson looked over at Kareem and asked, "How do you keep track of it? There are so many beers. I'm just learning and already feel lost. How do you know what you want to try and what you have already had? More importantly, how do you remember the ones you liked and the ones to avoid?"

Almost simultaneously the other three passengers said, "Untappd!"

"What is Untappd?" inquired Carson.

Ty spoke, "It is basically FourSquare for beer. Download it on your phone and check in beers as you drink them. You can type in tasting notes, select the location, and even take photos of your beer so you can remember them later."

"And you can make friends and see what others are drinking," added Tegan. "That way you can be alerted if there is a rare or new beer in the area."

Kareem stated, "I like to use it for tracking whales too, especially if I am traveling!"

The Chupacabra & The Bat Rastard

"Whales?" asked Carson.

"Yep – there be whales! You may hear them called whales or white whales. It's like Moby Dick, and just like Captain Ahab it's all about searching for a beer so limited and rare it's almost mythical."

Tyson spoke up, "In the words of Herman Melville, *such a portentous and mysterious monster roused all my curiosity.*"

Kareem continued, "As you have learned by now, craft beers are limited by production and distribution. So beer drinkers and collectors from other places where that beer is not available may go to great lengths to acquire beers. There are online beer retailers such as CraftShack or Inside the Cellar that have a limited inventory that rotates frequently. There are online communities such as BeerAdvocate and RateBeer.com that list what people have and want, and they also have online forums where members can list what they are in search of and what they have for trade. Facebook also has communities dedicated to trading."

Carson looked surprised. "I thought shipping beer would be illegal. Isn't that like bootlegging?"

"*Legally*, shipping beer to any state is riddled with… gray zones," said Tyson. "It is a federal offense to ship via the postal service. UPS and FedEx will not ship beer."

Tegan added, "They will ship other liquids such as 'olive oil' or 'marinade' or even other things like yeast samples – wink wink.'

"Hmm…sounds complicated," said Carson. "So, just download Untappd and start from there?"

"Yes," said Tyson. "You will need to create an account name and use your email address. Add me as a friend – TechieTyson."

Kareem spoke up, "KareemTheDream for mine."

Lastly, Tegan said, "AustinTegan."

"I might as well use the Wi-Fi and download it now, then we can search the area for mysterious beasts!" said Carson.

"Mysterious beasts, indeed!" said Kareem.

At precisely 8:23 a.m., the group pulled into the driveway of Fred

& Jess Dalton. Fred was standing in the enclosed front porch drinking his morning coffee and awaiting his visitors. As his guests slowly emerged one by one from the car, Fred opened the door and walked out to greet them.

"Good morning!" he spoke in an inviting tone.

"Hello, I am Carson. You called about some trouble?" Carson said as he stepped forward, extended a hand, and the two men exchanged a handshake.

"Yes, something got in with my cattle the other night, and a neighbor's a couple of nights before that. I caught the sumbitch on film!"

"You did what?" Carson exclaimed excitedly. "Can we see it? What was it?"

"I don't know what the hell it was – at first I thought it looked like a wolf or coyote, but then I wasn't sure it was a canine at all. I saw it with my own two eyes and have it on the trail camera."

Kareem asked, "And it killed some of your cattle? Times are pretty tough. That has to be difficult!"

Fred replied, "Yeah this farm's all we've got. We have to find out what that thing is and stop it – not just for my farm, but for everyone in the area!"

"Have you seen it since that night?" asked Tegan.

"No, ma'am," he said tipping the brim of his hat toward Tegan. "It's been a quiet couple of nights, but I am nervous it's ready to strike again. It may have had its fill for a while, but it could be hungry again by now."

"Did it eat the calf?" asked Ty.

"No, just drank the blood. Didn't eat the meat. That's the weird part! Damnedest thing I've ever seen."

Carson looked over the group and said, "What do you say we take a look at those photos!"

Excitement was in the air. Ty and Carson were familiar with the feeling from their college experiences. The cattle felt it, and Kareem and Tegan felt an uneasy, excited-nervousness that was equal amounts of anticipation and despair. Fred nervously opened his phone and showed it to the group, hoping for an answer.

"I have a few photos of the creature, but I went back and reviewed some video footage the trail camera also captured. We can see the trail camera videos on here." Fred pulled up a web browser and located a link in his favorites. The group drew in close to watch as the grainy video began to play. Mostly it showed just darkness and cattle, but then something else. An animal unlike anything they had seen before. It was seen initially in the darkness standing upright on slender hind legs, almost like a kangaroo – but then it dropped to all fours and moved quickly out of camera range. In that instance it somewhat resembled a canine, but it had a unique shape, almost like what a slender man would look like if he were crouched down ready to leap - and its head definitely was different.

"What the...!" Tegan said in disbelief.

"That's some shit!" said Carson. "Can you show us where this was shot?"

"Of course," stated Fred.

Fred told the group the photos came from the camera by the old fence post. The one by the barn did not turn up much. Despite the lack of photo evidence, Carson wanted to visit the barn location as well to see what the surrounding area looked like and if any evidence could be located.

Walking the grounds, the group didn't notice much by the tractor barn except some overturned bags of corn and the broken bale of hay.

"We keep small bales of hay here," said Fred. "The hay barn across the drive is where we keep the large round bales of hay that we feed to the cattle in the winter months."

As they started to walk past and head out toward the pasture to the other camera, Kareem noticed a small patch of dark fur sticking to a splintery side of one of the fence posts.

"Do you have a dog?" asked Kareem. Fred shook his head no. "I wish I had a baggie," stated Kareem. "Carson – get that McDonald's bag and a napkin. We can pick it up and put it in that for now."

Carson handed the bag to Kareem and said, "Whatever it is will smell like McGriddle now!"

Ty spoke up, "I thought you said the thing in the video was hairless?"

"Yes, mostly hairless, except for a patch of spiky dark fur down its back that resembled a spine or quills," added Fred.

As the group continued down the dirt path, Ty asked, "We saw a blurry image on the video, but how big is this creature?"

"Hard to say," said a puzzled Fred. "It was big from what I could see – maybe three feet tall and four feet long? But what we saw in the video standing on its hind legs, I don't know? Four to four and a half feet? He didn't do that when I saw him! The thing that really stood out though was the red eyes."

"Jesus! That's what's crazy," said Carson. "The description is like nothing I've ever seen before. Red eyes? Standing on hind legs? Canine teeth? What the hell?"

The group continued to the location of the other camera, walking amongst cattle paying little attention to them. Fred took them to the site of the camera that picked up a good visual of the creature, and near the spot where he himself had an encounter. Tegan and Kareem looked at the ground as they walked through the pasture.

"I doubt we find anything here. It's been a few days and the footprints are gone. Whatever was here is mixed with the hoof prints of cattle and washed away with rain from the other night," said Tegan quietly to Kareem.

"Yeah, there's nothing discernable here," added Kareem as he ambled and kicked at the ground.

Carson and Ty looked around at the landscape, cattle, and off into the horizon.

"It's a pretty nice place you have here, Fred," said Kareem.

"Thank you. It goes out a ways to those green metal fence posts. It's got a barbed wire and an electric fence – because the barbed wire isn't going to stop a two-thousand-pound bull if he decides he wants through there. The electric fence gives him another reason to reconsider – but it mustn't be too effective against that creature," said Fred.

"The pond and trees must be nice for the cattle," said Tegan.

"It's not bad for them. Best we can do. We have a lot of dead trees around the property. We had that drought a few years ago. It was really bad on us and we lost a lot of trees. The pond lost a lot of water during that time too. It has a natural spring feeding it, so even if she's low, she doesn't run dry. Of course with this heavy rain the past few nights the pond is doing pretty good," observed Fred.

"Hopefully not too much to wash away the grass for the cattle," commented Carson.

"We have some rolls of hills headed back toward the house. Those are water breaks to slow down the water so it doesn't wash the grass away," replied Fred.

Carson spoke, "I don't think we are going to find much here. Fred, can we take the photos and video link to the creature? I think it's best we analyze the photos you have and go from there."

"Yeah, and you mentioned it has been in the area – maybe we can talk to other ranchers in the area to see if there have been other sightings," added Ty.

"Right!" said Fred, "That's a good idea. See what they have seen. There was an incident just down the road a few days before mine and who knows where it may go next. Maybe I scared him off to somewhere else?"

Carson took the photos and had Fred text him the link. The group decided to review the information, set up a local meeting with the neighbors, and maybe learn more about what they were dealing with. Fred and Carson shook hands again, commented that they would each be in touch, and the four individuals returned to their vehicle, a little muddier and more confused than when they arrived.

As the car slowly navigated the driveway, Kareem looked at his watch and noted, "It's not even noon, we can't check into the hotel yet. Whatcha say we grab some lunch and a drink?" The car's passengers agreed. As Kareem looked at his phone and the Yelp mobile app, he suggested, "Southerleigh Fine Food & Brewery isn't too far from the hotel, and it's near the San Antonio Zoo. Maybe we can look at some animals?"

Carson spoke up, "Food & brewery sounds pretty good to me. That McGriddle is long gone after walking Fred's ranch."

"Done!" added Tegan. "Google me the directions."

Tegan took I-37 leaving Fred's ranch and headed north toward the next stop. Exiting the highway they briefly got lost on Avenue A and initially got exciting seeing a brewery on the corner. As the car pulled into the destination the group was impressed by the old outward appearance. An old silo bearing the name of the brewery looked much older than a newly opened craft brewery.

Still checking reviews, Kareem added, "This brewery moved into the old Pearl Brewery building. It just opened a few months ago." They walked inside and marveled at the interior of the building, an excellent integration of the old brewery with the new.

A tall, slender young man with curly blonde hair with a permanent cowlick approached. "Hello, I am Timothy. How are you this afternoon?"

"Hungry and thirsty!" said Ty.

"Well, we have twenty-one beers on tap – twelve of those now are house beers and the others guest taps - and our chef focuses on a contemporary take on Texas cross-cultural cuisine, especially Gulf Coast dishes," reported Timothy.

Kareem said, "We were digging that silo on the way in."

Timothy responded, "Can you believe that is a dining area? It is a private area that seats up to twenty people."

Ty looked over the drink menu. "Ooh, you have a rauchbier? I will have a Smoke on the Water." Kareem ordered the Darwinian IPA, Tegan the Seawall Belgian Wheat.

"I think I am going to stick to flights to learn my way around," said Carson as he continued to study the menu.

Timothy said, "We have a beginner flight of four or an advanced flight of eight – but you select four beers and get two of each."

"I am a beginner, so I will stick with that! How about the Dog Ate My Alarm, Putin's Revenge, Darwinian IPA, and Straight Outta Hopton."

"Nice choices," said Timothy, "I will give you a chance to look over the food options."

As Timothy walked away Carson addressed the team. "So what do you think about these photos?" he asked. "I've went on hunts looking for creatures for a long time and I haven't seen anything like it. Many times you don't get photos that you can actually make out. These are pretty good," he said as he flipped through the three photos Fred gave him. "And asking the people in the area for help is good, but how are we going to reach them? We only have a couple of days."

Tegan suggested, "We could contact the local radio station and see if we could get on for a few minutes, and maybe tonight we ask around at the grocery, restaurants, bars, or other stores in the area. Other than that just go door-to-door and see what turns up?"

"Speaking of turn up, I'm fixin' ta turn up on some shrimp boil with pork jowl & okra, and a side order of Gulf crab spiked mac & cheese!" replied Ty. Tegan selected the 44 Farms burger with bacon jam, Carson the cornmeal crusted saltwater catfish po'boy, and Kareem the 44 Farms Texas chili dog with hand-cut fries. Timothy returned with the beers, took the order, and disappeared toward the kitchen. Tegan grabbed her pint of Seawall and smelled.

"Hmm, it has a little hint of fennel I think." She took a sip. "Kind of like a hefe, but a hint of blueberry instead of banana. Not too strong. Could actually be a little stronger – but, yeah, definitely coriander of Belgian wheat. It's crisp and maybe a slight biscuit taste on the backend."

Kareem picked up the Darwinian. "Superbly hoppy!" he said after the first sip. "Mmm, that's a solid IPA, with just a hint of tropical fruit yogurt. The higher IBU's give it a nice bitterness, and maybe there is just a touch of mango?"

Carson looked at Tyson. "What type of beer did you say yours was?"

Tyson replied, "Rauchbier. It's an old German smoked beer that has a definite unique flavor created by using malted barley dried over an open flame." He took a sip of the Smoke on the Water. "Oh yes," he said as he sat back in his chair with a big, happy grin, "Big smokiness, hints of cherry at the start, clean finish. Some rye spiciness – this is going to pair well with that shrimp!"

Carson looked on his phone for some contact information at the radio station. He thought maybe Tegan could go to the radio station while the guys walked the town looking for people to speak to about any strange creatures in the area. He took a sip from the Darwinian IPA and agreed with Kareem's review. He found he liked the bitter-hoppiness flavor and concluded IPAs were much more flavorful and interesting than Lone Star. He moved on to the Dog Ate My Alarm, a milk stout with a luxurious chocolate appearance.

He was surprised the first sip was a little fizzy through the good thick head. Even though it was a milk stout, he picked up a good amount of coffee – a nice mixture of sweet coffee and chocolate. He looked at the menu and noted it read the beer was brewed with Café de Olla, a traditional Mexican coffee. Thinking of that ingredient, he thought it would have had a little cinnamon to it, but he loved the opaque dark color with the creamy brown head and chocolate flavor. "Man, this one is excellent," said Carson. Carson's call to K-BUC went through as Timothy brought the food. Carson walked away to make the call while the others reviewed the plates with anticipation.

A few minutes later Carson returned and told Tegan it was all set. She could go down to the station and ask for Jeff. He would get her on the air to make the announcement. He also revealed he just talked to the City Hall manager to reserve a conference room for the town hall meeting.

"Now, to dig into this po'boy!" he said with an eager grin. The portions were massive, which Carson thought was good because the menu price was a little higher than he anticipated. Kareem's gaze was momentarily diverted as another server walked by and delivered a pot roast sandwich to a nearby table.

"Damn, that looks good too," said Kareem – the sight and the smell distracting him. But he returned to his meal, satisfied with the Texas chili dog. The split bun gave a good appearance to the hot dog topped with chili and onions. "Not many things beat the simplicity of a good ol' fashion chili dog," he marveled.

As he took a bite, Kareem nodded in acceptance to the taste of the chili. Ty looked over the shrimp boil, unbuttoned his sleeves and slowly rolled them up. "Oh, it's on! On like Donkey Kong!" he exclaimed. Tegan looked at the thick hamburger and wondered how she could even eat it. The catfish po'boy was also amazing in size and appearance. The mac & cheese was rich and tasty, but Carson didn't really note any crab included. Maybe it meant flavored?

Soon Carson moved on to the Straight Outta Hopton, another IPA, but this one was over 11%.

"Wow – this one is dank and pungent," said Carson as he re-read the menu and noticed it stated the beer had a 134 IBU. "But it is amazing and has a wonder bitter finish…" Another sip and he concluded, "This might be my favorite beer so far!" Tyson looked over Carson's flight.

"You picked some really big ones. That last one is 11% and you still have Putin at 14%. Just that flight probably has more ABV than a full six-pack of Lone Star!" Carson shook his head in agreement.

"You're right – that Straight Outta Hopton was excellent, and I am looking forward to the final one. Leaving that one to last should improve the flavor as it has a chance to warm."

He took a sip and a smile crossed his face. "Whoa! Even better!" said Carson. "Rich, bitter chocolate, coffee, maybe a hint of bacon, creamy, yet it is so smooth and the high ABV is totally masked. Just from the taste I would have no idea how high it actually is." He took a final bite of the catfish and looked content. Carson added, "If we were finished for the night, I would have a full pint of that one!" Kareem threw down the napkin and suggested they get the check.

"We have a lot of work to do this weekend, so we should get to the hotel and get ready." He gave a wave and Timothy came over with the checks.

"The good thing is the hotel is just down the road," Carson added as he stood up.

"Before we head to the hotel," began Ty, "we should stop by one of San Antonio's greatest attractions, and it happens to be just a few miles away," he said.

"The Alamo?" answered Kareem.

"Nope. Not that one," responded Ty. "I'm talking about Barney Smith's Toilet Seat Art Museum," he said.

"Are you serious?" asked Tegan.

"Of course I am!" responded Ty. "This guy is in his 90s now, a retired plumber-turned-artist who has created a garage museum with over twelve hundred artistically designed toilet seats" Ty described. "These lids chronicle his life and the world around him. He has great stories, shows a little talk show video, and can tell you about any toilet seat that you look at - each of them come with a fantastic story. Where else can you see that? And, how can we possibly pass it up?" inquired Ty. Carson looked at Ty and turned toward Kareem and Tegan.

"I don't honestly know how we could skip that," he said. "And it is just down the street?" he asked.

"Yes, sir. And…it's free," said Ty.

"I'm sold," said Carson.

"Let's go check out these toilet seats!" Ty pulled out his phone. "Let's just see if he's in," he said. More softly he added, "You have to phone ahead first to check, according to the Yelp comments," he said as the phone rang.

Barney answered the phone and said he would open the museum up for the travelers. He was extremely accommodating and welcomed the opportunity to showcase his work to them.

Less than a four-mile drive down Broadway they pulled up to the museum and the doors to the garage were propped open. Barney

Smith greeted the group. He happily gave them a tour and in-depth description of many of his seats. Everything ranging from several toilet seats with automobile license plates to toilet seats decorated with everything from Troll dolls to a piece of the Berlin Wall to a portion of the Challenger space shuttle.

The group was in awe as they made their way through the garage with the slow-walking Barney, busy telling them stories about several individual pieces.

"Who knew a toilet seat could be so interesting?" said Tegan.

Near the end of the museum they stopped at a room to the far right. In the back corner a small television was set up with recordings of Barney's TV appearances on the Montel Williams Show, The View, and other news and radio shows. Each member of the group signed the visitor's log and even signed the toilet seat depicting the state of Texas. The detour to the museum took about forty-five minutes. The group left enjoying the stories of Barney, the pride he showed in his craftsmanship, and a passion and energy he displayed. It was well worth the extra time to see this unique museum. They climbed back into the car as Barney gave them a wave and called out "Thank you for stopping by," as they drove away.

Eight miles later, the group pulled up to the Red Roof Inn – a terracotta and white striped building with the American and Texas flags flying out front. Tegan and Ty waited in the car while Carson and Kareem went to check in the rooms. Quickly returning with keys in hand, the guys walked to the car and began unloading the travel bags.

"Looks like we are side-by-side on the second floor," said Carson. "Room 207 and 208." Ty examined the pool and the group walked toward the white iron staircases leading to their room on the second floor of the three-story motel.

"We might have to take a dip in that bad boy later tonight. I hope you boys and girls brought your swim trunks!"

Opening the door to room 207 Carson was pleasantly surprised. For the price he expected a small, dingy room similar to the roadside motel in *Joyride*. He was prepared not to answer the door if anyone knocked asking for "Candy Cane." But this room was nice: two large queen beds, a desk, a nice-sized small refrigerator, and a dresser with a good-sized television. It was not a flat screen, but it was good enough. Carson sat his duffle bag down.

"If you don't mind I think I will grab a shower and get ready for this evening," Carson said.

"Go ahead. I am just going to relax and watch some TV for a bit. Too bad we didn't pick up some shower beers on the way!" said Ty.

Carson grabbed a handful of clothes, a small back of toiletries from his duffel back, and disappeared into the bathroom. Turning on the shower he began to get undressed as the water warmed. He was impressed by the water pressure and sticking a hand in to check the temperature he found it to his liking. The base of the shower was a white plastic bathtub. As Carson pulled the curtain to the side and stepped in, the plastic tub make a loud "creak!" Carson instantly stopped and paused. As he fully entered the water stream and pulled the curtain back, the tub continued with the loud noise. He became nervously uncertain with each cautious step. The tub made him question his lunch choices and briefly, he wondered if a diet and exercise regimen was drastically needed. Then his thoughts turned to empathy for the people staying in room 107.

Fifteen minutes later, Carson reemerged wearing olive green cargo shorts and a navy blue t-shirt with orange text reading "Bigfoot saw me! But nobody believes him!" Ty looked him over from head to toe, shaking his head.

"I see you are with the guys at BroBible on the defense of cargo shorts. Where's the mandals? You're over twenty-five; you should stop wearing cargo shorts. What's next? The backward ball cap?" Carson shot a look back at Ty.

"Don't hate, bro. They are an American classic. Like blue jeans. Besides, they are comfortable!"

"Yeah, well maybe they didn't believe Bigfoot saw you because he said you were spotted in cargo shorts and it's 2015!" snarked Ty.

Carson tossed his wet towel at Ty and countered, "Don't ask me to hold any of your shit because you don't have pockets while we are out in the woods!" Ty took the wet towel and snapped the end at Carson's bare legs.

"I'm going to get ready, fool."

"I can't wait to see that fashion show," mumbled Carson.

"One thing's for sure, we're not going back in time, Dr. Brown!" quipped Ty.

Ty returned from his shower in a pair of black pants, a solid dark blue dress shirt unbuttoned and the sleeves rolled up, black belt, and black shoes. Carson just looked on silently. Tyson crowed, "Trunk club!" Carson shook his head.

"Maybe we should check on Tegan and Kareem?" suggested Ty.

Carson and Ty knocked on the door to find Tegan already dressed and ready to go. Kareem was still in the bathroom getting ready.

"What's the delay?" asked Ty.

"You know Kareem," said Tegan. "He's more of a diva than me! It takes him forever to get ready!"

Finally, Kareem came out brushing product into his hair. He looked around the group. "What? We are going out. We should look good!" said Kareem.

"Tegan, are you ready for the radio station? I think if you drop us around De Leon's Grocery & Market we can make our way through there, Tejano Taco House, the Elmendorf First Baptist Church, and some of the neighbors. Maybe something will turn up. We will hold the town hall tomorrow at the Elmendorf City Hall. I already cleared that with the clerk," said Carson.

"Maybe we can create and print some flyers downstairs in the business center to hang up around town?" suggested Tegan.

"Good idea. Let's take Fred's photos with us," added Kareem. "Maybe someone will recognize that animal."

Downstairs in the business center, Carson took a picture of the image in the photos with his smarphone, then emailed them to himself. "I can use Paint to crop it and add an image to our sign," suggested Carson. He was quite proficient with Paint and in a matter of minutes had a decently designed flyer with the image and his cell phone number. They printed twelve copies to post on area businesses. The town hall was set for tomorrow evening at 6 p.m. They decided that would be a good time after most folks got off work and had a chance to get to the building. They hoped hitting the radio station and businesses along the nearby streets would generate some leads from the locals who maybe saw the unknown beast. A few minutes later Tegan dropped the three men off at De Leon's Grocery and Market. Saying her goodbyes, she drove off to make her appointment at the radio station and told the boys she would meet them back at the hotel later that night.

De Leon's Grocery looked like a small town general store, and that's what it was. A moss-green building with darker green trim, the name spelled out in yellow text outlined in the same green trim. The yellow writing also revealed the store had groceries, fresh produce & deli meats, and freshly prepared sandwiches. The outside Vivco Ice upright outdoor ice merchandiser would serve as a good home for one of the newly printed flyers. Ty suggested they go inside and see if any workers or customers recognized the animal in the brochure. Once inside, they found the story mostly empty.

As they walked through the aisles they found one man stocking shelves. Frank Jackson turned eagerly to see if the men needed assistance. Frank was the cashier and night time stock clerk at DeLeon's. In his early forties, he was below average height and average weight with hard features. He had short, straight, strawberry blond hair, and dark hazel eyes.

"Can I help you boys find anything?" asked Frank. Carson and Ty looked at each other.

Carson turned and said, "I hope you can." He handed Frank one of the flyers. "Have you seen anything unusual around the area the past few weeks? Anything that looks like this?"

Frank studied the blurry image for a moment. "No, sir. I haven't seen it…but…but I heard something was going on in the area. Something with a couple of ranchers losing cattle and some chickens. Folks come in here and talk, so I hear things, but so far I haven't seen nuthen. I didn't believe it at first, but it was in the papers. It's mighty scary thinkin' somethin' is out there killing folks' livestock. That's their livelihood!"

While the men listened to Frank, another customer walked in and looked over the potato chip selection. A Hispanic man of somewhat short stature, he had a plump, round figure and curly brown hair with a thick beard. He nervously looked over at the men and made his way toward the soda, but was obviously listening intently.

"I wish I had seen that thing," said Frank.

"Well, if you hear anything else can you give me a call? I will leave you my number," said Carson. Kareem looked over at the soda and saw the plump man quickly glance back down at the selection. Kareem walked over.

"Excuse me, sir?" he said as he extended a hand. The man looked and slowly extended his hand with caution. It was apparent he was awkward and shy around strangers. "Have you seen anything like this photo?" Kareem inquired as he presented the man with the same flyer he showed Fred.

Jorge Villa studied the picture and his dark features seemed to turn a little paler. He looked up at Kareem with dark gray eyes and bushy eyebrows. He didn't say anything as he looked back down at the paper.

"Sir?" repeated Kareem.

"Si! I saw it!" said a nervous Jorge with a strong accent. Ty and Carson overheard Jorge's comments and briskly walked over to join the conversation.

"What did you see?" Carson asked excitedly. Jorge seemed reluctant to continue, but Ty assured him it was okay.

"I like to do the wood carving and got a little shed behind my house." He paused.

"Go on," coaxed Kareem.

"And three nights ago…Monday evening it was…I was working in my shed when I heard a noise. It was a sound I hadn't heard before so it caught my attention," reported Jorge.

"Did you see what was making the noise?" asked Ty.

"Yeah – I got up and walked outside. It was nearly pitch black, but I saw this large animal under the moonlight standing over by a tree at the corner of my property. It looked at me and then turned and ran down a trail and into the woods behind the lot. I was scared! It was night so I couldn't make much of it, but the moon was out and I could see it had big teeth. But the thing I remember most was the red eyes!" The three men looked at each other.

"Red eyes?" clarified Carson, "That sounds like the same animal we are looking for! Have you seen it since?"

"No, not since that night – and I hope I don't see it again. I think it was el diablo!"

Frank joined the group and said, "That must have been some fright!"

"Siii! Tengo pesadillas toda la semana!" said Jorge. Kareem placed his hand on the man's shoulder.

"It's okay, señor. We're looking for it and hopefully we find it. Can you call us if you see anything else?" Jorge looked up and shook his head, obviously still nervous from the encounter. Jorge walked to the cash registered with a six-pack of RC Cola and a bag of pork rinds. After he paid, Carson wrote his phone number on the top of the receipt.

"Thank you…you've been helpful! We are having a town meeting tomorrow at 6 p.m. over at City Hall if you two guys want to come out. Maybe hear what others are seeing and share your stories," added Carson.

He shook both men's' hands and headed back outside. Ty walked back in and purchased a roll of Scotch tape for the flyers. He handed it to Carson who hung the first sign on the outside ice machine.

Heading from the driveway of De Leon's the group walked down FM 327 toward Tejano's Taco House. Carson looked around as they walked.

"With this area that thing could be almost anywhere! Almost all of these places have trees and a thick brush that a sucker like that could hide," said Carson dejectedly. The night air was warm, but not humid, which was a relief because the walk to Tejano's was a little further than they thought. When they arrived they were a bit surprised – it was actually a house. Outside of the house they found a newspaper rack with advertisement papers supporting local businesses. Kareem picked one up and flipped through it. Inside he found a Tejano's coupon for 60% off one entrée.

"Who's hungry?" asked Kareem. Inside only one customer was dining.

Jackson Lewis sat alone at a table eating a three enchilada plate with rice and beans. He had a thick afro and a clean-shaven face, medium height and lean build with smooth features. He had a quiet confidence about him. The server from Tejano's was in the back leaving Jackson alone in the dining room. Ty approached, apologized for interrupting his meal, but asked if he had a minute. Jackson nodded his head up but didn't say anything.

Ty showed him the flyer and asked if he had seen the animal in the area. Jackson quickly tilted his head and confirmed he had seen the creature in the photo.

"I am skeptical about strange things," he confessed. "I think life has purpose and meaning. I hate that science fiction shit and I don't much care much for strange people or things either…but I can't explain the creature I saw Sunday night," he explained.

"Sunday?" replied Carson. He and Kareem looked at Ty.

"That's just the day before Frank saw it," said Ty.

Jackson told the story of driving home late at night. "I came around a corner on Old Corpus Christi Road. As I turned the corner the light shined on the road ahead and this thing ran across the street. Damn near hit it!" said Jackson.

"Did you see what it was?" asked Carson. "I just saw the ass-end of it, but the damn thing was big – like about three feet tall. It had long legs, was slender, and had a long tail," remembered Jackson.

"Like a wolf or coyote, you think?" asked Ty.

"Naw, man. It was taller than that – and longer. He disappeared into the weeds and trees. I stopped the car and tried to shine the headlights on it, but he was gone."

Carson told Jackson about the town hall meeting the next evening and wrote down his phone number in case he saw anything unusual again.

"I don't think we're going to get those tacos," said Ty. "We are getting some leads and need to keep going. Whatchu boys think?" Carson and Kareem agreed. "We could go to the Baptist church or turn back the other way and check out City Hall and Rail Logix," suggested Ty.

Carson said, "Let's go toward City Hall. We can finalize details on the meeting for tomorrow." They thanked Jackson for the information, hung a flyer on the bulletin board in the taco house, and headed back down the street.

Walking down the street toward City Hall, the men rehashed what they learned earlier today. "I think we are making good progress," said Ty.

"This thing is still here in the neighborhood and has been spotted as recently as a couple of days ago!" Let's hit up that mechanic shop, then finish up at City Hall," suggested Carson.

The bay door to Rail Logix was open and a pair of legs extended from under a gray minivan. As the men walked up a voice from under the car greeted them.

"Howdy! It'll be just a minute," the voice said.

"Take your time," said Carson. "We're just here to ask a couple of questions."

The man rolled on the creeper from underneath the vehicle and looked up at the three men. "You fellas cops or somethin'?" inquired the man. Ty and Carson chuckled.

"No, not those kind of questions!" reassured Carson. After rolling entirely from under the car, the man stood, wiped his grease-covered hands on his pant legs, and shook their hands.

Phillip Cooper was tall and slightly chubby. He had round cheeks and gentle, warm brown eyes. His light brown hair was concealed underneath a John Deere cap that was also slightly stained with grease and oil. He spoke with a slight accent and down-home country charm that undoubtedly made him well-liked in the community.

"We're looking for an animal," said Kareem, again showing the photograph. "Can you help us out? Have you seen anything?"

"Well shit fire!" exclaimed Phillip. "Last night…sure did!"

"Here?" asked Ty. "Nope, but not too fer. Just down the road a piece. I was working late here the past few weeks. We've been busier than a than a cat coverin' shit on a rock pile, then it's dark when I get home ta work in my garage…I'm restoring a '67 Nova, two-door hardtop coupe – real nice!" He bent over to pick up a plastic Burger King cup on the floor and spit his dip onto the paper towel inside.

"Anyways, I just got out from under the hood and was fixin' to fetch a cold one from the house. That's when I saw it in my yard eating some apples that had fallen from my tree." Carson was intrigued. This was just yesterday!

"How big was it? What happened next?"

"It was every bit three foot tall and maybe four foot long. I thought it was one of them feral pigs and I thought about some nice bacon. I went to get my shotgun, but that's when he took off."

"A pig?!" Kareem sounded baffled. "Are you sure it's the same animal?"

"Yep, that's him – that spiky fur on the back is the same. It wasn't quite like a pig – it was either hairless or short, close hair like a pig. It was shaped kinda like it from the back, but it was skinnier than a rail. It had long legs in the back, but the front looked more like a wolf or one of them hyena," said Phillip.

"Well one thing's for sure," said Carson, "there aren't…or shouldn't be…any hyenas around here!"

Ty looked at the guys, "well whatever it is, when we find that thing, it won't be around here either!" Phillip shook his head while he spat in the cup again.

"Yep, that thing had some fierce-looking teeth. I am sure it could do some damage to whatever it gets a-holt of," said Phillip. Carson told him about the cattle over at Fred Dalton's ranch and the neighbor's ranch before that. "Well you boys better bag him then!" said Phillip.

Carson replied, "Hopefully the people in the area can sleep once we figure out what it is and take it out of here!" "I'm sure everyone will be happier'n a two-peckered dog when you do," replied Phillip.

"Indeed they will!" said Carson. He invited Phillip to the town hall the next day.

"One more stop and let's call it a night?" asked Ty.

"I think we have enough from the talks tonight to set up an investigation," said Carson.

"Yep, and who knows what'll come from Tegan's radio spot," added Ty. "We are going to need some equipment if we stay out here. Some tents, some cameras for sure. Maybe headlamps, walkie-talkies, and a thermal camera. I will make a couple of calls tomorrow and I think I can get them for a few days while we investigate," said Ty.

The final stop was City Hall; however, it was already closed by the time they arrived. The doors were locked and the parking lot was empty. They were surprised that it looked like a bricked mobile home and that also contained the police department.

"Since the police department works from here I would've imagined the building to be open," said Carson. "I guess they're out patrolling." Meanwhile, Kareem stepped aside to call a cab. They taped a flyer on the front door and waited for the cab to arrive for the return trip to the Red Roof Inn. Ty looked at his cellphone while waiting.

"Tegan texted. She made the announcement and everything is on for tomorrow," he said.

"Great!" said Kareem. Slapping the palm of his hands against the top of his legs he asked, "Who's thirsty?"

The trio returned to their rooms and shared a bottle of Jester King's Black Metal Farmhouse Imperial Stout Ty had brought in his duffle bag.

10 TOWN HALL

Friday, June 19, 2015

The crew arrived at City Hall approximately 4:30 p.m. to set up for the town hall meeting. Carson began to get a little nervous as they walked toward the building.

"I don't know about this," said Carson hesitantly. "I was all fired up about it yesterday, but maybe we are in over our heads. I mean, it's been years since you and I did this stuff in college, and maybe I am just not good enough to do it," said Carson dejectedly.

"Snap out of it, man! These people need us. As Fred said, they are out of options and they think we can help. You and I used to have fun doing this, and that was just for shits and giggles. Now we can actually help people. You always were so confident on our hunts before and I admired that and looked up to your leadership. I know the past few years have been difficult, but you got this! I am proud of you for getting out of the house, trying new things, meeting new people, and taking the chance on this adventure. Now let's go in there, kick some ass, and take some names," Ty said encouragingly.

The pep talk appeared to work as a determined look crossed Carson's face.

"You're right. Let's do this!" he said he said with a new sense of purpose.

Entering the building they met Natalie Simmons to review the room's layout and discuss the evening's events. Natalie had worked with the city for nearly twenty years and thought there would be a good turnout.

"Folks 'round here are plenty scared. This isn't the first time there's been strange animals in the area."

"That's right," said Ty. "About ten years ago there was a creature spotted and they called it the Elmendorf beast. It turned out to be coyote with severe mange."

Kareem said, "Well after what we heard last night, who knows what we are dealing with. The descriptions ranged from wolf and hyenas to pigs to kangaroos. That's why this meeting is going to be so important."

Tegan suggested that they open the meeting up with only a brief background of why they were there.

"We don't want to give too many details that could inspire their stories. I think we should keep it vague and see what the people have to say." "That's a good idea," agreed Carson, "We can take notes and ask some of the people with better leads to stay behind and schedule individual interviews over the next day or so."

Ty and Tegan finished setting up some tables that included soft drinks, water, and snacks donated by De Leon's Grocery.

"That should about do it," said Ty.

Soon the door opened and the first people began arriving. A couple at first, but then a few more. Minutes later a steady stream entered. Soon, the one-hundred-fifty person-capacity seating was full and a few people stood in the back of the room. It was a larger turnout than they expected.

"Hopefully we can get some good leads from the room," said Carson.

The crew looked at each other with anticipation. What would the evening bring? It was all new for Tegan and Kareem and they were looking forward to hearing from the people of Elmendorf. Carson gave a quiet, single clap and rubbed his palms together as they began to sweat. He looked at the others and took a deep breath. "Let's do this," he said.

Carson approached the podium and adjusted the microphone to his level. He surveyed the crowd, cleared his throat, and began to speak. The crowd murmurs quieted down as he stood at the podium ready to begin.

"Wow," he said, then quickly turned to look at his crew. Turning back to face the audience he continued. "I'm really beside myself to see the turnout here today. This is great! We didn't expect this many people. We want to thank you all for coming and taking time out of your evening to come to our meeting. We really appreciate your time and assistance. My name is Carson Quinn and I am one of the field researchers for the group. Along with me today are Tyson Carr, Kareem Ortiz, and Tegan Stone. I would like to start things off by saying a special thank you to Natalie Simmons from the City Hall for providing the space and helping to set this town hall meeting up on such short notice. We appreciate your hospitality and the generosity of working on getting this together."

The crowd looked on eagerly. Natalie stepped slightly forward and gave a quick nod of her head as the crowd applauded. Carson began again after the applause died down.

"Ty and I started this group a few years ago when we were in college. We wanted to go out and do scientific research and investigate unique North American creatures that were as of yet unrecognized by mainstream science. We've heard reports of such an animal in the area, and we brought Tegan and Kareem along to assist in the investigation. We are interested in speaking with anyone here who may want to share their stories with us, and we'd be happy to talk with you one-on-one. You can always count on the fact that any information you give us will be strictly confidential. We will never share your identity, your whereabouts, or anything else. So with that in mind, we'd like to invite you to share your stories, anything you've recently witnessed – even if it seems minor. The information you share can maybe help to identify what this creature is and hopefully capture and remove it before anything else happens. You know, meetings like this are great because it gets people thinking 'oh, I'm not crazy!' 'Cause there are people in here who have seen tracks, heard noises, and caught glimpses of this creature. So maybe hearing their stories and experiences can reassure you if you have seen something and perhaps quickly dismissed it as your imagination."

A hand slowly raised in the second row. Ty pointed at the man. "Yes, sir?" The man stood and used his elbow to nudge the woman beside him.

"This lady here has had a sighting," he said. Ty perked up.

"Outstanding! Would you like to tell us about it?"

Lily Shaw shot her husband a quick, aggravated look. "Jonathan! You tell 'em!" she softly objected.

"No, you!" replied Jonathan.

As she nervously stood, Carson reassured her. "It's okay, ma'am. Any information you have is fine. Even the smallest detail." Lily gave Jonathan another irritated look before beginning. She was an average woman of medium height and lean build. She wore a small gold earring in each ear, her blond hair placed in a bun, and light brown eyeshadow around her green eyes. Reluctantly she began.

"About two weeks ago we had an incident on our farm where we had a young calf come up missing. We live in a farmhouse on several acres of well-preserved land and have a herd of cattle, some chickens, and a dark brown horse. We later discovered the calf had been killed by something."

Jonathan interrupted, "Tell 'em what you seen before that."

"Well, a few days before that," she nervously continued, "I was out picking apples beyond the barn. It was just starting to get dark. I finished up and was just starting to walk back to the house looking at the apples in my basket and planning which ones to use for pie later the next day… and as I walked back I heard a russlin' in the brush behind me. I looked up and turned…I saw this thing standing beside a tree about maybe sixty yards away. It was dark in color and tall. I couldn't tell if it had fur or what not from that distance, but what stood out most was the red eyes. I hadn't seen anything with eyes like that before. It just stood there looking at me. I felt hypnotized for a moment, then I just took off running toward the house and said to myself don't stop until you get to the door."

"You said it stood?" clarified Kareem.

"Yes, on two legs," responded Lily. "It had two front legs too, but the back ones were longer and it could stand up but was kind of hunched over," added Lily.

Jonathan stood. He had a medium, solid build, long face, creased brow with hazel-blue, bagged eyes, and a prominent Adam's apple. "I think that's the same thing that took to our calf a few days later!" he said.

"What did you notice about the calf when you found it?" asked Carson.

"Well, there were puncture marks on its neck, and some deep scratches on its back, but otherwise it was intact. Whatever it was didn't eat it like you would think a wolf or coyote would do. The weird thing was all of the blood was gone from it," reported Jonathan.

The guys in the group looked at each other recognizing Jonathan's story fit with the other sightings of the same animal.

Tegan asked, "Have you had any more sightings since then or had any more incidents on the farm?"

"No, ma'am. Just those couple of days. A few days later I heard my neighbor Fred had some of the same things happen to him on his farm." The group again turned and looked at each other.

Ty spoke to Carson in a hushed tone, "This family lives close to Fred. We're definitely gonna to want to meet up with them later and get more information." Carson turned to the Shaws.

"Thank you for the information. We would like to speak afterward and see if we can talk to you in more detail privately if that's possible." Jonathan Shaw nodded in agreement.

Another man stood in the middle of the audience. He had a large, massive body with strong muscles, cold, narrow brown eyes, well-kept black hair, and a thin chinstrap. He appeared to be a fan of Latin jazz, as he was wearing a Tito Puente t-shirt and jeans. He also sported a fancy watch which gave Carson the impression he was hard-working and career focused.

Taking the microphone he said, "Hello. My name is Ronaldo Amaya. I saw the animal just last week."

"Last week?" repeated Ty as he jotted some notes on an index card. "Go on. What did you see, Ronaldo?"

"Well, it was in the woods by my house, and it was dark. I had a long, stressful day at work and I wanted to relax by spending some time in the woods. I get re-centered in the woods," reported Ronaldo.

Carson quoted John Muir, "The clearest way into the universe is through a forest wilderness."

"Yes, but this night I couldn't shake an uneasy feeling I had," said Ronaldo. "I felt like something was closing in on me. I pulled out a flashlight from my back pocket. It was dark and creepy, and I started to sweat. I was really scared. As I scanned the landscape with the flashlight, that's when I saw it! It was hideous – the most grotesque thing I've seen in my life! It was greenish-brown in color with a scaly, sparsely fur covered hide. But the scariest thing was the huge red eyes! And, an equally large mouth, crowded with long fang-like teeth!"

"What was it doing?" asked Kareem.

"It just stood there with its left clawed hand resting on a tree and the right clawed the air toward me. The only thing I could think was to get out of there. I dropped the flashlight and hauled ass toward the house. I turned a couple of times and looked over my shoulder, but it wasn't following. Didn't matter- I continued to run until I made it back to the house. I remember the low growl and hiss-like noise it made. That's still fresh in my mind!"

"What do you think it was?" asked Tegan.

"I don't know – it looked like a hellhound or something. It was tall, but hunched over. On all fours it looked like it would have been big, but standing on its hind legs it was frightening!" added Ronaldo.

Carson replied, "Have you been walking in those woods long? Have you ever seen anything like it?"

"I have lived there for over five years and have always enjoyed walking in the woods...but now...now I haven't been out there since. I haven't seen it again, but I haven't went looking either," stated Ronaldo.

"Hopefully we can find the creature, remove it, and you can get back to enjoying the woods," added Ty. Ronaldo shook his head affirmatively and returned to his seat.

"Do we have any others who want to share an encounter with us? After we conclude the meeting we will remain here for some time and can talk to you about any information you have if you do not wish to share in front of the group," said Carson.

After a few seconds with no one speaking up it seemed as if the meeting was about to conclude until another man decided to stand and speak. Just below average height and lean with soft features, Dexter Allen was in his mid-thirties, had long, wavy brown hair, and pale brown eyes.

"If we have time for another story, I'd like to share my experience. I also have some photos that I took," revealed Dexter.

"Photos?! We definitely would be interested in seeing any photographs you have!" said an excited Carson.

"I work for a company just on the edge of town. It a fairly rural part of town - quiet and usually very little traffic. I was making some collection calls in the evening about a week ago and was leaving the office around 8:45 p.m. As I walked across the parking lot to my car I was looking at Facebook on my phone and texting to my friends to see if they wanted to meet up for a drink. I looked up and paused because it struck me that it was quiet. Like deathly quiet; no birds, no barking dogs, no frogs or insects making noise. That struck me as odd. There is a pond not too far behind the building and there are always frogs or some insect making noises in the evenings," said Dexter.

"As I scanned the area, I didn't see anything at first, but then I noticed a shadow walking around the pond. It walked like a wolf but was longer and taller than any wolf I had ever seen. It was also slender – like a malnourished extra-large Mr. Bigglesworth. Then the creature heard a noise and it stood up on its slender hind legs. It stayed in that position for a while smelling the air and looking around," reported Dexter.

"Wow, that's incredible!" said Kareem.

"Yes – and I still had my phone out, so I clicked on the camera app and zoomed in. The photos came out a little green and grainy due to the natural lighting, but the images can be made out," said Dexter. "I clicked the video camera and filmed a few seconds as the creature stood on his legs, then dropped down, and ran into the woods beyond the pond."

"That had to be scary," added Carson, "What happened next?"

"Well, I just stood in disbelief trying to run through possibilities in my head to explain what I just saw. I had never seen a large animal that was equally comfortable on two legs as it was four," recalled Dexter.

He described that when it stood on its hind legs it was not fully erect, but hunched over like an old Hollywood monster movie. He recalled even after it ran off he cautiously walked toward the pond, passing his car by a couple of feet, yet close enough to reach its safety should the strange animal return. But the beast did not return. It disappeared into the rapidly falling darkness that engulfed the woods. He stood in wonderment and a little fear.

"I'd love to take a look at those photos and video!" said Ty. Carson called Dexter up to the podium to review his evidence. Kareem assisted by plugging the USB cable to Dexter's phone and Carson's computer. Once connected to the computer and the running projector, Dexter pulled up three photos and a short ten-second video taken of the creature. A couple of photos showed the creature standing on its hind legs and one on all fours. Dexter had zoomed in when taking the photo so the creature was larger, but the photo quality was grainier. Still, the features and size of the beast could be seen.

The crowd gasped in shock and awe when the images opened and a low chatter continued as people talked to their neighbors about what they saw on the screen. Looking at the photos the creature didn't match any animal the group had seen before. It was easy to tell how the reported sightings ranged in comparison from wolf and coyote to boar, alien, devil, and even kangaroo. It surely resembled a combo of each animal – like a Texas platypus. The video showed the animal drop from two legs down to all fours, then turn, and disappear into the wooded area.

"Wow, I don't know what to say," said a stunned Carson. "Can you email me a copy of those pictures? We'd like to take a closer look and begin to determine what this might be. We're up against something that truly looks unknown."

After a minute or two of soaking in everything they just witnessed, Ty stepped up to the podium. "Well…I think that is a good way to end the session…Wow, I am still shocked. If you do have any other information or want to talk to us we will be here for a while longer. We would also like to have a couple of you stay, and get some details from you. We want to speak in further depth with those people and work to set up an investigation to hopefully capture this animal. Dexter, if you could stay and also the Shaws. If you do want to meet further with us you can stick around, or you can also write your name, number, and a description of your encounter in the notebook on our table up here. Thank you for coming out and sharing your experiences with us. We hope to have some answers as soon as possible," concluded Ty.

The crowd stood and slowly began to file out, others waiting around to see who else might come forward with a story they could eavesdrop on. The Shaws remained, as did Dexter, and a couple of other individuals. The small group lingered around hesitating in the balance of stepping forward or walking out. Ty began to unplug the computer and break down the presentation equipment as the other investigators began to pack up and prepare to leave.

Jordan Phillips was a man with deep-set blue eyes, a scratchy unshaven beard, and long blonde hair. He had a tall and narrow build kind of like Shaggy from *Scooby Doo* with an equally charming and easy-going personality. He approached Tegan and Ty near the snack table and shared his recent encounter.

"Hello," he said nervously, "My name is Jordan, and I recently saw that animal." Ty and Tegan stopped what they were doing and listened intently.

"You did?" asked Tegan.

"Yes, I am an amateur astronomer and I saw the creature one night while stargazing… I like to get out of the city limits and look at the stars where it is darker. About six weeks ago I went out to watch the Eta Aquariids meteor shower. The peak activity was in the predawn hours the morning of May 7. Even though the shower is better viewed in the southern hemisphere due to the later sunrise, I thought with an average near-peak activity of more than forty meteors per hour, I stood a good chance of seeing some before heading off to work. So, I drove out to one of my favorite spots, out at Braunig Lake Park."

"The lake? What did you see there, Jordan?" asked Carson as he walked over, joining the others.

Jordan continued, "I walked along the sidewalk and although there were some campers in tents, it was unusually quiet. There are some animals that live there like white-tail deer, some smaller mammals, and a large number of migratory and wading birds like tri-colored herons, common moorhen, red-winged blackbirds, and Harris' Hawk. There are some tree-lined areas and tall reeds along part of the lake."

"Sounds like a nice spot to view wildlife," replied Carson.

"It is. And a nice spot for channel cat fishing too. Well, as I came around a bend and into one of these more secluded areas, I heard a rustling noise from the reeds. I had been looking up at the sky the whole time, so I stopped and looked toward the noise. That's when I saw, about twenty feet away, the animal that was in that guy's photos."

"Dexter's photos?" inquired Tegan.

"Yes, ma'am! It was on all fours and appeared to be feeding on a small deer."

"Did it eat the deer?" asked Tegan?

"No," replied Jordan, "it wasn't eating it, but it looked like it was biting it on the neck. Like a vampire or something."

"I froze with fright when I saw it. It looked up, dropped the deer's neck, and gave a hissing-like noise. It was still early and the sun was just coming up – I remember the bright red eyes it had as it looked at me. I didn't know what to do – I was far away from the car at that point and not even close to the campers. I thought I might be next, but it turned and disappeared into the reeds. I gave up on the meteor shower after that and didn't even go to work. I called the boss on my way home, hold him I wasn't feeling well and went back home to bed. I hoped to not see that beast again, but when I heard about this meeting I wanted to come and see if I was crazy. It's nice to know I am not, but I am spooked by all of the people here today that have reported seeing it. Makes me nervous going back out at night. I certainly hope you guys find it and kill it or at least get it out of here!"

Kareem had a map of the town and drew a red X on the map in the location Jordan reported his sighting. He added an X to the site of some of the other stories they heard in town yesterday and earlier in the meeting. He called Lily and Jonathan Shaw over to add their location to the map.

"We want to map out all of the sightings so we can see if there is a pattern. Maybe then we can narrow down the search area and get a realistic search radius for our investigation," said Kareem.

Lily pointed to their location on the map, and Kareem added their neighbor Fred Dalton's ranch. He drew a circle around the region with his finger.

"With two sightings right there, this seems like a strong possibility. Some of the others are not too far away so it could be a good sign the animal is staying in that area," analyzed Kareem. Jonathan wrote down the couple's phone number and address in the notebook.

"We'd love to have you come out and take a look around. See if you find any more clues or hopefully find the animal," said Jonathan.

"We will call and set something up in the next day or two," assured Kareem. After an exchange of handshakes the couple left the town hall hopefully something could be done to return the community the peaceful life it knew only weeks ago.

Two other attendees awaited an opportunity to speak to the team. A short, thin woman with mousy-brown hair, gray eyes, and dark freckles across her nose identified herself as school teacher Sharon Chapman. The other woman, a tall, thin lady whose multiple tripping episodes walking to the podium led Carson to believe she wasn't particularly graceful introduced herself as Sophie Thompson, lab assistant. Despite the clumsy nature, Carson picked up on her kind-hearted, dedicated to helping others quality. Plus her rosy cheeks and her ability to blush easily added to the appeal of her straight, neck-length red hair and sparkling emerald eyes.

Carson was pleased with the number of leads that they received in the meeting as he prepared to talk to the two ladies. He glanced over at the notebook on the table, and although he could not see how many names were written, it looked like there were at least a few. He thought ahead to the process of narrowing down the potential interviewees and investigation sites. The anticipation made him both nervous and excited. Maybe with all of this information they could find and remove this predator.

Sharon spoke first. "I teach third grade at Freedom Elementary School."

Ty asked, "Where is that located in relation to these other locations on the map?"

"It's about seven miles away, out South Highway 181. Just under three miles away from Braunig Lake. I arrived early to school one day about six weeks ago. It was still dark outside," said Sharon.

"Three miles, plus the animal would have to cross that highway," said Carson looking at the map.

"Our school is just off Liedecke Road and it is quiet out there. Some small businesses, but mostly rural," said Sharon. "I only caught a quick glimpse, but I saw what I thought was a coyote running across the back of the parking lot."

Carson asked, "Have you seen coyotes there before?"

"No, I've seen coyotes, but not by the school. This animal was taller than what I have seen before, and after hearing these people today, I think it may be the same animal. I remember it was fast too. It had long, thin legs, but it was agile and quick for its size," recalled Sharon.

"Have you seen it since then?" asked Tegan.

"No, just the one day," said Sharon.

"That's extremely helpful," said Carson. "The other stories didn't talk about how quick it was, so it's good to know what we are up against when we go out to investigate," he concluded.

Turning to Sophie Carson asked about her sighting. "I have not seen the creature," she said. "And I hope not to see it alive! I do work as a lab assistant, and I thought if you capture or kill this creature, you will need someone to run tests on it to help identify it. I can help you all with the lab analysis if you need that," she offered. Ty was obviously excited.

"Yes, we need some assistance with that. I hadn't actually worked through the problem that far ahead. I think with this information we can set up a pretty good investigation and if he is still here I think we can catch him. When we do, we will need your help," replied Ty.

Carson added, "Yes, for sure. We appreciate your offer! That will be important in solving this mystery." She wrote down her information in the notebook and left.

Kareem looked at the group and at Natalie Simmons who remained behind to help with the cleanup. "I think that went surprisingly well," said Kareem.

"Yes, better than I expected," said Carson. "We had some good stories and we have some other people to follow-up with tomorrow. Tegan, how many others signed the book?" asked Carson. Tegan pulled the notebook toward her and looked it over.

"Looks like four new people we didn't talk to this evening, plus we have the contact information for the Shaws, Jordan, Sharon, Dexter, and Sophie."

"Well, we've got our work cut out for us," theorized Carson. "What do you say we call it a night?"

He turned to Natalie. "Do you need us to do anything else?"

"No," she said, "Everything has been put away and ready to lock up for the night."

"Thank you for all of your help in getting this set up," said Ty. "We could not have pulled this off without your help." Natalie smiled and acknowledged the gratitude. They walked out together into the dark parking lot.

Kareem said, "Hey, what do you say we hit up a bottle shop on the way back to the hotel? I used Untappd and found some Lone Pint Yellow Rose not far from here. Tegan agreed, acknowledging how helpful that will be when reviewing the notes from the evening and planning the next step.

"Let's do it! I'm down for a couple of bottles," said Carson as the group headed back to Tegan's Verano.

11 INTERVIEW PROCESS

Saturday, June 20, 2015

It was just after 10 a.m. when Carson dressed and headed down to the Red Roof Inn pool where the others were already discussing the plans for the day. "Mornin', ladies," he said as he wiped the sleep from his eyes.

Ty spoke, "There's Sleeping Beauty! 'Bout time you got your ass up. We've got work to do." Kareem tossed Carson a packaged blueberry muffin as he sat in a white plastic chair with his face to the sun.

"Have some breakfast. Complements to the Chef at Valero."

"Yum. Gas station muffins," Carson said sarcastically. You didn't happen to get any more of that Yellow Rose, did you? That was delish!"

"No, 'fraid not," said Kareem. "They don't carry it at the Valero, but I can get you more of that Lone Star you used to love." Carson looked up and grinned.

"I'm good, thanks."

"So, what's the plan for today? Are we going to meet up with some of the witnesses from yesterday?" inquired Carson.

"Yes," said Tegan. "I have called Jordan, he's the astronomer guy,

Sharon the school teacher – because the school isn't too far from where Jordan had his encounter at the lake. We're also going to meet up with Dexter. You remember his awesome photos? And then there are the Shaws - that couple who live next to Fred Dalton. Since he called us in the first place, that should be a good area to start," concluded Tegan.

Kareem added, "We can meet the Shaws at their farm. Since we have already been to Fred's we can get a closer look at that land. Jordan can meet us at the lake, but Sharon isn't working today since it's Saturday, so she isn't in the same area. I set up a meeting with her at Las Coronas Bar & Grill off the Loop 1604. It's a little closer to town, but she lives out that way and we can grab some lunch. We'll wrap up later this afternoon with Dexter over at a place called Papa Woody's Roadhouse on South Presa Street." Carson pulled the old black straw hat down over his eyes to block the sun. His opened shirt fell to each side of his stomach as he slouched down in the plastic chair.

"Sounds like ya'll got it figured out. When do we get started?"

"It's time to get started now, slackass," said Ty. "We have a lot of people to interview, and I am sure the Shaws are up and ready for us now. So button up your shit and let's get ta stepping, Skippy."

Carson stood and arched his back as the group made its way to the Verano.

"I want to get some good information that leads to catching this creature, but hopefully it hasn't caused any more damage to anyone in the area. Especially the Shaws and Daltons. They have already been through enough and it will be a difficult year for them with the loss of revenue from the ranch," said Ty. "When you are running a tight business with a lot of debt, every little piece of the puzzle is an important one. We have to get this thing before any more incidents happen. Another head or two might just put one of those ranches under!"

The sun was quickly approaching high-noon when the investigators pulled into the Shaw's "L.J. Ranch". Jonathan approached extending his hand to Carson first. Lily smiled and quietly shook Tegan's hand.

"Thanks for letting us come out and look around," said Ty.

"We visited Fred Dalton's farm a few days ago. Actually he is the one who called us down here," said Carson.

"Is that right?" asked Jonathan.

"Yes, he lost a couple calves as well and saw a brown creature out around the creek. Even put up a couple of trail cams and got a few photos," revealed Carson.

"Well, I hope you get the sombitch since he's done got three calves right here in the same area," said Jonathan.

Kareem looked at Lily. "Now you say you were down here by below the barn?"

"Yes, I was down picking some apples to bring up and bake a pie for Sunday dinner. First I heard the russlin' in the bushes, and when I looked up, he was down by that tree over yonder. He was up on the hind legs and sniffing the air," recalled Lily. "I dropped the apples right quick and turned back toward the house. I didn't run, but I moved quickly and kept checking to see if he was followerin' me."

"That must have been scary," said Carson. "What would you have done had it came after you? That's a long way to the house!"

"Yes, it is. I wouldn't have made it running. I figured I would have to jump our old brown horse Bandit over there," suggested Lily as she pointed toward a tired-looking horse grazing in the pasture.

"Well I am glad you didn't get hurt and that you haven't seen the animal again" said Ty.

"Me too!" said Jonathan, "but the rest of the area doesn't sound so lucky. Those sightings have been fairly common over the past few weeks. Do you guys have any idea what kind of animal it is?" asked Jonathan.

"Not yet," admitted Carson, "We are still piecing everything together. We have only a handful of blurry photos, a couple of eyewitnesses like yourself, but we haven't checked them all out yet. We're going to get through a few more today and then come up with a plan to do some investigation. Maybe spot this creature with our own eyes," said Carson.

"Are you prepared to kill it?" asked Jonathan.

"We would rather not, especially if this is something no one has seen before," said Kareem. "We will if we have to, but I think I speak for us all when I say we would rather capture this thing alive and see what we have."

"Well I am fine if you kill it," said Lily, "I don't want to see that thing again!"

Carson and Ty looked around at the distant trees, the barn, and the field where the cows, chickens, and old Bandit lived. "Do you mind if we walk around and see if there are any clues still here?" Jonathan approved.

"Sure, let's take a walk – but it's been two weeks now. I don't know what we could find. It has rained a few days since then, so I am sure any clues are long gone."

"Maybe, but we could get a feel for the land and maybe see how this thing is traveling the area," suggested Carson.

The group walked along the barn and down a path leading to the apple trees. The cattle remained distant while Bandit raised his head to check out the new visitors but seemed to have little interest in actually checking them out. The walk wasn't too far from the barn to the trees, but far enough that Carson wondered if Lily had mistaken it for another animal. The black bear had been eradicated from Texas in the 1950s but had been seen re-emerging over the past thirty years. Since 1983 the state made it illegal to hunt bears, and recently sightings had increased. Since the sightings were uncommon maybe she wasn't expecting to see a bear. It could have stood on its hind legs to maybe reach up for some apples. The group continued walking and Carson didn't mention the possibility of a bear.

As they approached the trees Ty and Kareem searched the ground for clues, but as Jonathan thought, the recent rains left the area smooth with no signs of tracks. Tegan and Carson looked at the trees and did notice some scratches on the trunks.

"Carson, do you have a tape measure?" asked Tegan. There were some scratches near the base of the tree, but Carson was surprised to see there were also some as tall as him. Tegan held the tape measure at the base of the tree while Carson extended it toward the scratches.

"These are just over five feet, almost six feet tall!" said a surprised Carson. Still, in the back of his mind he thought it could be a bear at that height. He remembered at the town hall Lily did say it was a dark animal, which again could be a black bear. But she wasn't sure it had fur, and that sounded unusual. Plus she mentioned the eyes were unique. "You said something yesterday about the eyes?" inquired Carson. Lily grew attentive.

"Yes! Those eyes were like nothing else I have ever seen. Bright red like they were glowing," said Lily. That eliminates a bear thought Carson.

"And you said it was dark in color?" asked Ty.

"That's right. It was dark – like a dark gray or maybe brown," recalled Lily.

"Was it furry?" asked Kareem.

"For some reason I don't think so. There it looked smooth, but there was some spikey fur that was even darker kind of down his spine," said Lily. Caron kicked at the ground covering while he ran through his mind of what the creature could be.

"Some of the other people who saw it said it looked like maybe a boar or a wolf. One guy said a kangaroo of all things," said Carson.

"Well I don't know about a boar or a wolf because it was on two legs and those walk on four. Plus it was really slender, not stocky like a boar. And a kangaroo? I ain't never seen a kangaroo except once at the zoo," said Lily.

Carson chuckled, "Yeah, the kangaroo threw me too!" he admitted.

As they continued to walk Ty did notice some of the brush was trampled down and made a slight trail through the back of the trees and off of the Shaw's property. "What's that direction?" asked Ty.

"Down that way about a mile or so is Fred Dalton's ranch," said

Jonathan. The group turned and looked at each other. "Looks like whatever was here was using that trail to get between ranches. Maybe we should follow it down to Fred's and see where else it goes?" suggested Tegan.

"You are welcome to use the 4x4 if you want to drive it down along the path and see what you can find. Beats walking it". Carson agreed. Lily remained with the group while Jonathan went to get the vehicle. A few minutes later he returned with the 4x4 and a couple of bottles of water.

"You better take some water. It's getting warm out," suggested Jonathan. All four got in with Carson driving and Ty riding shotgun while Tegan and Kareem sat in the back.

"Let's see where this thing goes," said Ty.

With the crew settled into the 4x4, Carson started driving down the path of trampled grass and brush that ran along the property line. The trail down to Fred's ranch was reasonably straight, but Carson had to drive slowly due to the rough undergrowth. It took nearly fifteen minutes to make it down to the boundary of Fred's ranch. Fred was outside working on fence repairs as the unknown vehicle entered his property. Pausing work, he laid down his hammer and raised his rifle toward the unknown trespassers. As they moved a little closer he recognized Carson and lowered the weapon.

"What are y'all up ta' this mornin'?" inquired Fred.

"We met up with the Shaws about their incident with the creature. You see anything else of him since the other day?" asked Ty.

"Nope. Nary a sign," disclosed Fred.

"Well that's good, but he's still around somewhere," said Tegan.

"Any leads?" asked a hopeful Fred.

"Quite a few witnesses. We are out today meeting with a few of them to see what we can discover as far as clues," said Carson. "But chances are we won't find much due to the rains."

Kareem suggested, "Most likely we will have to camp out and do a field investigation to try and locate the creature."

"Well I'm glad this ain't your first rodeo. The feller I spoke to about you said you guys were good at catching things like this," confided Fred. Ty and Carson turned and looked at each other with a non-confident glare.

Tegan broke an uncomfortable silence by speaking up. "If the creature is still out there, we'll find it!" assured Tegan.

"I hope so!" wished Fred. "Where you headed to next?"

"Well we just wanted to take a look at the land between the Shaw's and your place. We are headed out to Braunig Lake, but that's a little far in the 4x4. We are going to head back and get the car, then meet our next witness out at the lake. After that we're going to visit the school, even though our witness can't meet us there. She did say she saw the creature, so we will look at the area first, then meet up with her later," reported Carson.

"Sounds like y'all've got a long day ahead of you," acknowledged Fred. "Better get to it I reckon." The quartet waved as Carson turned the vehicle around.

"We will be in touch," said Kareem as the vehicle started on the trip back to the Shaw's ranch.

Arriving back at the Shaw's ranch Carson drove the 4x4 up to the barn and talked to Jonathan and Lily. "Well we didn't see much, but it is a clear shot between farms. That path was beat down, so it is likely it followed the tree line right down to the Dalton place. We are going to head out to the lake to see our guy out there, but I want you to call us immediately if you have any new sightings or find any clues," said Carson. Lily assured they would call if anything happened. The group made their way back to the car and headed out to Braunig Lake to meet Jordan.

As Tegan pulled into the lake's parking lot, Jordan was standing in a ramada not too far from the water. The team exited to greet him. "Is this where you were?" asked Kareem.

"Yeah, about. I was walking down the sidewalk here. Usually on the weekends there's tents set up along this side over yonder," Jordan said as he gestured with his right hand toward the dirt area past the ramada. "As I said yesterday I was out looking at the sky for the meteor shower and the creature was over in the reeds there just barely in the water. When I heard the sound of the reeds rustlin' I looked down to see what was causing the commotion," recalled Jordan. Carson looked on.

"And you said it was about twenty feet away?"

"Yes, that's about right," confirmed Jordan.

"You mentioned it had red eyes, which we have heard from a couple of other people too, so I think it's the same animal. But you said it hissed at you?"

"It sure did! I was scared and thought after the deer it was feeding on I might be dessert!" said a nervous Jordan.

"It's still got you shook up pretty good, doesn't it?" asked Ty.

"Yes, sir! Those eyes I see in my nightmares. I don't know how fast it would be if it came after me, but those long back legs looked like they could scoot on down the canyon!"

Ty asked, "Did you get a look at his teeth? You said he had a deer and bit the neck like a vampire?"

"I didn't get a good look at 'em, no. I just saw he wasn't eaten on the deer but was biting it on the neck. Then he dropped it when he saw me and thankfully skedaddled on into the reeds and off ta who knows where next."

"Well that was about six weeks ago you saw him, which is around the time when Sharon saw it at Freedom Elementary in the morning. That's about three miles away, so it probably stayed between the lake and there I imagine," said Carson.

"Well, all of the sightings aren't too far apart," said Tegan. "All are within a seven to ten-mile radius, and that isn't too big of a range for an animal of that size." Ty glanced around.

"Let's walk down to the lake's edge and have a closer look at where that creature was when you saw it," suggested Ty.

The five made their way down the sidewalk and stopped on the water's edge. Looking around they got a good view of the area and headed further in the direction Jordan saw the creature. Several of the reeds were broken and the group could see there was some struggle that took place, but there were no signs of the animal or remaining footprints of the creature.

"A dead animal like that won't stay out here long," said Carson. "Other animals will come and pick apart that carcass and clean it up pretty quick." Ty looked around the weeds just past the grassy edge of the lake.

"They may pick the meat clean, but the bones won't break down that fast. In six weeks' time? Something larger may have drug it somewhere, but I am sure we might find it around here somewhere," replied Ty.

Laying on the side of the lake, the deer would feed a lot of other animals in the ecosystem: ravens, flies and their maggot offspring, coyotes, and other larger birds of prey such as buzzards would all take part in feeding on the body.

"The circle of life," said Ty. Carson looked up.

"It's the wheel of fortune…," replied Carson.

"The coyotes are likely to drag the body off the path and into the underbrush. As they say, Mother Nature is the best clean up for dead animals."

The group disbursed a little to search for the body, and after a few minutes, Kareem stumbled upon the mostly decayed body of the fallen deer. The skin and meat were gone from the neck down, but some skin on the head and neck were still present.

"Do you have any of those pecker-checker gloves?" asked Carson.

"Do you mean latex gloves?" asked Tegan. Tegan handed Carson a pair of chalky latex gloves from her purse as Carson smiled. Using the antlers to drag the body into the opening a little more, Carson examined the remaining elements of the body.

Examining what remained of the neck, the puncture wound was surprisingly still intact. There were two large gashes in the neck, and one slightly smaller in the middle - but the skin around was not torn, showing the killer did nothing more than drain the victim. The other damage occurred later by the other local predators after the deer was slain. Carson was puzzled. An animal would have to eat to survive. How is this creature surviving only on the blood of its prey? All of the reports mentioned biting the neck of an animal and draining blood, but not eating the animal.

"Unique," said a puzzled Carson.

Ty pulled out his cell phone. "Let's get a few photos of this. Maybe we can have Sophie look at these and she can get some clues from that."

"Yes, great idea! Take photos," said Tegan. "Because you are not putting that dead animal in the back of my new Verano!"

"So, Jordan," said Kareem, getting Jordan's attention, "After the animal saw you and hissed, dropped the deer, and disappeared this direction?" he asked as he pointed toward the reeds at the back edge of the lake.

"Yes, he turned and moved pretty quickly," replied Jordan. "That's why I was glad he went that way instead of coming at me. He can move pretty quick and there would be no way I would outrun him." Ty looked on.

"So far we haven't heard any stories of it attacking people, so maybe it's not interested in humans?"

Carson agreed but added, "With those sharp teeth and claws as well as quick, long muscular legs if he changed his mind I think a human would be in trouble. Just because he hasn't yet doesn't mean he wouldn't."

Wading through the reeds and flats, the group headed in the direction the creature was last seen. The grasses and cattails were thick along the backside of the lake. The shallow water, dense wetland plants, Craneflies, and humid June afternoon around the lake made for slow progress. Looking around to survey the area Carson pointed off to the distance.

"What's that big building over there?"

"That's Braunig Lake Power Plant," noted Jordan.

"Power plant?" questioned Carson.

"Yes. This park and lake are a reservoir owned by City Public

Service Energy. Back in the mid-1960's San Antonio was rapidly growing but the increased need for power coincided with a six-year drought. Before that they had been using water from Edwards Underground Aquifer, the city's sole source of drinking water to generate power. But now they were forced to find a way to increase power but reduce the usage of the city's drinking water. In producing electrical power, it takes a lot of water, so they came up with the idea to build a reservoir. Actually two – this one and Calaveras. The power plants are cooled with recycled water which is then released into the lakes. The two lakes provide cooling for five power plants and also provide almost five thousand acres for recreational use as well as creating a fish and wildlife habitat," reported Jordan.

"There's no danger of contamination to the lake? There are a lot of people out here fishing," questioned Tegan.

"Fishing is popular here. It's definitely a major pastime of a lot of folks," said Jordan. "There have been reports of mercury in the past. CPS has taken a lot of precautions to reduce the amount, but about five years ago low levels of mercury contamination were found in fish at Calaveras, here at Braunig, and in the upper San Antonio River, but the city said they are considered safe to eat. This lake is about the best around for catfish. Even in winter, around the hot water discharges next to the jetty and under the bridge at the end of the west end of the reservoir are great fishing spots. Good red drum and bass fishing too," said Jordan.

"Seems like a lot of smoke," said Ty looking up at the sky.

"That mercury gets blown from coal stacks, gets in the waterways, and is absorbed by fish that can end up on the dinner table," continued Ty.

"Or a bird eats the fish, then something eats the bird and it can get into the ecosystem," said Carson. "You hear stories about mutated animals all the time," said Carson. "Has to be some truth to all of the legends. You never know. This animal we are looking for might be a mutated coyote or something due to the water and animals eating fish here," theorized Carson.

"I've been fishing here since I was a tyke," said Jordan. "I think it's fine. I've never come down with anything from eating the fish."

Finally coming to the end of the reeds and back to dry land, the group faced a small wooded area. "What's out that way?" asked Kareem.

"Nothing for a bit," said Jordan. "But out that way there is Community Baptist Church in that direction, Nando's Ice House toward this way, and if you keep going there is the Pilot Travel Center and Freedom Elementary."

"Freedom Elementary?" repeated Tegan, "That's where Sharon works and saw the creature in the morning before school."

"It's about four miles from here," said Jordan. "Is it mostly backcountry out through there?" said Carson.

"Mostly. There's a couple of small roads, and the San Antonio River runs out there," said Jordan. "But he would also have to get across I-37 to get there."

"Unless he used the river and went under the highway," said Ty.

"Well I say we get there using the car," suggested Kareem. "I'm not walking four miles through a river only to walk four miles back! Plus, I'm getting hungry."

"Sounds like someone needs a Snickers!" quipped Ty.

"You can drive along Frontage road. There's a Whataburger and Bill Miller's BBQ right next to the Best Western and Pilot Center," said Jordan.

"Let's get the BBQ," suggested Kareem.

"Aren't we going to meet Sharon at a restaurant?" asked Ty.

"Las Coronas Bar & Grill…we can skip the grill and just have the bar!" said Kareem.

"Let's go check out Bill Miller's, then we can walk around the school and head out to see Sharon after that. With this heat some cool drinks always hit the spot. And Bill's is a chain, but it's barbeque so it's good," said Carson.

The quintet walked back toward the parking lot where they shook hands and parted ways with Jordan. Getting back into the car, it was a short drive to the restaurant. "They have a drive-thru," mentioned Tegan.

"Let's go inside and side for a bit. We can look over what we've seen today, plus plan for the two more interviews later this afternoon," plotted Carson.

Tegan found parking right in front of the entrance sign of the brown-brick building. Exiting the vehicle, Carson stood and stretched in the shaded area underneath the covered entrance. Inside they were ushered to a booth by a young waitress wearing the name tag "Alana". Alana Iglesias was a young Mexican woman, about 17-18 years old working at Bill's during summer vacation from school. She was average height with a heart-shaped face and small nose. Her thick black-blue hair had faint signs of purple and pink as if it had been previously dyed. She had dark brown, close-set eyes and pink eyeshadow, dark well-shaped eyebrows, and rosebud mouth with pink shiny lip gloss. A small tattoo on left forearm and a septum piercing suggested she was a little edgy.

"Can I start you off with something to drink?" asked Alana in a silvery voice. Looking over the menu all four selected sweet tea. "Why don't I bring you a bucket? That's only $3.99 and will save you a little money," suggested Alana. The guys looked over the menu and discussed what barbeque they wanted. Tegan stood up to go to the restroom, requesting the guys order for her.

"I know you all want barbeque, but I have been craving fried chicken. Can you get me the three-piece?" asked Tegan.

"That has fries and bread. You good with that?" asked Ty.

"Yes, that's fine. Thanks," said Tegan as she exited.

Soon Alana returned with four cups and a bucket of sweet tea. "What did you fellas decide?"

"She wants the three-piece fried chicken. And I will have the Rancher plate with mashed potatoes and cole slaw," said Ty. Carson ordered the Rancher plate as well and Kareem with his big appetite ordered the Rodeo plate.

"Since you all want barbeque and are choosing the same sides, you might instead go for the large Bar-b-q Family Order. That's $28.95 and you get a pound and a half of barbeque that you can mix and match, a quart of potato salad, pinto beans, and coleslaw. Plus you get pickles & onions as well as two loaves of French bread. It's cheaper than you ordering separate and you'll probably have some left over," suggested Alana.

"Perfect!" said Carson.

"Can we get brisket, chicken, and ribs?" he asked?

"Oh, and I want a couple of hot links," added Ty.

Tegan returned, sat down, and removed a small notebook from her purse. "Okay, so what do we know? Should we make a sketch?"

"I don't even know what we would sketch," admitted Carson. "We know it's about three feet tall and four or four and a half feet long, thin but muscular back legs, slender, kind of darkish-gray in color and either hairless or just a little hair on the body except for the dark spiky fur down the back. We know it has big teeth, red eyes, and makes a hissing sound. But we don't know what it looks like. We have heard canine creatures to boars to bears, and don't forget that crazy kangaroo description. We heard he looks like an under-fed Mr. Bigglesworth too. It can move on four feet and at least stand upright on two, but possibly even walk as a biped. We know a lot of characteristics, but not the overall general picture," pointed out Carson. "All of the photos we have seen have been too blurry to really know what we are dealing with, but maybe we can use it as a start and add the details we have learned. At least that might be clearer than what we've seen."

"One thing we have seen from Fred's photos, from what Dexter showed us, and even what we learned from Jordan, it seems the creature typically moves on all fours, but when it is checking out the area like catching a smell, looking for the source of a noise, or scouting the area, that's when it goes bipedal. It can probably walk like that short distances, but for longer distances I bet it drops back down," suggested Ty.

As the food arrived, Tegan decided maybe two drawings would be better – one walking and one standing. "So maybe the four-legged one I can have a body like a boar, but a head like a coyote or dog. The back legs are long, thin, and muscular, with the front legs a little shorter. That is going to make it hunch forward. And the tail we know is a long one," said Tegan as she sketched a rough draft.

"Where did you learn to draw like that?" asked Carson.

"The Art Instruction Schools…you know, from the television commercials and comic books? I used to draw Tippy the Turtle and that pirate. I just kind of kept practicing," replied Tegan.

"Really? I didn't know anyone actually did that," replied a surprised Carson.

"Yep. Charles Schultz is a graduate, thank you!" added Tegan.

"No shit?" Carson asked rhetorically as he took a bite from a meaty rib.

Tegan paused long enough to take a few bites of the fried chicken. Her facial expression indicated the chicken met the anticipation and cravings she had in the recent days.

"There really is nothing like good, southern fried chicken," said Tegan as she took another bite. Putting the drumstick down she wiped her fingers on the napkin and went back to adding details to the four-legged version of the animal. She added the spiky hair along the creature's arched back, added pointy ears, and sharp teeth to the gaping mouth. Alana walked back to the table to check on her guests. She looked down at Tegan's sketch.

"Whatcha drawin'? The chupacabra?" asked Alana. The table's occupants looked at each other.

"Chupacabra?" asked Ty. "You don't believe in that, do you?" Alana gave a surprised look back.

"Yes, they're around here. Been here for years," said Alana. "They drink the blood of small farm animals like chickens, goats, and so forth. And nothing else but a vampire really drinks the blood of its victims," she said matter-of-factly. With plenty of food and drink still on the table she dropped some more napkins and returned toward

The Chupacabra & The Bat Rastard

the kitchen.

Kareem looked at the drawings. "Now that she mentions it....," he said pausing. Carson took the bipedal drawing and stared at it. Tegan had not yet finished the detail on that drawing, but Carson tried to picture it completed.

"Sonofabitch!" exclaimed Carson. "The stories we hear about here in Texas, and the so-called chupacabras that have been reported in the past look like dogs. The Texas chupacabras always look like a canine; a Mexican hairless dog or a wolf or coyote with severe mange. Even a raccoon with mange recently was thought to be the chupacabra. But that's not what the chupacabra originally looked like when it was first reported in Puerto Rico in the 1990's. Madelyne Tolentino described it like a Hollywood monster with big alien-like eyes on the side of its head, large back legs, short hands with three fingers, about five feet tall, kind of monkey-like in shape with spinal quills. They said the eyes were large oval red eyes that sometimes glowed and the skin blueish-gray. It had a snake-like tongue, fangs, and a foul, sulfur-like stench. It was more demonic, like a cross between a vampire and a gargoyle. Come to think of it, the Puerto Rican reports did say it hopped like a kangaroo," recalled Carson. "The common feature the creatures share, apart from their name, is their lust for the blood of livestock."

Ty looked at the two drawings. "You know...the sightings between the Texas and Puerto Rican versions sound like completely different animals, and someone might wonder how the story changed over the years. Why was the chupacabra like you described and now people think it looks like a dog? Well these drawings may explain that. When it is on all fours it looks like the Texas version, and upright it does look like the Puerto Rican version. That creature caught in Cuero, TX that was said to be a chupacabra also had three toes. Maybe there really is something to this chupacabra," said Ty.

Kareem said, "Chupacabra means 'goat-sucker' and they say it drains the blood of its victims, just like our creature."

"But why blood and not eat the meat?" asked Tegan.

119

"That is a puzzle," replied Carson. "Maybe the creature has evolved to where it needs that nourishment…maybe it is deficient in a mineral or something that it gets from blood?" suggested Carson.

"Iron!" said Ty.

"Maybe it's deficient in iron and gets it from the blood. That's the only thing I can think of that would be significantly present in the blood."

Finishing up the meal Ty called Alana over. She instinctively brought a couple of boxes and the check. "Thanks for your help with that drawing," said Ty. "That does look like the stories of a chupacabra. Have you ever seen one?"

"No, not personally, but a friend of mine said he saw one a few years ago," replied Alana.

"Well keep your eyes open," said Carson. "We are just checking out the story of a teacher over here at Freedom Elementary who says she saw one about three weeks ago." Each person dropped $10 on the table and Ty threw in an extra $5 for an added tip.

"What do you say we give a quick drive by the school to look at the landscape, then head down to Las Coronas? We are supposed to meet up with Sharon in about an hour," suggested Ty.

Tegan took the road in the parking lot, turned right on 1604, then a quick right onto Liedecke Road. The school had two large parking lots up front, and one on the side. Ty speculated those were not where Sharon saw the creature because of the higher levels of traffic.

"She said she caught a glimpse of it running across the back of the parking lot. What's behind the building?" asked Ty. Tegan drove to the side parking lot and saw the driveway continued past a basketball court and behind the school. Continuing on the road they saw two large round parking areas well behind the school.

"That's a little far to park and walk to the school for work," suggested Carson.

"Yes, but she could park here at the far right of the parking lot and she would have a clear line of sight back there. That could explain the distance she said it was," said Kareem.

"Those areas actually look like playgrounds, and look – behind them it's just green woods and what looks like a little dirt road. Perfect spot for the…I guess…chupacabra…to hide," said Carson.

"Oh, so that's what we are really going to call it now?" questioned Ty.

"Why the hell not? We don't know what it is and that's just as good as anything. We said it fits the legends, so let's go with that until we find out otherwise," suggested Carson.

"No wonder she didn't get a good look at it," said Tegan. "That's quite a distance out to that lot and if it was just dawn it would be hard to see it clearly."

"Well let's head out to the bar and see what Sharon has to say," said Carson.

"Yeah, let's see how she reacts when we spring 'chupacabra' on her!" chuckled Kareem.

Three miles later the crew turned down an unnamed dirt road with a cow ranch on one side and a goat ranch on the other side and headed toward a lengthy building with yellow aluminum siding. There was some shade from a large tree out front and a large outdoor dining area. That would be good in fall evenings, but not a hot June afternoon like today. Opening the door underneath the watchful eye of two faux geckos chasing each other around a "Welcome to Las Coronas" sign, they found Sharon was already inside. The dining area was also quite large and being early afternoon wasn't too busy.

"Definitely a nice little hideaway bar," said Carson as he walked around heading toward Sharon's table. Piñatas hung from the ceiling and cowboys sat at the bar. Two dart machines, a pool table, bar-top video games, and six televisions scattered around gave more of a Giddy Ups vibe than the craft breweries Carson had been visiting recently with his friends, but it was comfortable. And during happy hour the drinks were $1.50.

As they walked in, they made their way to the table Sharon where sitting. "Hello! Nice to see you again," she said in a friendly voice. "Are you hungry? They have some pretty good T-bone steaks."

"That does sound pretty good," said Carson, "but we just had some barbeque down the road. We will probably just order drinks. How are you today?" Sharon revealed she was doing well and grateful they were there to help get to the bottom of the creature.

"We did visit the school before coming here," said Ty. "Where was the creature when you saw it? We were thinking you parked on the side and it was in the back at those playground areas."

"That's right. It was a good distance, but I could see it. I was afraid for the kids because you know we have some small children and an animal that size is definitely a threat. It was early in the morning before the kids got there, so I don't know if it would be afraid of humans or not. You know kids are noisy, so that could scare it away," said Sharon.

As they spoke, Carson was momentarily distracted by the sounds of a fiddle on the television. The bar was showing a channel of music videos on the television, and the sound of the fiddle stood out over the prior background songs that hadn't captured Carson's attention.

"Huh," he thought to himself, "Alabama was right – if you want to play in Texas, you gotta have a fiddle in the band!" The others at the table continued their introductory conversations while Carson watched a four-member Spanish country band called 8 Segundos play their self-titled song. He was impressed with the speed and artistry of the fiddle player. "Wow!" he spoke aloud drawing the attention of those at his table. "This guy is really good!" said Carson.

"You know Spanish?" asked Kareem.

"No...my high school Spanish is a bit rusty, but I am diggin' this song and that guy reminds me of Charlie Daniels."

"How do you like it if you don't understand Spanish?" asked Ty. Carson's comparison was even more visible as the next song up was another song by 8 Segundos, *Cuando el Diablo bajo a Georgia*, a Spanish rendition of the Charlie Daniel's song *The Devil Went Down to Georgia*. The fiddler flipped the bow behind his back and twirled it in his fingers with an artistry similar to Doc Holiday and the tin cup in movie *Tombstone*.

Looking back to answer Ty's question Carson said, "You don't have to understand the words of the song to enjoy it. Karl Jenkins proved that with *Adiemus*." Puzzled, Kareem asked, "What's *Adiemus*?" "What? Besides amazing?" replied Carson. "*Adiemus* was a concept focusing on music. When we hear a song we are distracted by many things, including the words. Jenkins sought to remove that and basically created a new language. Singers performed the song in the created language, which instead of distracting us with the words – since we don't know what the words mean – the voice becomes an instrument itself. So, the songs and album were very popular, even though people didn't understand the words," revealed Carson. "I'm gonna have to add these guys to my BandsInTown app," he said.

The discussion was broken up as a young waitress named Letty approached the table and asked if the newcomers wanted anything to eat or drink. The group looked over the menu, not seeing many craft options.

"Well…when in Rome," said Kareem. "I'll have a Bud Light." Tegan looked over the menu and saw not many options.

"Yes, I think a Bud Light for each of us," she suggested. Ty and Carson agreed, and Letty disappeared toward the back. Soon she returned with a cold round for the group. A few weeks ago an ice-cold Bud Light would have been refreshing to Carson, but now he was already starting to dislike it, but internally hoped he wasn't turning into one of those beer snobs he heard about since trying to learn more about craft beer. He tried to remind himself of the two best types of beers. The first being free, meaning if a friend offers a beer, take it regardless of the style or brand. Second: cold, and this Bud Light, although not free, was cheap and it was cold.

"So…," started Carson, "This creature, have you seen it since that day?"

"No, I only saw it that once," admitted Sharon.

"You said about six weeks ago. Do you remember the day?" Sharon paused and thought about the incident. It was a Thursday, because I remember it was pizza day at school," she recalled. Looking at her phone she scanned the weeks.

"Thursday May 7," she said.

"May 7?" questioned Carson. "Just like we thought, that's the same morning Jordan saw it out at the lake. He said it disappeared into the reeds, and that was early morning. The lake is just a few miles away so it is possible that it headed here next," replied Ty.

"Do you have any idea what it is?" asked Sharon.

"Well, we are not certain," said Kareem, "We have a few leads and a lot of clues…"

Ty spoke up, "We think it might be…" he paused as he scanned the faces of those at the table, reluctant to say the word.

"A chupacabra…," interrupted Carson. The group looked at Sharon awaiting her reaction. She was slightly surprised, but not as much as they expected.

"I have heard of the chupacabra…but I didn't think I would ever see it," she said.

"You don't seem overly surprised," said Ty.

"Well, there have been rumors of chupacabras around here for years," said Sharon. "I thought it might just be one of those urban legends, but it seems every year or two someone is saying they encountered one, so I guess I thought it might be a possibility. Especially being in that town hall meeting and everyone talking about what they saw, but not knowing what it was," she stated.

"Well we aren't completely sure yet," admitted Carson. "We do have another guy to meet with this evening, but after that we are going to do an investigation and see if we can find this creature before he does any more damage to the local community and ranches," Carson replied.

"Do you think it's a threat?" asked Sharon.

"So far it has not hurt any people," said Tegan. "It has only attacked farm animals – a couple of cows, and there may be some chickens. Small animals like goats could be at risk too," continued Tegan. "Historically the chupacabra is known to attack those type of animals," she concluded.

"We are going to meet our last contact then make some calls to our friends at the university. We are going to set up camp and investigate this creature. We aren't going to leave until we get it. One way or the other," said Carson.

"That's a relief!" said Sharon. "That will at least help the community rest knowing the creature is either captured or killed. Maybe life can get back to normal," she said.

After a few more minutes of small talk, Carson spoke up and said they had a lot of information to go on, but needed to get to their final meeting of the day and prepare for the upcoming investigation. The beers totaled $6 for the four of them, but he also picked up Sharon's tab. Twenty dollars covered the total check. The next stop was Papa Woody's Roadhouse and that was just about twelve miles away. Ty said they would be in contact if any additional information were needed. Returning to the car Tegan set the GPS for Papa Woody's and they headed up US-281 North.

Late afternoon and Papa Woody's wasn't too full yet, but later in the night it appeared likely to fill up as the Motley Crüe tribute band Looks 2 Kill would be taking the stage. Closer to concert time it would be a $5 cover charge, but right now it was free entry. At a small round, wooden table close to the stage the group located its final contact for the day, Dexter Allen. Carson thought Dexter's long, wavy, brown hair fit with the hair band genre, but the mid-thirties seemed a little passed the peak of Motley Crüe. The band wouldn't play for a few hours so he wasn't sure Dexter was planning on staying for the band.

Reaching out for a handshake, Carson sat down.

"We were really impressed with your photos yesterday," said Carson.

"Thank you," returned Dexter.

"I know they were a little blurry, but you can get an idea of the size and characteristics," he said. "You said you were working late that night when you caught the creature on your phone?" asked Ty.

"Yes, that's right. I was making some calls and came out around 8:30 that night. Trying to set up a get-together with friends I noticed that creature as I walked to my car," recalled Dexter.

"You said it was near a pond?" asked Carson. "What's interesting is you saw it near a pond, Jordan saw it at a lake, and two other contacts Fred and Jonathan have a creek that runs through their ranches. We also think that it moved from the lake to the school where Sharon saw it by traveling along the river. So, it appears to like water," said Carson. "You described it as a Hollywood monster," recalled Tegan.

"Yes, the way it was hunched over and walking. It was a slower deliberate walk on two legs. It appeared able to move pretty quickly on four legs," said Dexter.

A young waiter walked up to the table as the group was talking.

"Are you all ready to order?" asked Dexter willing to offer some guidance.

"The wings are pretty good here," he added.

"Oh yeah?" asked Kareem.

"Hungry again?" inquired Ty.

"There's always room for wings," retorted Kareem.

"And they also have the absolute BEST homemade chips in town," added Dexter.

"This place is fairly nice," Tegan said to Dexter as she looked around the spacious dining room. She also noticed the large outside patio with multiple televisions and a big fan. "It looks like a popular place," she added.

"Yes, it is. Especially when a good game is on or in the evenings when a band is playing. It gets pretty packed," he said. "It's been here just over four years now and definitely has its share of regulars. Me included," he said. "And, the beer is cheap - $2 for beers, including Shiner," said Dexter. Each member of the group placed an order of wings and a Shiner.

As the group awaited the drinks, Carson filled Dexter in on updates to the case.

"I want to thank you for those photos yesterday. They really helped. We had seen some trail camera footage from Fred Dalton, but they were grainy and hard to see. Although yours were a little grainy, they were the best we've seen," commented Carson.

"They came out pretty good for catching me by surprise," said Dexter. "Had I been prepared for and looking for a creature I could have maybe taken some better pictures, but when you are preoccupied with your phone and then just happen to see an unknown creature out of the corner of your eye, photo quality isn't the first consideration," said Dexter.

"We've looked at the photos, and we've talked to a few witnesses," said Ty.

"This may sound a little crazy, but from what we have seen and heard, we think this might be the chupacabra," explained Ty.

"Chupacabra?" responded Dexter. "I've heard stories of the chupacabra, but it's always been described like a coyote. Not like this two-legged creature," he added.

"That's true," admitted Carson, "That is the typical description here in Texas...but the chupacabra sightings, the first sightings, from Puerto Rico describe a different creature," said Carson. "That creature stood on two legs, looked like an alien, hunched over with spiky hair on its spine, red eyes, and fangs. We think with those big legs the creature is capable of standing either on two legs like a kangaroo or running on all fours like a coyote or boar. That would explain the descriptions of each type of animals in the sightings," concluded Carson.

"Well, damn," said Dexter.

"What's the plan? How are you going to catch a creature that has never truly been caught or identified?" asked Dexter.

"That's a good question," said Carson. "We are going to make some calls to get some equipment and we are going to have an investigation to try and see this thing for ourselves. If we can catch or kill it we have a lab assistant that was there at the town hall meeting.

She will analyze it and see what it really is," explained Carson.

"When are you going to investigate?" asked Dexter.

"We start tomorrow," said Kareem.

"Yes," said Ty, "I am going to make some calls here in a bit to friends at the college and get some equipment. We will also stop by and get some tents from buddies in the area who are into camping."

"That's the plan," said Carson. "But tonight we can hang out, have some beer, and listen to some good local live music."

The group stayed for a few more hours drinking $2 Shiners and listening to the tribute sounds of Motley Crüe. Except for Tegan. She decided to switch to sweet tea since she had to drive the boys back to the hotel. The conversation faded as the band took the stage. The loud speakers were pumping screaming guitars that made talking impossible. Even the lights seemed to distract from the ability to talk as they pulsated brightly around the group's table. The crowd size increased as the band played on throughout the night. As the evening concluded to the sounds of toasting bottles and *"Kickstart My Heart"*, Carson was glad they didn't have to get up early in the morning.

12 BASE CAMP

Sunday, June 21, 2015

Mid-morning a white Bronco pulled up in front of the group's hotel. It was an old 1993 model that had seen its better days. Two individuals rode inside, but it was not Al Cowlings and OJ Simpson. It was Tomo Watanabe and Fahim Al-Razi, two friends of Ty's whom he met at a teacher's conference in San Antonio a couple of years ago. Al-Razi was a thirty-two-year-old Iranian male, tall and skinny, with a background in science and technology. He exited the Bronco wearing dark blue jeans, a short-sleeved dark blue button up shirt, black cowboy hat and boots. He hadn't shaved in a couple of days and his dark black facial hair showed a shadow that was closer to 8:30 than 5:00.

Tomo Watanabe worked with Fahim in the science department at St. Philips College in San Antonio. Tomo was 5'9", clean shaven, and slender. He too was wearing jeans on his weekend off, with a black Japanese t-shirt of Kirby dreaming of hamburgers a backward New Era Rakuten Eagles hat, black with a purple bill, and black boots. John Michael Montgomery's *I Can Love You Like That* stopped playing as Tomo turned off the vehicle. The two stepped out looking more like Japanese and Iranian cowboys more than scientists.

Fahim made a call to Ty as the two stood outside of the truck.

A few minutes later Ty, Tegan, and Carson greeted Tomo and Fahim in the parking lot. Tegan moved her car next to the Bronco.

"We brought the stuff you asked for," Fahim said to Ty.

"Good! Thank you!" replied Ty. Carson introduced himself to both men as Tegan opened the trunk on the Verano.

"What do we have?" asked Carson. Tomo removed a large item from the backseat of the Bronco.

"Ty said you guys were going camping and needed some supplies and hi-tech equipment to search the woods," said Tomo. "We brought a Black Pine Freestander Turbo six-person tent that should be big enough for everyone," Tomo said as he handed it to Carson.

"We also brought four North Face Wasatch sleeping bags," said Fahim. "And what's the most important part of camping?" asked Fahim.

"The cooler?" asked Ty.

"The cooler!" said Tomo.

He pulled out a Coleman forty-eight quart chest in the standard red with the white top. "And, of course we brought it filled," said Tomo as he removed the lid showing a couple of bags of ice engulfing twenty-four various cans and bottles of local Texas craft beer.

"Now we're talking!" said Tegan as she looked on.

"Oh, and you will need this," said Tomo as he handed a long metal object to Tegan.

"What the hell is this?" she inquired. The metal object was just over twelve inches long with a twisted middle and a harpoon edge. The other end had a downward turn.

"That is a WhaleSlayer™ – and Ty, don't lose it or it's your ass!" threatened Fahim.

"WhaleSlayer™?" questioned Ty.

"Yes, it's a handcrafted bottle opener forged out of half-inch steel by this guy out of Mississippi. It's about $60 for a small one, but the larger one like this is $120. The challenge is since it's handmade the wait list is about nine to ten months long," said Tomo.

"I've had that one about two years and I absolutely love it. I would recommend getting on the wait list now and forget about it until you get the confirmation from him that it's almost ready. Join the Facebook group and fill out the online form. Then forget about it until he contacts you when you make the short list," suggested Tomo.

"He makes them in several different styles and all of them are incredible. I can't imagine drinking beer without using my WhaleSlayer™...so you better make sure I don't have to!" said Fahim as he gave a steely gaze to Ty.

The camping equipment and cooler were loaded into the Verano, but one large box remained. Fahim said, "Now for the fun stuff!" The group looked on with anticipation as Fahim sorted through the large cardboard box. "We have a couple of audio recorders – just standard handheld mini cassette recorders, a few sterile collecting bottles in case you run into some fecal samples, a box of latex gloves so you don't contaminate the DNA, a yellow rigid one-foot wooden ruler for measuring footprints…," Fahim said as he voice trailed off.

"I would recommend if you split up to stay in pairs," suggested Tomo. "So we brought two walkie-talkies for communication, four headlamps, a small parabolic mic, two cameras with thermal imagers, two sets of night vision goggles, a time-lapse camera and tripod, and finally a remote controlled drone with an infrared camera."

Fahim told Ty they could keep the stuff for a couple of weeks because school was out for summer and the semester's low enrollment meant they wouldn't really need anything back until the end of July.

"What are you guys hunting?" asked Tomo.

Ty and Carson looked at each other before Carson answered, "the chupacabra."

"Are you shitting me?" asked Fahim.

"I wouldn't shit you…," said Ty. He left the rest of the one-liner unsaid.

"Do you think that thing really exists?" asked Tomo.

"If it does, this stuff should help us find it," replied Carson. "And we've had a lot of eyewitness reports with similar sightings, so something is definitely out there," he added.

"We plan to camp out between these two ranches where recent sightings have occurred, then we are going to walk the woods and see what's out there," revealed Ty. Tomo and Fahim looked at each other.

"Well if you need any more toys, give us a call," said Tomo. The two shook hands with the trio and said their goodbyes.

"Be safe out there," said Fahim through the open Bronco window as the backed out. "If that beast is out there, who knows what it's capable of?" As Tomo turned toward the driveway he reached down between the seats.

"Here," said Tomo, "You might need this. Just in case." He handed a revolver to Carson. "Just in case it comes down to it," Tomo said. Fahim reached into the glove box and passed a box of ammo to Tomo, who in turn handed it to Carson.

"You might need this rifle too," said Fahim as he removed one from the gun rack in the truck. The Bronco drove off as Carson and Ty looked at the weapons and realized shit was about to get real.

Tegan, Ty, and Carson returned to the hotel room after loading the car with the newly-borrowed equipment. They found Kareem looking over the map of the Elmendorf area and measuring distances with a small ruler.

"What's up?" asked Ty.

"I am looking at the map and trying to see where we might set up base camp," said Kareem. "We have Fred Dalton and the Shaws just over Highway 181 off of Elmendorf Lavernia Road. They are kind of close to Calaveras Lake. Then you have all of the sightings we had around the town of Elmendorf, just a few miles on the other side of Highway 181. A little further past that is Jordan's sighting at Braunig Lake and Sharon just a few miles away at Freedom Elementary.

Basically a total radius of thirteen to fifteen miles. One thing that is common is water. The two lakes, some ponds in town, and the San Antonio River closer to the elementary school. Water not only attracts it but attracts other animals that it might feed on. Just down from Fred & Jonathan there is an area by a few ponds where the ranches stop and it turns into a few houses down by the Valero. That gets a little busy because Highway 181 is right there, but there are also three big ponds close together between the highway and Fred's place. Those lakes are not only close to Fred & Jonathan's sightings, but they are on the way to the other sightings. I think we should camp out right around that area because there will be plenty of water that will draw potential food for the chupacabra."

"That sounds good to me," said Carson. "We can leave the car at Valero and walk over to the pond. I think I saw a for sale sign there recently so it should be vacant land."

"Let's roll!" said Ty. "We can be there this morning, set up the campsite, and maybe take an afternoon nap. It's going to be a long night I think.

Leaving most of their belongings in the hotel the crew headed down to the car. "We are paid up for the rest of the week," said Carson, "so we might as well leave the stuff in the room. Tegan has all of the equipment in the car. I think we are good to go. Maybe we can stop by Fred's on the way to let him know, then head down to Valero's." Everyone headed to the car as Carson locked up.

"I am kind of excited," admitted Tegan as they got in the Verano. "I've never been on a night time investigation before. But I always see them in Ghost Adventures and those type of shows. Have you seen Ghost Brothers? I love that one," she said. "Makes me wonder though, do ghost only come out at night?"

"Well I don't know about ghosts," said Carson. "I've never seen one. But animals typically hunt at night, so for us it makes sense to be active when they are active."

It was nearly twenty miles from the Red Roof Inn to the Valero. Tegan parked the car near the back of the parking lot. "Do you want anything from inside before we set up camp?" asked Tegan.

"I'm good for now," said Carson. "It's literally like three hundred yards to the front of that first pond. We can definitely go back to the store if we need something."

The group decided to begin unloading the car and set up the tent on the east side of the first pond. There is a small strip of land between it and the next small pond was flat with a few bare areas perfect for a tent.

"Let's back up here to the pond so we have a good water source," suggested Carson. "It's a little shady with the trees, it's a flat surface which makes it good to set up the tent, and we are not too far from where the reports have been. Fred's ranch is just about a mile or mile and a half down that road, and it's a good chance the chupacabra passed by here to head toward the town where the other sightings occurred."

"Right," said Ty. "I think the first thing we do is set up the tent and secure our base camp as it were, and we have to also be mindful of our environment. Being close to the pond we might encounter snakes, ants, and the bushes are kind of bristly and thorny. We probably should all wear pants to protect our legs from the briars and thorns," he suggested.

Each member grabbed items from the car and headed toward the pond. It was fairly quiet out with the humid temperatures, so not many onlookers were around to wonder what they were doing. The walk to the pond and the campsite location did not take long. It wasn't a far distance and within two trips from each member the car was fully unloaded.

Carson and Ty began working on erecting the tent by dropping the stakes and unfurling the tent from the bag. With the help of a nearby flat rock Carson began banging the stakes into the ground and within a few minutes he and Carson had the tent in place and ready for the evening. Once erected, Kareem moved the box of equipment inside the tent, and Tegan brought the cooler. Just outside the tent they found four large, flat rocks that they could use as chairs while planning the evening's events."

"Let's see that map again," said Ty. "Here on our right we have the other small pond, and just past that two more small ponds. A few hundred yards east we have a long, narrow pond that's almost like a canal, so when we are out walking around tonight be careful of all of these little ponds. I don't want to fall in one," said Ty.

"I think we head out as a group first," suggested Carson. "That way we have each other's back and there's protection if we run into the creature."

"I agree," said Kareem, "and an afternoon nap does sound pretty good so we can be alert tonight, but I think first we need to check out this cooler your boys brought," he said as he looked at Ty.

Tegan said, "This humidity is making me thirsty! And it's important to hydrate."

"Well knowing those boys, who don't forget came equipped with this awesome WhaleSlayer™," said Ty, "there shouldn't be any Budweiser in here!"

Opening the cooler the group gasped as if they just opened One-Eye Willy's treasure chest. A mixture of San Antonio bottles and cans were surrounded by a glacial amount of ice stared back at them. "Look at this haul!" said Kareem.

"I told you my boys wouldn't let us down!" said Ty. Reaching a bare hand into the icy waters, Carson moved in a counter-clockwise motion causing the cans and bottles to dance in the icy bath.

"I haven't had any of these!" said an excited Carson. Busted Sandal's Slippery Rock IPA and 210 Ale, Ranger Creek Brewing's Oatmeal Pale Ale, Strawberry Milk Stout, Red Headed Stranger, Love Struck Hefe, and Purple Rhine Berliner Weisse, Freetail Brewing Company Bat Outta Helles, Yo Soy Un Berliner, Texicali Brown Ale, and a couple bottles of #Whalezbro presented the group with a variety of local beers and enough to get through the afternoon and probably morning after the investigation.

"Wow! I am excited to dig in!" said Tegan eagerly.

"Well let's finish unpacking and getting set up, then we can start the pre-game," suggested Ty.

"I think when we go out this evening we should go as one group," suggested Carson.

"That sounds good," said Kareem. "That way we have some protection in case we do run upon this creature. We have to remember that night time is when it is active, so it's used to the area in the dark. We are entering its terrain during its peak time."

"When you say it that way it sounds a little scary," admitted Tegan.

"Right. That is why we should stick together. And this night vision equipment will help us even the playing field a bit" said Carson.

"We should set the time-lapsed camera's tripod right here around these ponds," suggested Ty. "The water might draw him in and he likely will be curious about the tent that is new in his area."

"We will divide the other equipment up among each of us," said Carson.

"How about we divide some of these beers up amongst us now?" suggested Tegan.

"I like the way you think!" said Kareem as he shoved a hand in the icy water of the cooler. He pulled out a white and silver can of 210 Ale from Busted Sandal.

"Hmm, I've heard good things about San Antonio blondes," Kareem said as he popped the top and took a swig. "A little nutty. Kind of reminds me of a lager. Smooth. A little sweet, but the bitterness from the hops keeps it from being too sweet. I could do this at a beer league softball game all day," said Kareem as he tossed a beer to Tegan.

She reached up and two-hand caught the bottle headed at her. "Aww, aren't you a sweetie?" she asked as she caught a Ranger Creek Brewing Berliner Weiss. "You know I love Berliner Weiss! Cute purple label too. Hand me that Whale-thing?" she asked as she leaned toward Carson and pointed at the WhaleSlayer™ bottle opener. "How the hell do you use this?" she asked as she looked it over. She took the hook end and easily popped the top off as she softly sang Prince's Purple Rain. The beer was a nice sour with a hint of lavender, a tart flavor she loved, and an aroma that was amazing. "I love this!" she said with a smile. "Nice fruity notes, a little carbonation, maybe a bit of pear and honey," she said. "When you are really thirsty nothing quite cuts through that like a nice sour beer," said Tegan.

"You ready for one too?" Carson said to Ty.

"Ooooh yeah, hit me, brother!" Ty said in his best Macho Man Randy Savage voice. Carson tossed Ty a Ranger Creek Oatmeal Pale Ale and pulled out a Ranger Creek Love Struck for himself.

Ty sat down and grabbed the WhaleSlayer™, quickly opening the bottle. Taking a sip, Ty decided it was a good brew – somewhere in between hoppy and bock, but a clean hop flavor with a little bitter finish. He picked up the oaty tones that balanced out the hops before declaring it smooth and tasty. Carson used the WhaleSlayer™ on the Love Struck Hefe and was love struck himself after the first sip. Nice and light with the traditional banana and clove tones, a slightly dry finish, descent carbonation that he thought made the beer refreshing and easy to drink. He thought he even picked up some mild pepper and a hint of lemon zest in the mix.

"This stuff is pretty good!" said Carson.

"Better than your Stars?" joked Kareem making fun of the San Antonio Star's recent loss in overtime Saturday night.

"Yeah, well they are struggling," admitted Carson. "They started the season losing all six games they've played, but I am still a fan and have hopes they will turn it around. Have any of you ever been to a WNBA game?" asked Carson. Everyone shook their head no. "Depending on when we wrap this up we should go to a game. Next one is Thursday against the Phoenix Mercury," said Carson.

"Sure, why not? Hopefully we will be finished with this creature by then. And when we get back to Austin we have to get ready for the Jester King release in a couple of weeks," said Tegan.

"Oh yeah, you mentioned Jester King and their releases when we were at Black Star last week," said Carson.

"When is the next one?" he asked.

"Friday, July 3, I believe," said Ty. "It is their spring beer, the Vernal Dichotomous. That's a farmhouse ale that is a blend of a November 2012 beer barrel-aged in oak barrels. It has barley, hops, lavender, and spearmint. The other beer was brewed just a couple of months ago with kumquats. There is always a crazy line, so we have to get there early. They usually limit it to three bottles per person per day," revealed Ty.

"I'm pretty sure I've never even seen a kumquat," admitted Carson.

Kareem and Tegan finished their beers and were on round two – Tegan the Ranger Creek Strawberry Milk Stout and Kareem a Ranger Creek Red Headed Stranger.

"This is also really good," said Tegan. "Nice stout with dark chocolate, strawberry, some vanilla, and maybe even coconut," she reported. This was one of the best milk stouts she had in a long time. The Red Headed Stranger was an IPA – a red IPA, which was something new to Kareem.

"A little sweet and mild," he said. Malt, grapefruit, lemon, floral notes and hops gave it balance. Nice tribute to Willie Nelson, he thought. Ty grabbed a Yo Soy Un Berliner but decided to put it back in the bath. He knew Tegan loved Berliner Weiss and decided to save it for her. Instead he took a Texicali Brown and tossed Carson a Bat Outta Helles. Ty stopped to admire the artwork on the can; a nice Day of the Dead motif. He was equally impressed with the beer. A nice brown ale with coffee notes. The coffee was a little robust and toasty. Carson's can was also smooth and flavorful. It had the aroma of wheat, grass and earthy hops. The mouthfeel was thin with a sweet wheat and honey flavor with a sweet finish.

"Okay, so what's the plan?" asked Kareem, "Are we out to catch this thing today or just try to find it for now?"

"We aren't in a position to cage it right now, and I don't want to kill it. That is unless we have to do it. Hopefully we can spot it tonight and get a feel for what it truly is. Where it goes, what it does, and what it's capable of so that we are prepared for later. We will have to build a trap or get something to hold it once we know exactly what we are dealing with. We think this is a good area based on the prior sightings, but it's not guaranteed. The sightings from Fred and Jonathan are going on three weeks now. Our more recent sightings have been in town, so if we don't find anything we may have to relocate. But I think we get a nap then see what's out there tonight," suggested Carson.

"Yes, that's what I was thinking too," revealed Ty. "That's kind of how we did it in college – get the information then head out with the intent to catch later. We can't catch what we don't really know is still out there," he said.

As the group sat in the tent working on the contents of the cooler, Kareem noticed it was getting darker outside. "Looks like it is getting cloudy. I hope it doesn't rain tonight while we are searching for that beast," he said.

"Not getting much rain during the year makes me a bit of a pluviophile," said Carson. "But rain would kinda suck tonight. From my experience a little light rain wouldn't hurt that much and might keep it cooler, but if it rains hard like it usually does during May and June that will definitely slow us down and make spotting the animals that much more difficult."

Tegan took the final sips of her beer. "Speaking of experience," she said, "how did you and Ty first get into this?" Ty and Carson looked at each other trying to recall.

"The idea came about over a bottle of gin and a jarful of pennies," quipped Carson. "Ha! Actually, I think it was…Dr. Thompson's social science class, wasn't it?" Ty recollected.

"Dr. Thompson? Yes. Yes, I think that's right. I was in the back of the room, not paying much attention to the lecture. I was looking out the window in class and drawing sketches in my notebook instead of taking notes," recalled Carson.

"That's right! I remember Bigfoot peeking out from behind a

tree!" said Ty.

"And wasn't there an alien?"

"Yeah, most likely," said Carson. "I was always drawing aliens," he said.

"You were definitely into that shit. Like *Project Blue Book* or something," said Ty. "That's because I had a weird sighting once when I was a teenager. Well not a first-hand alien or spaceship sighting, but my aunt did and called us out the next day to her farm. The ground was scorched in a circle and there were four indentations in the ground like legs or something. I remember taking pictures of the grass. Although I didn't see anything else it still sparked my interest so I started spending more time outdoors and watching the sky," said Carson.

"I thought you were weird at first," admitted Ty. "I hadn't seen anything usual and didn't really believe in it, but we started talking in the back of the class every day and you kept sketching animals and aliens. You suggested we go out and look for something after I asked you if you believed in that stuff," said Ty.

"Remember we went out in the woods behind the college and tried to find some mysterious animals?" recalled Carson. "Haha – yeah, the jackalope!" Never did find that sonuvabitch either, did we?" asked Ty.

"Nope, but they are out there," said Carson as he finished the beer, "They are out there…."

As he crinkled the can a light rain did begin to fall, the sound hitting the top of the tent was a little relaxing. "Welp, boys and girl…I think I'm going to catch a few hours of shut eye. What say you?" asked Carson. Tegan unrolled her sleeping bag.

"I think that is a good idea. It will be a long night and I am a little sleepy now anyway. A few hours should do the trick," she said as she scooted inside the top of the unzipped sleeping bag.

"Never thought I would be sleeping and dreaming behind a Valero," said Kareem.

Within a few minutes all decided to unfurl their sleeping bags and take a nap. The late afternoon clouds rolling in and the rhythm of the falling rain put each to sleep quickly. They continued to sleep as afternoon turned to evening and darkness began to fall.

13 NIGHTIME INVESTIGATION

Sunday, June 21, 2015

One by one the group awoke from the afternoon nap, with Carson being the first to rise. He walked to the front of the tent and looked out as the sun neared the horizon, leaving the sky a bright orange. The rain was still falling, but lightly, and he concluded it would not be an issue to take the electronics out with them. Since they were not his he wanted to be more cautious. The headlamps would be fine, the microphones and cameras they would have with them, and the drone they would leave in a duffel bag until needed. The only equipment that might be at risk would be the time-lapsed camera that would be out in the open for an extended period. Perhaps he could locate it under a tree that would provide some break to the rain?

As the others began stirring, he turned to start separating the equipment for their scouting mission. "Remember tonight we are heading out for information. We want to try to locate the animal, see how big it is, where it lives, how it interacts with the environment, then we come back to put together a plan for later. We will need to

The Chupacabra & The Bat Rastard

get some traps in place once we know more," said Carson. He grabbed the duffel bag and drug it toward the equipment, placing the Phantom 2 remote-controlled drone into the bag.

"Nice sack!" said Ty, "Where's that from? The Gap?" Carson turned with a sharp look.

"As Jacob said in *Crazy, Stupid, Love*, 'be better than the Gap,'" remarked Carson. "For your information, kind sir, it is from my monthly subscription box from Bespoke Post. It's the *Standard Issue* box, and I can earn $25 if I send you an invite and you join the club. Maybe then you could get a monthly box of awesome," said Carson with a snarky response.

"How many damn subscription boxes do you get a month? I suppose you do Taste the World and Barkbox too?" Ty shot back.

"No – I don't have a dog," replied Carson. "I just have the two for right now. But I am thinking of joining the Dive Bar Shirt Club if you must know."

"Guys, the sun is down and maybe we should get started," suggested Kareem.

Kareem joined Carson down on the ground to split up the equipment. "There is a headlamp for each of us," said Carson. "We have a parabolic microphone and a couple of Olympus voice recorders. Why don't you and Tegan each take one?" Carson said to Kareem. "Let's throw the sterile collecting bottles, latex gloves, and wooden ruler into the duffel bag also. I have my cell phone. Anyone else bring a camera?" asked Carson.

"I brought my GoPro camera. We can use that. It has better low-light performance, outstanding 4K video capability, and super-smooth slow-motion, so we shouldn't get those notoriously blurry photos we see of Sasquatch," suggested Kareem.

"That's sweet," said Ty. "We also have these night vision goggles."

"What the hell is this thing?" asked Carson.

Ty said, "This stick? Well we have one rifle and one pistol. We might need more protection. This is an O-mega Star Warrior Stun

Baton – it's capable of packing a whopping legal maximum of 150,000 volts. If that beasts attacks this is a good, non-lethal way of stopping it in its tracks," said Ty. "Put that in your pretty little duffel bag, grab the firearms, and let's get to hitting these woods," suggested Ty. Carson grabbed the pistol and Ty the rifle. With the equipment split up the group decided it was time to head out.

Stepping out of the tent, the group assessed the situation. As Carson looked around he recognized that while the rain was not hard and would not damage the equipment, it did pose some challenges. Having rained for a few hours, the ground would be wet which would cause footing to be more challenging.

One benefit to that wet ground was an increased chance of footprints. Witnesses reported the tracks of the supposed chupacabra were different than those of canines such as the coyote. Instead of four distinct toes, the chupacabra's two middle digits were said to appear joined, almost as if the animal had three toes. The long toenails also were more prevalent than other animals in the area.

Carson knew that on cloudy nights it was essential to hunt with your ears because you can't see with your eyes. The deep shadows and the unseen animals lurking in the brush made the thrill of being outside hunting for such a mysterious beast even more dangerous, but also exciting.

With the sun now fully submerged, the group left the opening of the tent and entered into the rough terrain south of the two ponds. Medium height thick grass, roots, and brush on each side surrounded the banks of the pond. The night was filled with the sound of frogs around the water, katydids in the bushes, owls, and other miscellaneous bugs that brought the night to life.

As they made their way through the darkness, carefully walking around the water's edge, Kareem felt nervous. The idea of looking for the creature, the interviews, and everything that transpired up to now was exciting but didn't quite feel real. At this moment hiking around the dark Texas landscape with technical equipment, lights, and firearms, the realism suddenly hit him. He indeed had never been

The Chupacabra & The Bat Rastard

part of such an expedition, and even though camping is an often embellished experience guys glorify when telling others, Kareem had only been camping a few times as a kid, and none of the experiences were positive.

From his first experience camping in the middle of summer outside of Austin where their campsite had no grass – only rocks. And ants. Tons of ants. He remembered a restless night attempting to sleep on the hard ground in the hot Texas air and listening to the unknown sounds on the other side of the tent. He remembered some of those sounds belonging to at least one raccoon who entered their camp and ate all of the food because Kareem left it out, even though his father reminded him to put it away before going to bed.

Another camping experience when Kareem was about ten saw an unexpected, horrible thunderstorm popup on the second day of a camping trip with his family. He remembered the lightning flashing before his eyes and the thunder crashing so loudly that he was scared and hiding in his tent screaming his lungs out.

The terrifying night was interrupted by the sounds of sirens. An ambulance. A person camping in the same campsite had been struck by lightning and was unconscious. As the rain now had fallen to a slight drizzle those memories of camping in the thunderstorm brought those nervous feelings back. To this day thunderstorms still scare him. Hopefully there would be no storm tonight, thought Kareem as he remained close to Tegan who was just in front of him in the group's march through the darkness. While Kareem did have a couple of other non-eventual camping experiences, the two negative ones stood out more in his memory than they did.

Kareem snapped back to the present moment as the group continued around the pond in the light rain. He began to scan the ground looking for any footprints, but especially the odd prints described as belonging to the chupacabra. There were still sounds of night animals, which usually indicated a predator was not around. The group continued slowly as frustration grew. The animal had been spotted around the area recently and the proximity of water seemed to be a good attraction, but as each member continued to look and listen, the creature was nowhere to be found. Carson wanted to ask if anyone had seen anything that could be the creature they sought, but he knew the answer. He half expected if he asked aloud he was likely to get a response similar to the trooper in *Spaceballs*, "We ain't found shit!" He elected to leave the question unasked and continue walking.

Another fifteen minutes and the group came full-circle around the pond. "Okay, this isn't working," said a frustrated Carson. "Ty, what do you say we split up? We have enough equipment. Kareem and I can go one way while you and Tegan can go the other way," suggested Carson.

"Sounds good. We can cover more ground that way, and we have radios in case we get in trouble or spot something," replied Ty.

"We have highway 181 to the east and Elmendorf Lavernia Road to the south/southwest. Chances are he won't want to cross the road unless he has to. It isn't too busy at night, but there may be enough cars to scare him off. That leaves the woods to the west and the woods to the north. I think that is as good as a place to look as any. What do ya'll think?" asked Carson.

"Sounds like a plan," said Tegan.

"There's a lot of wooded areas around here where it could be hiding." "Let's make a plan to meet back up in say three hours if we don't find anything," suggested Carson. "Stay in contact on the radio. They are all fully charged and should get us through the night."

"See you soon, bro. Stay aware and be safe out there," said Ty to Carson. After a fist bump, the two groups went separate ways. Carson and Kareem to the west and Ty and Tegan to the north.

"It is a little creepy out here at night," Tegan said quietly to Ty as they made their way toward the darkened tree line ahead.

"Per audacia ad ignotum," replied Ty. "Through boldness into the unknown." Tegan knew Ty and Carson used to go on frequent camping expeditions hunting for these unknown creatures while in college, but this was new for her. She was startled by every noise, and equally nervous when there was no noise – just waiting for something to jump out. While this "chupacabra" had not yet attacked a person, she wondered what if this is the night it decides to try a human snack? She stayed close behind Ty and continued toward the woods and as ground brush grew thicker.

Just then, she saw something out of the corner of her eye about the same time that she heard it! She detected the crash and just *barely* caught sight of something running through the persimmon trees parallel to her. Barely because it looked like a huge, brown dog. At first she thought it was a buffalo, but she knew that a wild one wasn't possible in Texas. The beast crashed through the thicket and she heard it hit water from where they just came. It sounded like a herd of hogs plowing the trees.

"Did you see that?" she excitedly whispered to Ty. Ty didn't see the animal but turned hearing the noise. After the initial loud crash the animal continued running toward the campsite. He thought he heard the faint splash of animals across the thicket in the pond. The duo turned back toward the direction they came from and ran cautiously toward the water.

As they got closer to the pond, the sound got louder, and even Ty begin getting nervous. It was so weird because in all of this expeditions he had never felt that way before. Maybe it was because it had been several years since going on this type of adventure and his adrenaline was pumping. What he thought could be a group of animals turned out to be one single animal. When it was within a hundred yards, he could hear it plain and clear.

Whatever it was, it was in no hurry and stayed in the brushes out of sight. Earlier in the day the group had scouted the area and Ty knew the water the creature was in was about waist deep on him. He could hear the *splash, drip...drip...drip...splash* as the animal put one foot in front of the other, real slow like it was trying to be quiet. He thought it might be another person till he remembered how deep that water was. He would never point a gun at a noise or anything he wasn't planning to shoot, but as that noise got louder he found himself raising the rifle and looking down the barrel. He was actually shaking.

The creature eventually got to the edge of the water with about forty yards of thicket before the open ground between where it was and Ty and Tegan were approaching. It crashed about ten or fifteen yards and then went quiet. Deathly quiet. No frogs, no crickets, no birds, nothing. Ty thought he might have imagined it, but Tegan did say she saw the blur of something from the corner of her eye, and they both heard it crash through the brush and undergrowth.

As Ty scratched his head and turned looking for the animal, he thought he could hear something now and then, like it was sneaking up on them. But as they stopped at the pond, there was no sight of the animal. Ty lowered the rifle and searched the ground. He no longer saw or heard anything from the animal, but did find tracks on the ground. Prints with a nearly combined third digit fitting the description of the mysterious creature. He and Tegan were both shaken but excited by the chase.

"I know it was the beast," said Tegan, "and we tracked it here to the pond...but where'd it go?" she wondered.

"Beats the shit out of me," responded Ty. "But we should get some photos of these tracks while they are fresh. Look at the distance between them he was covering some serious ground quickly," he said.

Tegan grabbed the radio. "Hey guys, over?"

Kareem replied, "Hey Tegan. You guys finding anything over there? It's quiet over here, over."

"Keep your eyes peeled. We just had some excitement over here. I saw the creature run back toward our camp, but it was hidden in the covering. We ran after it and we could hear it, then just when it sounded like we were right on top of it, we came out of the brush and there wasn't anything there, over." Kareem looked at Carson in disbelief.

"What do you mean there was nothing there? Are you sure you saw it? ... Over..."

"We definitely saw it, and something was here because we are standing in a group of footprints. That animal was running fast and had a large gait from the location of these prints. They dug deep in the mud too, so it's a big beast. Shocking something that big moves that fast. Over," replied Tegan.

"Did you take photos of the tracks? At least we have something to go on. Some type of proof. Over," responded Kareem.

"Yes, we got 'em. But the animal disappeared, so it might be headed your way. Over," Tegan added.

"We will be on alert. Thanks for the heads up. Over and out," concluded Kareem.

Carson suggested since the animal could be headed their way maybe the parabolic mic and thermal camera might help them identify if the creature was near. Reaching into the knapsack, Kareem removed the camera and handed it to Carson. He kept the mic for himself and returned the bag over his shoulder. Scanning the open grass and low-ground covering brush, nothing showed up on Carson's camera.

Kareem scanned the area with the mic looking for any unusual sounds. It was surprisingly quiet. He would have expected to hear owls, maybe some frogs around the wet areas, and the night insects. A coyote or even a fox would be expected, but the silence was unsettling. It could be that a something the animals considered a threat was in the area. Maybe the chupacabra was near?

As Carson scanned the camera back to the left he saw a red, orange, and yellow figure moving quickly from right to left. Much of its body was red indicating it was warm, likely from running. It was distant and mostly covered by the trees and brush.

"I can't tell what it is, but it's in a hurry," said Carson. "This could be the creature the other team saw. Let's go!" Kareem and Carson hurriedly put the equipment back in the bag and turned to pursue the creature. They loped awkwardly through the dense underbrush, attempting to avoid rocks and roots protruding from the ground. Sweat ran down their foreheads as they continued along, Carson attempting to keep his breathing in tune with his steps. The damp grass brushing against his legs, the puddles soaking his feet as he led the way into the darker recesses of the woods. He quickly realized months of day drinking and lounging voided any cardiovascular fitness he enjoyed in his youth as a basketball player in high school.

Now struggling to breathe and talk he managed, "Shit... I need to put that Shaun T workout DVD on when we get home," gasped Carson. Kareem was having an easier time and could converse easily with the slow-jog pace.

"Which one? Hip Hop Abs? Tilt, Tuck, and Tighten?" asked Kareem.

"No – Insanity. I bought it a while ago but never used it."

Brushes smacked his face as he continued following the trail of the animal. Soon the ground covering became less and they were in a small area of open field. The animal was not in sight and once again the night air was silent. Taking the camera back out of the bag Carson scanned the horizon, but nothing showed on the screen.

"Damn it!" he murmured. "I know it went in this direction," he said assuredly. He picked up the radio and called over to Tegan. "Hey guys, let's meet back up. We just saw it run by off in the distance. I think we're closing in. Over," said Carson. He gave their location to Tegan and approximately fifteen minutes later the groups were reunited.

"So what's the plan?" asked Ty.

"It could keep running to God knows where," said Carson. "But I'm hoping it stops and rests somewhere and we can catch up to it. I couldn't get a feel for the size of it because it was so far away on the thermal.

"Well from what we saw," said Tegan, "it is large – and fast!"

"Oh it was definitely fast," replied Carson. "He shot across the tree line not worrying about the rocks and branches that slowed us down. He definitely knows the area."

As the two groups continued walking as one they searched the area for clues with Ty and Carson taking the lead. "Let's hope this investigation turns out better than that jackalope," Ty said with a chuckle. They continued through the open ground and back into a wooded area, denser than the first.

"Not much human traffic through this area," said Carson. "Some patches of grass, but mainly dirt," he said looking down as the moved slowly through the area.

Carson's headlight shone down on the ground and he noticed footprints. They looked like the ones Tegan described near the pond. Each print had four toes, but the middle two were combined. The claws were long and the tracks were deep from the size and speed of the animal as it ran across the dirt floor of the wooded area.

"Let's get some more photos of these so we can compare it to the ones you took earlier," said Carson. "But I am sure they are the same. Wish we had some plaster that we could have made some casts to get a good size. Where's that yellow ruler?" asked Carson.

Bending down to take a good look at the tracks Carson concluded they were similar to a canine species. He turned toward Kareem and Tegan, who he knew had never tracked an animal before.

"The claws help to identify this as a canine track," he said. "It is possible to see claw marks in cat tracks – like a mountain lion or bobcat, but this is usually when the animal is running or pouncing. Also, the leading edge of the heel pad on a cat has two parts, or lobes, but you can see in this one a lack of a third lobe on the hind edge of the heel pad. That is another clue it is a canine. A canine track does have a third lobe, but as you can see shape of the leading edge of the heel pad is a single lobe. You can also see at the top of the track the alignment of the front two toes. They are side-by-side, or very close to it, in dogs tracks. There are exceptions, such as when the animal is making a turn or walking on a slope. Here he was likely running in a straight line, so they are side-by-side. But you can see the second and third toe are conjoined, which matches our eyewitness reports of the creature. These outside toes are consistent with canines, almost triangular in shape of the pads. Canines have a little point where the heel pad turns. One thing that is unusual with these, front tracks are usually larger than hind tracks. These larger ones appear to be the hind tracks, which would support the reports that the creature has strong back legs that allow it to stand on its hind legs. They have to be muscular to support its weight," said Carson.

Kareem took several photos of the track with the ruler laid out beside the print. "From the heel to the toe that's about four inches long and five inches wide," said Kareem. "The average adult cougar tracks average three-and-a-half inches tall by four inches wide, so we are looking at something bigger than that," said Ty. "Male coyotes are about three inches by two inches and a standard walking stride is about forty or forty-two inches apart. This guy was running so the stride would be longer. We also know this creature is nearly five feet long, so running stride is likely around eighty inches," calculated Ty.

"Let's get moving while he still may be in the area," suggested Carson. Looking at the surrounding trees, there were occasional branches that were bent, indicating something large passed through. The tracks continued in the same direction. Continuing walking in the same direction as the evidence, the group eventually came to an area that looked like a large field. There were trees in the distance and there was ankle-high grass, but it was more maintained.

"This might be someone's property," said Kareem. "It looks like a field, but it's too dark to see if there is a house." Ty stopped and looked around. There was no indication of a building, but it could be the backside of a large plot of land. He did want to continue following the tracks to see if the animal was still in the area.

"Let's dig in the bag and get that drone out," suggested Ty. "We can fly it over the area to see if the creature is still there and maybe we can see buildings as well."

Kareem removed the Phantom drone equipped with FLIR Vue Pro Dual thermal and E/O cameras. The thermal imaging was helpful for spotting livestock on large ranches – or in this case feral animals such as the chupacabra. Some of the high-tech ranchers also used drones for crop inspection and monitoring field irrigation. With the control the images could be quickly toggled between thermal and regular camera, making it useful in ranch management.

"We can also stream live thermal images as well as capture photos and video," said Ty. "I got to use one of these bad boys after a conference last fall and I would love to have one – but they are pricey. About $3500 – so don't break it or Tomo and Fahim will have my ass!" replied Ty.

Soon a light humming sound was heard as Kareem brought the propellers on the four arms to life. The drone slowly rose up and glided out over the open field. "We can get about seven-hundred meters distance with this before it gets out of range with the radio transmitter," said Ty. Carson pulled up the app on the smartphone to watch the video and guided Kareem toward the search area.

The drone disappeared into the darkness as Kareem guided it toward the distant trees. A couple of large images appeared, but from the video Carson identified them as horses. A barn was also seen near them.

"It looks like this is a small ranch or farm," said Carson. "Just a couple of horses, but there is likely a house closer toward the road. We can check that out later."

Dark trees appeared in the live stream and under the cover of them a bright red and orange figure was seen. It was panting and standing next to a tree, on two legs with one of the front legs on a tree trunk as if to prop the animal up.

"That's got to be him!" said Carson. "It's not a bear and I haven't seen another animal stand against a tree like that!" he said excitedly. "Let's go!" He turned to dart off in the animal's direction, but Ty reached an arm out to stop him.

"If this is someone's property we can't just run across it. This is Texas – we might get shot for trespassing!" Ty said.

"We are close to the creature and we are well behind the house. And besides, the owner is probably asleep. I am sure we won't get in trouble. We will be in and out before they know it," responded Carson.

"Right – and if we catch it, then what? How are we going to

extract the animal from their land?" argued Ty.

"It might not be trespassing," said Carson. "If we didn't have that drone we wouldn't know it was someone's property. It might just be an open field," he offered.

"I don't know, but I know someone who would know," replied Kareem.

"At this hour?" asked Tegan.

"Yeah, he's always around and available. Let me give him a quick call," responded Kareem. He took out his phone and dialed a number. Seconds later thunder crashed and a bolt of lightning struck a nearby tree and it sounded as if an eagle shrieked. A man with a tattered gray suit and ash marks across his face walked toward them from behind a tree.

"SOMEONE JUST CALLED ME!" he bellowed as he continued walking toward the group. The other group members looked at Kareem, then at the man.

"Are you the Texas law eagle?" asked Tegan.

"RYAN PILSON! THE TEXAS LAW EAGLE!" screamed the man.

"Um…Mr. Law Eagle…can we go chase that creature hiding over there in the trees?" asked Carson.

Calmly the man replied. "You could be charged with criminal trespass and more serious property crimes throughout San Antonio, Bexar County, and the surrounding areas in Texas under Texas Penal Code Section 30.05. Under the penal code criminal trespass includes the following elements: the person enters or remains on or in property of another; without effective consent; and when the person had notice that the entry was forbidden or received notice to depart but failed to do so."

"Well…we did see on the drone there is a barn, so it likely is the property of another, and we will only remain there long enough to get the animal…but no one told us we could not enter or were forbidden. So we're good, right?" asked Carson.

"For purposes of the criminal trespass statute, the term *entry* is defined as the intrusion of the entire body. And notice must proceed the criminal trespass allegation," replied the man.

"Yeah, like I said, no one gave us notice," retorted Carson. "It's not that simple," said the man.

"*Notice* is defined to 'include an oral or written communication by the owner or someone with apparent authority to act for the owner'. That can be the property is surrounded by 'fencing or other enclosure obviously designed to exclude intruders or to contain livestock', replied the man.

"No fence here, or at least if it is then it's broken and none right here where we might realize it is someone's land," said Carson.

"A second form is a sign or signs posted on the property or at the entrance to the building, reasonably likely to come to the attention of intruders, indicating that entry is forbidden," said the man.

Scanning the trees and surrounding area with the flashlight from his phone Carson replied, "no signs here…"

Looking at Carson the man continued. "The visible presence on the property of a crop grown for human consumption that is under cultivation, in the process of being harvested, or marketable if harvested at the time of entry also is considered notice."

"Just grass over there. No crops that can be seen. Looks like we are good to go," replied Carson.

"A final method of notice can include the placement of identifying purple paint marks on trees or posts on the property," added the man.

"Purple paint?" asked Carson.

The man stated, "(HB 793) took effect in September of 1997, under the Texas Penal Code 30.05 Criminal Trespass, section 1, subsection D. The law requires that the purple paint markings must be vertical, at least eight inches long and one-inch wide. The bottom of the mark should be between three and five feet above the ground. The markings can be no more than 100 feet apart in timberland and 1,000 feet apart on open land, and must be in a place visible to those approaching the property. Ranchers all across the state at that time were contacting their state representatives and stating that they were having problems with getting trespass cases filed because signs were torn down and fences were cut; thus, rendering the property not properly posted. The presence of purple paint is identifiable and unique. Purple paint should be taken seriously. Trespassing is a Class B misdemeanor in Texas unless the intruder is carrying a firearm, which you have, then it stands as Class A misdemeanor. Both are punishable by fines and imprisonment," added the man.

Ty shone his phone around the area where the field began. He noticed on two nearby trees a vertical stripe about ten inches long. "Well, there's your sign," said Ty.

"Best to go knock on the door," suggested the man. He walked behind a tree. Another lightning bolt struck down. A hawk screamed again, and the man was gone.

Looking down at the phone app Carson noticed the animal was gone. Dejected he said, "Better fly that drone back in here before we lose signal. I guess we should return to camp and visit the house tomorrow. It's too late to knock on the door tonight. Besides, the animal is gone, so...."

"We had some excitement tonight, didn't we?" said Tegan as the group turned and slowly walked back toward their campsite.

"Not bad for our first time out," smiled Kareem.

"I am tired," said Ty. He continued, "Plus all of that excitement did get me thirsty. Who's up for a beer?" "I could use one before bed. Maybe two. Let's finish off those beers and hit the sack," said Carson as they continued walking.

14 FLUTTERS IN THE BASEMENT

Monday, June 22, 2015

Tegan awoke to the smell of cooking bacon. She looked around to assess the situation and saw the guys were already awake. Ty and Carson were cooking over a campfire and Kareem was looking at the footage from the time-lapsed camera left at the camp last night while the groups hunted for the creature. She looked at her watch. It was 8:45 am.

"Good morning, guys. What's up?" she asked sleepily.

"Just getting a little grub going," said Carson. "We walked over to the Valero and bought some bacon, eggs, bread, and orange juice. Had to get the paper plates, forks, and a pan too."

"Wow – that's a pleasant surprise," said Tegan.

"So what's on the camera," asked Ty.

"Mostly nothing," said Kareem. "A lot of darkness, but there are a couple that have some promise, and one that is the best photo we've seen of the creature yet," he said.

"Let's have a look," said Ty. He scrolled through dozens of photos before coming to one that showed a blurry animal close to the camp in the water. The next one was amazing. Something must have made a noise – maybe it was Ty and Tegan as they were running back toward camp – but the animal was standing still, upright, and looking upward toward the camera. It was a clear photo that showed the animal. The red eyes that had been described in prior encounters were clear, almost as if they were glowing. It had one foot in the water and one on the muddy ground outside of the pond. Its mouth was slightly open. Enough to where the front fangs were visible and the group could see that they extended long almost like a sabretooth tiger. The night vision of the camera made the animal look green, but they could tell it was dark in color and mostly hairless. There were patches of fur along the spine, and while it stood erect, it was hunched over.

"Holy shit. That's our guy! It's just like all of the reports said. I can see why they described it as anywhere from a cat to coyote, an alien, and a kangaroo. It has features of all of those and if you just see it for a second I think you could imagine it was any of those," said Ty.

"That proves this urban legend is a real animal, and it's here in these woods. Imagine the scientific aspect of this find and what it would do to bring cryptozoology to the forefront of discussion," said Carson.

"Or we could get eaten," said Kareem pensively.

"I'm sure he won't eat us all," Ty said snarkily, "Someone has to live to tell tale in the movie." That didn't make Kareem feel any better.

The group continued to eat breakfast and look at the photos. Carson picked up a piece of crisp bacon with his fingers. He savored the moment as he took a bite. "Damn, I love bacon," he said with an ecstatic smile on his face.

"So, plan for the day… we need to visit that house down the street and see if we can talk the owner into letting us check out that area past the barn. Once there we can look for clues and begin to figure out how to catch it and where to go from there. Agreed?"

Carson asked.

"I had a hard time getting to sleep last night," revealed Ty. "I didn't used to feel that way when we were in college, but then we never really were that close to finding something. Yesterday each group saw it and then we found it again at the end of the night. My heart was racing, my mind was spinning, and my blood was pumping all night," confessed Ty. "When we used to do it before I think what we felt was mostly us psyching ourselves up, but last night was real. We now have the photo to prove that," said Ty.

"We know he is big, we know he is fast, and he is familiar with the terrain. He's going to be a hard beast to catch," pondered Carson.

"Do you think that homeowner will even be home now?" asked Tegan.

"It is Monday morning. He or she is probably working." "Good point," said Ty, "What can we do?" Carson looked at his phone.

"I don't know about now, but tonight Whitesnake is performing at the Majestic Theatre," said Carson. And with that he went into an air guitar motion and began singing "*Here I go again on my own…*I used to love that song," he said.

"I say we just go over, knock on the door, and see what's up," suggested Ty.

"Maybe wait until noon or so. I don't want the trail to get too cold," confided Carson.

After finishing the breakfast they decided to check out the house. "We should at least see if someone is there," suggested Kareem.

They cleaned up the breakfast remnants and other trash in the campsite, running it over to the trash bin behind the Valero, then walked along Highway 181 to the driveway of the house. Walking down the long driveway between rows of trees they saw a single-family house that looked to be built in the late 1980's. A brick house with an asphalt roof it looked to be more than 2500 square feet. Carson knocked on the door and waited. He turned, talking to the group, and after a few minutes knocked again. Still no answer.

Another pause, then Carson said,

"Third time's a charm," and knocked again. "Well, looks like no one is home," he said. "Let go back to camp, then maybe head into town and think about traps and where we can put it since we can't get on this property."

As the group turned to walk away and took a couple of steps in the driveway, the front door opened. A lean, average height man with striking features, medium, curly, light brown hair, and blue-green eyes stood in the doorway.

"Can I help you?" he asked. Carson and the others stopped and returned to the front door.

"We are investigators in town checking out reports of a mysterious creature in the neighborhood," said Carson.

"Oh, the guys from the town hall meeting?" the man asked.

"Yes – we met with some of the people after that meeting, checked out the areas they reported seeing the creature, and we set up camp yesterday in the woods out by those ponds behind the Valero," said Carson.

"Yeah, I meant to go to that meeting, but I got busy at work and couldn't make it out," the man said. "Sorry I didn't hear when you first knocked. I was out back in the beer cellar with a couple of friends." Carson looked back at the group with a raised eyebrow.

"Beer cellar?" he inquired.

"Yeah – I'm a graphic designer and work from my home office. Well home office/man cave/beer cellar/garage," he said. "A few of my friends who also have flexible schedules came over for an early-week, near-mid-day bottle share," he added.

"Right on!" said Carson.

"Last night that creature was in the woods around here and we chased it, but it crossed over into your property. We didn't want to trespass so we came to ask permission to check it out," said Ty.

"Sure, no problem. I have almost nine acres out back. A barn, a couple of horses. And I don't want it attacking my horses. I heard a few ranchers lost cattle because of that thing. Hey listen, you guys want to come in and meet the friends? I don't know if you are into beers, but we're about to dig into these bottles? We have several and they are all pretty good ones the man added. He stuck his hand out. "I'm Freddie Marshall." Carson shook his hand, as did the others, as he introduced each one.

Freddie led the group into the three-bedroom house, into the kitchen, and through a door that led into a converted garage. A life-sized Fathead poster of Tim Duncan and another of Manu Ginobili graced the wall of his man cave. A sixty-inch television, a PS4 console, and a framed poster of the USFL San Antonio Gunslingers logo completed the wall on that side of the room. A desk with a computer monitor rested in the back of the room behind a yellow beanbag chair. The other long wall continued wooden shelves and two double door wine refrigerators. A leather sofa, love seat, and chair completed the room. Another man and two ladies were sitting down each with a glass in hand.

Freddie introduced the group of investigators to his friends, mentioning they were searching for an unusual creature in the area. Ellie Barnes was the first to introduce herself to the group. A young lady in her late thirties with a small, delicate build, dark brown eyes, and thin dark eyebrows. A light, natural tan and shoulder length straight brown hair with straight bangs. She mentioned she worked as a realtor and just a few weeks ago she saw the creature while out showing homes.

"It was off in the distance, so I didn't get a good look at it," she admitted. "It looked dark gray and I thought it was a coyote, but it was a little skinny. Like it was malnourished."

"I am amazed at how many sightings have happened in the area," said Kareem, "It is surprising it has been seen this frequently, yet it hasn't been caught or properly identified."

"We are hoping to end that this week," said Carson.

"I hope you guys do put an end to it," said the other lady.

Caitlin Turner had dark black hair with platinum streaks and hazel eyes. She was medium height, thin, and a small birthmark on her wrist. Carson could tell she was probably creative. Maybe an artist or a musician he thought. As they continued to talk he perceived her to be eccentric, maybe a little weird, but lovable. She said she was in her mid-thirties and currently between jobs.

"I too am between jobs, although it has been some time since I was in one," said Carson.

"What did you do before?" he asked.

"I've tried a few jobs, but not many fit. I'm jobless 'cause I feel lost in this world. I don't want to work in an office. I don't want to do any paperwork, and I don't want to work with a computer. I want to work with animals or plants or do something helpful for our Earth or something like that. I also like to write poetry and occasionally play the guitar and sing at local bars," said Caitlin. "I like the freedom, but it doesn't come with much of a paycheck," she said. "I have thought of opening my own business. Having my own teahouse with a hippie-style shop sounds appealing. That thought brings peace and satisfaction to my mind. But I have no money to start. Continuing to performing songs around town in the evenings would make me happy. But an artistic career is always difficult and uncertain," she concluded.

"Moving from a science teacher job to a mysterious animal hunter is hard and uncertain also," replied Carson. "A lot of people are reluctant to talk about what they've seen because they are afraid of what others will think," he continued.

"I haven't seen the creature, but I do enjoy hanging out with these folks and having the occasional bottle shares," replied Caitlin.

"This is my first bottle share, so I look forward to it," said Carson.

Caitlin described the rules: everyone brings at least two bottles of a barrel-aged beer or something with limited availability. "Or at least not available here," spoke up the yet-to-be-introduced man. "It can be a shelf beer from another state that isn't distributed to Texas," he said. "Hi – I'm Emiliano Rivera," he said with a strong handshake.

"Look at you, talking to strangers!" quipped Freddie. "Normally

Emiliano takes a while to warm up to others. He is usually serious, quiet, and has definite loner tendencies. He enjoys solitude and tends to sit back and observe. He's private, rarely talks about his feelings, and can be insensitive to the hardships of others…but when he gets comfortable and opens up, he is knowledgeable and funny. I always invite him to bottle shares because he dutifully shows up, is consistently punctual, and always follows the rules," said Freddie.

Emiliano was in his forties, gestured quickly in talking with his hands, had a long stride, was diminutive in stature, and had a soft tending to rounded build with tanned dark brown skin.

"It's essential to follow the rules," said Emiliano. "The purpose of the bottle share is to introduce the group to new beers, so that's what I try to do. I try to find beers that none of the others have had so that we can enjoy the experience."

Freddie added, "We like to hold these bottle shares regularly. Sometimes they happen because we like getting together with friends, some of whom we don't get to see often otherwise, or, as in today, it is a good way to meet new people."

"I wish we brought some beers along, but we didn't know anyone was home," said Ty.

"Please. You are our guests and welcomed to share. We also have a few random extra beers that are not as limited. You know, just in case we run out and are still thirsty! We also have some food. Any good bottle share host knows you need a foundation – we have some platters of cured meats and veggies, cheese plates, and of course Texas barbeque," said Freddie.

"Let's get our cups! I will go first," said Caitlin.

"There is a half bath just outside the door so we can rinse the glasses," said Freddie.

"First up, I have a 2013 bottle from Freetail Brewing here in San Antonio," said Caitlin. "I love ales, and I love sours…I also love wine, so this is a combination of all of them."

She passed around a bottle of Ananke, an American wild ale aged in wine barrels. With the unexpected increase in attendance, it meant each pour was just under three ounces. Not enough for a solid drink, but enough to enjoy a taste of something new.

The beer poured a hazy, golden straw hue with a small ring of pure white head, even in the small vessel. With her love of sour beers Tegan was excited to try it.

"This is surprisingly fantastic!" said Freddie.

"Oh my God, this beer is amazing," said Tegan. "This definitely has a little funk, lemon, white wine, hay, and sweet tarts smell to it. I can taste the oak flavor coming through too," noted Tegan. Kareem smelled it and agreed with Tegan's notes.

"Sour with some tangy citrus notes. A touch of oak with some nice brett presence. Light to medium in body with a puckering finish. Pretty tasty!" decided Kareem.

"It's interesting because a lot of the barrel-aged programs use whiskey or bourbon barrels," said Emiliano. "This use of wine barrels really stands out."

"I get a little vanilla in the aroma too," said Ty. "Sour light fruits and a bit of citrus, oaky vanilla... and a bit of coconut."

"It has a dry finish like a white wine," said Carson. "It is definitely refreshing and could see myself really enjoying it on a hot Texas day."

"Two years and this is drinking well," Ellie said. "I wonder what another year would do with that oak and wine."

"Let's go light to dark," suggested Freddie.

"Then I think I am next," said Ellie. "Since we started with a wine barrel-aged beer..." She produced a brown growler and introduced the beer as being from a new, hot spot. "It's from Red Horn Coffee House & Brewing Co. in Cedar Park," she said.

"Hmm. I haven't heard of them yet," said Freddie.

Ellie responded. "These guys just opened March 11, but I really enjoy it. This is a Belgian-style red ale that aged in red wine barrels from Hilmy Cellars in Fredericksburg. It's called You Be Forty. It's only aged for only three and a half months in the Hilmy barrels, but I think it really brings out the wine in aroma and the flavor."

Each participant received their share, swirled the small glass, and placed their nose above the rim. Ty took a sip and offered,

"Nice twist on a Red Ale. Dryness of the Cab barrel balanced by the malty Red Ale."

"Hmm...tastes like a slightly sour dark beer," said Carson.

Caitlin enjoyed the beer as well adding 'I'm getting a lot of 'dark berries, cinnamon, and toffee,'" she said.

"The amber color is nice, but for me the red wine is a bit strong and makes it kind of a slow drinker," said Tegan.

The group took a quick break to wash out the glasses and prepare for the next tasting. Emiliano picked up a brown bottle with a white label and poured for his new friends. This is a bourbon barrel-aged imperial brown ale from Ranger Creek Brewing and it was bottled November 2014. Kareem looked at the glass of jet black beer with light cocoa colored foaming head and smelled. He noted a warming bourbon aroma, with hints of oak and vanilla before taking a small sip.

"I get some heat on the palate, with a pleasing warming caramel and vanilla flavor," he said.

"That one spent time aging in two barrels," noted Freddie. "First a Four Roses barrel, then Ranger Creek .44 & Rimfire Barrels."

Ty took a sip and reported, "the bourbon dominates but doesn't overwhelm the base beer, which I don't think seems like much of a brown ale; there's no nuttiness or English brown malts. Instead, I find dark malts, faint tobacco, toffee, cream, and a hint of dark malts."

"Man, I love the bourbon on this. I bet this gets better as it warms up," said Carson.

"Wow. It really has everything you look for in a barrel-aged brown, so smooth! Not too much bourbon, although using two different ones gives the different notes that adds to the flavor," said Caitlin.

As they finished up the Imperial Brown, Freddie looked over at Carson and Ty. "What are you going to do when you find this animal again?" he asked. The guys looked at each other briefly.

"Ideally, we would like to capture it alive," said Ty. "We want to take a look at your land and see where it has been traveling, what's in the area, and where a good place to put a trap might be."

"We've seen it in a photo and from a distance, but not up close to fully understand its size," said Carson. "That could determine our trap plan. But once caught we hope to have it analyzed to see what it is and maybe where it came from," finished Carson.

"I hope you catch it," said Ellie. "A lot of the ranchers here live on tight budgets and losing part of their herd is difficult at best. And for me, if word got out a monstrous creature was in the area that would reduce the number of real estate showings I would have. Not many people would want to move into an area like that," she said.

Freddie offered a tray for each participant's glass. He took them into the kitchen for a quick wash and returned to continue the party.

"Hopefully my first bottle won't be as scary as that monster," said Freddie with a grin. He held up a dark bottle with an artistic label. "Being a graphic designer, this label really stood out to me," he said. "The label has a nice graphic, eight colors (which is unusual for graphic print), and an interesting name. This is Branchline 5 a.m. To Midnight Dark Ale," said Freddie.

Carson looked at the bottle and agreed with the review of the label design: A graphic of a number like those on an old alarm clock or gas station pump in the process of rolling over from 4 to 5. He was curious about the name – 5 a.m. to midnight. What is a 5 a.m. to midnight?

A note on the label stated it contained cocoa, espresso, and mint. Espresso and 5 a.m. could indicate a cup of morning coffee, and perhaps the mint and midnight related to a relaxing cup of mint tea to end the day around midnight? But then why not chamomile? That sounded more night time tea-like than mint. He pondered for a moment, then turned the bottle.

The commercial description provided the answer: "In order to brew beer you need to be both an early bird and a night owl. Get up early, drink coffee, eat tacos, drink beer, brew beer, clean up, drink beer, fill kegs, drink beer, stay out late, drink beer, drink beer, and tomorrow do it all over again. So here at Branchline we brewed a seasonal beer to make it a little easier to wake up so early and stay up so late. You are holding a sweet, dark ale brewed with mint, cacao, and locally roasted espresso beans. A wonderful espresso aroma and milky mint on your tongue awaits. So stay up late, or wake up early, or both from 5am To Midnight."

"Clever!" Carson said as he returned the bottle to Freddie for the pouring.

Freddie poured a serving to each guest and awaited the results of their review.

"I like the dark brown hue with small fizzy fully diminishing head," said Ty. Taking a sip he continued, "Initial flavor is moderate sweet with a light bitter finish. It has a lot of tastes in this one - chocolate, light mint, molasses, brown sugar, espresso, and dark bread, a medium bodied with light carbonation."

Caitlin smelled the glass and noted a minty, fresh-brewed coffee, and Mexican chocolate with a faint smell like Kahlua. "I really like this," she said, "I think it's really well done. It's well balanced; nothing is dominant. It's not overly sweet, and the mint tastes like fresh mint rather than cheap candy or flavoring. There are even black pepper and chili overtones that blend in nicely, as well as a creamy texture and a long, smoky finish."

Kareem agreed with Caitlin. "Like an Andy's mint but refreshingly smooth," he said. Emiliano offered "This is a super interesting, unique beer. I think it's perfect to share with others as the flavors are a little strong. Not sure I could drink a whole one myself, but definitely a solid coffee kick and light mint. Good balance to those two flavors."

"I definitely enjoy the darker beers the most," said Ellie.

"Me too!" spoke Carson. "I just recently started into the world of craft beer, thanks to these guys, but I have enjoyed the dark beers more than anything else," he concluded.

"That beer is a good transition into the next round of beers we have," Ellie said. "These are smaller bottles, 12.7 ounces, so I brought two of them," she said as she removed two brown bottles from a paper bag. This is one is also from Ranger Creek and part of their barrel-aged small batch program. This one is marked as bottled November 26, 2012 and is Small Batch Series No. 4." She passed one bottle to Kareem, Tegan, Emiliano, and Freddie while she did the honors of pouring her Caitlin, Carson, Ty, and herself.

"Ranger Creek does have some advantages over others in the barrel-aged program," Ellie said. "It has a whiskey distillery side and always has barrels available to use for aging beer. These bottles are 10% ABV so it packs a little kick."

The beer gushed when opened, indicating a bit of over-carbonation.

"Cleanup on aisle two!" said Emiliano. Freddie quickly grabbed a towel from the dryer in the other room and used it to wipe up the spill.

"Looks like we have a little less now," said Ellie. A hard pour into each of the snifters generated a decent-sized head, even for such a small pour. Ty took the glass and let it rest a moment.

"Good head retention on this, likely due to the carbonation. A nice thick head of khaki," he said.

"What type of beer is it?" Ty asked.

Ellie responded, "The label doesn't say, but at the brewery the said it was an imperial mesquite smoked porter aged in Ranger Creek bourbon barrels."

Tegan agreed, "It has a nice medium body but the high carbonation leads to a pure foam mouthfeel all the way to the finish, a bit over-carbonated."

"But it tastes pretty good," said Kareem. "The mesquite gives some woodsy and herbal flavors. I've had the base porter before and it is simple with some light chocolatey notes. The mesquite smoking actually compliments the base beer quite well, without being overbearing."

Caitlin agreed it wasn't overbearing, but added, "The barrel notes are lacking, leaving this feeling like a smoked imperial porter - not a barrel-aged one. I would have liked to see a little more oak and bourbon in this."

"I was definitely looking forward to it," said Carson. "This was a nice concept but I don't think that they got enough influence from the barrel to match up with the smoke of the base beer."

"Let's have another rinse break and I will pour my second one," said Caitlin. Carson took the time to review the pitching match-up for the Houston Astros vs. Los Angeles Angels game. Emiliano took notice.

"Are you an Astros fan?" Carson looked up and smiled.

"Yes. Since I was a kid and they were in the National League. Nolan Ryan. Cesar Cedeno. Ken Caminiti. And later Craig Biggio, Jeff Bagwell, Billy Wagner…but my all-time favorite was Jose Cruz. I used to try to do that high leg kick when I played little league. Emiliano agreed with the historic choices."

"After a couple of rough years transitioning to the American League I am glad to see they are doing well now. What about that Carlos Correa kid? He's off to a great start in his rookie year. I think he's definitely the shortstop of the future. He's shown he can hit at the major league level, and with power."

"We've got some good, young arms too. Collin McHugh is pitching tonight and already has seven wins," Carson stated.

"Okay, I wanted to rinse the cups before this one because it should have a little different taste and I wanted to see how it stands up," said Caitlin. "This is Lakewood Brewing Company's Mole Temptress Imperial Milk Stout. Bottled in earlier this year, so not a lot of age, but it should be good. I've left it out on the table to get closer to room-temperature, so it should open up nice."

Tegan's eyes lit up and she smiled as the dark liquid poured into her snifter. "We might need some tacos to go with this," Tegan said. The pour was a dark brown/black, but not pitch black as Tegan was expecting.

"I am a big fan of mole," noted Emiliano. "In cooking there are many variations of recipes, but common ground includes chiles and nuts along with a touch of chocolate to tame the heat of the chiles." Taking a sip, he paused with a surprised stern smile. "Vanilla and cinnamon at first, changing to smooth chipotle spice with chocolate. The chocolate also has some cinnamon with it, but then the chile peppers hit you at the end along with what seems to be nutmeg."

He took another sip. "I've pretty much tried any pepper beer and this is quite possibly the most well balanced I've ever had. This is my favorite of the night so far!" said Emiliano with a satisfied smile.

"That Temptress smooth chocolate milk stout base is solid, but then a nice earthy flavor profile hits you in the middle – which I expect from mole. At the end it finishes off with a slight burn from the dried chilies. The only chile I can pick up is adobo and maybe some poblano. The spicy finish is nice and not too powerful, which is a good thing for me," said Freddie.

Tegan continued the positive reviews, following close to Emiliano's comments, "It balanced the earthy spices, peppers and chocolate extremely well without overpowering any of the three. This may be the best pepper-ish stout I have tried," she said.

"Cinnamon is one of my favorite spices," said Carson. "The pepper is really light while it goes heavy on the cinnamon and sweetness. There is some chocolate and the slightest bit of roast. This would be a great nightcap. What's the alcohol on this one?" he asked.

"That's a 9.1%," said Caitlin.

"The alcohol is covered up nicely in this, and I agree with the guys. I think this is the closest I have come yet to finding the 'perfect' pepper stout," said Ellie.

Still smiling, Emiliano looked around at the group enjoying themselves. "It will be hard to top that last one," he said. "But we are getting down to the end so let's go. That last beer was 9.1%, and as Emeril said – *let's kick it up a notch!*"

He reached into a brown paper bag of his own. "Boom!" he said as he grabbed two twelve ounce bottles with his left hand and dropped the now-empty bag with his right. "How about a little Russian Imperial Stout?" he asked. Carson set up tall in his seat. That last beer was good, but from his brewery tours earlier in the week he knew he liked Russian Imperials.

"Even though these pours are small, I'm starting to feel it," Carson said – but still extended his glass for the offering.

As Emiliano poured he said, "This is St. Arnold's Bishop Barrel 8. They take the Divine Reserve No. 5 Imperial Stout recipe as the base beer in this one."

Carson looked like a child at Christmas unwrapping a new PlayStation console. Immediately he smelled it, taking in the Chocolate bourbon aroma. He could only mutter a "mmmm" as he inhaled. Tegan commented that it also smelled like raisins, toasted coconut, and vanilla.

Emiliano added, "This was then aged in Woodford Reserve barrels." Everyone commented positively on the smell, Carson lingering a little longer than others, just taking it all in.

Ty tasted it and revealed, "There is plenty of bourbon up front giving it strong flavors of barrel juice, charred oak, caramel, and toasted coconut. The dark chocolate mixes with fig and date, along with a hint of toffee & coffee, the finish gives flavors of toasted nuts with hints of caramel and straight bourbon on the linger."

Carson looked over at his friend. "I'm not sure what barrel juice is, but I hope it's tasty." With that Carson took a sip. "Oh my. Electricity on the tongue! The barrel aging plays quite well with this one!" he said with happiness. Freddie suggested the taste included molasses with a little bit of peat and charred malt. While Caitlin felt that what set it apart from the other stouts was the rich thick body and excellent mouthfeel.

"I think there's some bakers chocolate," said Ellie. "For the high alcohol content and the bourbon smell, the taste is silky smooth; no hint of alcohol," marveled Freddie.

Ty looked at his watch and noticed it was well into the mid-afternoon hours. This drinking party turned into a longer-than-expected event. Freddie saw Ty looking at his watch and felt the group might be ready to get going. After all they did come to just ask permission to check the back yard for the animal. He commented that there was one bottle left.

"Why don't we crack this last bottle," then I can walk you to the back to look around. But there is plenty of beer to go around as long as you want to stay after we come back," said Freddie. "We can get some pizzas from down the street, watch the Astros game, and make a day of it," he offered.

"Last, but not least, I offer up Freetail Brewing Co's. Old Bat Rastard. This one a 2012 bottle," said Freddie. "I admit that I have had this before. Actually, I have it every year and usually buy a few bottles. It comes out on New Year's Day and is classified as a winter warmer. I know kind of unusual to have a winter warmer in the middle of a humid Texas summer, but it is one of my favorites," said Freddie.

"I love the name," said Ty, "My dad used to say things like 'bat rastard' instead of rat bastard when I was growing up."

Carson looked up and said, "mine said 'tig ol' bitties," with a smirk.

Freddie poured the drink and Carson took a deep breath as he prepared for the final round. His head was already lightly tingling, which he speculated should make searching the woods more interesting.

"Hopefully the chupacabra doesn't pick that moment to attack," he thought. "So, what's with the label?" asked Carson. "It looks like a bat in a leisure suit." Freddie proceeded to tell him and the group the tale.

"Every New Year the Old Bat Rastard unfurls his withered wings and stretches, feeling for any sign of the sun warming his would-be thumb. If there is no warmth, he's in for a long winter; if however he feels a sunrays' warmth, he folds his leathery appendages back, content to know spring is not far."

"So, kind of like Groundhog's day?" said Tegan?

"Yes, but grumpier. An old curmudgeon is how the brewery describes him," said Freddie. "They release the regular version on New Year's Day then typically come out with a barrel-aged version in early February. That one has been limited to around two hundred bottles, so it is hard to get."

"Have a whiff of this," Freddie said to Caitlin as he poured the first taster. She sniffed and had a pleased look on her face.

"Smells bready and nutty, like almond butter spread on toast," she said. He passed one to Emiliano who enjoyed the malt aromas and caramelized sweetness.

Tegan took the smell in and found a lot of bread and caramel malt along with a lot of fruits with an almost port-like smell. Kareem caught the caramel sweetness but thought it followed by notes of grapes, figs, and apples. Ellie thought the smell was tough for me to pick out, but certainly fruits and dark roasted malts.

Ty smelled and asked, "It's a winter warmer?" He thought it could almost pass as a barleywine with rich molasses, licorice, and caramel giving it a big aroma. Not quite barleywine material but in the vicinity. Carson found the smell to be enjoyable and complex. He detected smells of dark fruits, raisins, figs, caramel malts, bready malts, and toasted malts. He eagerly took a sip. His mind raced trying to place some of the lingering tastes coming forward. Almost like burnt sugar, a tangy dark malt, some type of metallic roastiness, but a big chocolate mixed with a mild spice, caramel, fig, and plum.

Others noted it had a nice hop hit in the middle, but also a great mouthfeel with a slight boozy taste making it feel big. Ellie called out a smooth herbal earthy bitterness and nuttiness. While others enjoyed it, Carson was extremely pleased.

"This has flavors of caramel, cocoa, cherry, brown sugar, raisins, roasted malt, and herbs with a somewhat dry finish. It's really complex with all of the subtle undertones," he said. "It is full and slightly bitter, not too strong, but I can get the alcohol and I think if a winter warmer means giving you a nice warm feel on a chilly winter day, this would do the trick. I did like the other two beers, but this might be my overall favorite. Nectar of the Gods! I think those tones of apricot, cherry, and currants make me look forward to spring and to hope…new beginnings!" he said as he raised his snifter.

Freddie was glad his friends enjoyed the beer event, and Carson especially liked the Old Bat Rastard. "Freetail makes a lot of excellent beers," Freddie said, "But that one might be my absolute favorite in the lineup. I look forward to it every year."

"I definitely don't blame you," said Carson. "I am new to the craft beer scene, but that was one of the best I have tried so far."

"You are new? How new?" asked Freddie. Ty spoke up.

"About three weeks now. He was a regular beer drinker at a dive bar when we found him. We introduced him to a local brewery in Austin and blew his mind. Now we are stuck with him and I think have to hit up some bottle releases around Austin. Maybe a beer festival or two to give him the full experience," Ty said.

"Do you have a beer cellar yet?" asked Freddie. Carson chuckled.

"Definitely not. I need to learn about cellaring and beer trading. It sounds so foreign to me, but also interesting," he said.

"Tell you what. Since you are here to help the community and find out what the animal is that is wreaking havoc here, and you are a nice guy who is just starting out, let me give you something," said Freddie. "A little thank you for your work and a welcome to our world. Something to start your beer cellar," he said.

He walked to the far temperature controlled refrigerator. "We can keep it here until you are ready to go back to Austin, but since you enjoyed that Old Bat Rastard so much, I will give you one from my collection. He pulled out a bottle and handed it to Carson. It's one of the 2010 Barrel-Aged Old Bat Rastards," he said. "As I mentioned, they only make about two hundred per year, and this one is now five year's old, so that greatly reduces the number. I still have one left, but you are welcome to have this one," he said.

"Wow! I don't really know what to say. THANK YOU! I appreciate your generosity – inviting us into your home, to the bottle share, introducing us to your friends, and now this. I am very grateful," Carson said humbly.

Freddie smiled, slapped Carson on the shoulder and said, "No problem. Now....let's go out back and look for that chupacabra!"

Carson, Ty, Kareem, Tegan, and Freddie walked out the back door and into the ankle-deep grass out back. The walk was slightly more challenging than it would have been earlier in the day when they first went to the house. Even though the pours were small, eight of them added up thanks to the variety of beer and the alcohol volume.

The horses were off to graze behind the barn and didn't come around to see what the group was up to. Walking past the barn the group eventually made it to the backline of the property. Ty looked around and toward the west.

"This is where we were yesterday," he said. "We came from over there, saw it on the cameras, and chased it over the property line. We did fly a drone over the area and saw that it was propped up against a tree back here somewhere," he said.

Walking around, searching the ground for clues, the group – including Freddie, looked for any clues to the animal. Kareem kicked some of the fallen leaves looking for tracks the animal may have left.

"Look here!" he said. He pointed with his shoe to a pile of scat that laid on the ground. "We know the animal was here. I bet that is his droppings," suggested Kareem. "Did anyone bring those bags?" asked Kareem.

"Actually, I happen to have a couple of bags and a pair of the gloves," said Tegan. "I like to be prepared for anything." She put on the gloves, bent down, and collected the sample. "We can save that for Sophie and the lab," said Tegan.

Ty shined a flashlight around the trees. "Look over there – claw marks on the tree. Those are higher than most animals," he said. Freddie looked at the evidence in disbelief. He didn't frequently spend time in the back of his property – just enough to tend to his two horses, but to think an animal such as the mythical chupacabra was that close to him made him nervous.

"What is that?" Freddie asked as he continued to help the group. "My God – that looks like a nest," said Carson.

The limbs from saplings, leaves, dirt, and other materials were collected together and formed into a large matted down area. Something that looked like where the chupacabra definitely slept.

"Some of the recent chupacabra findings have come back after analysis saying they are raccoons with mange or scabies, but this nest…whatever slept here is bigger than a raccoon. And that animal we saw last night definitely wasn't a raccoon," said Carson.

"Bigfoot supposedly sleeps in nests, but does the chupacabra?" asked Ty.

"Coyotes are one thing the chupacabra has been speculated to be, but they don't usually live in nests. They use dens to give birth to their offspring and to sleep," said Carson. "Some have described this animal as looking like a boar, and boars and other wild pigs do sleep where they are covered by thick brush," continued Carson.

Kareem started looking through the nest and found feathers similar to chickens, leaves, twigs, more scat, and footprints matching the animal Tegan and Ty encountered around the pond. There was also the body of a small chicken. It was still intact, but puncture wounds around the neck drained all of the blood from its body, matching the accounts on other larger animals. "Looks like it was here recently and it is definitely the nest of the chupacabra," said Kareem.

"What will you do?" asked Freddie.

"We have seen it and know it is big. We have seen it run and know it's fast. It is also strong and knows its way around these woods. We have to trap it, but the trap also has to be strong and fast," said Carson.

"We could dig a hole and cover it with leaves," suggested Tegan. "Then it would run across it and fall in," she said.

"We would have to dig a deep hole, then it may still jump out. It is about six feet tall and with those long legs who knows how high it could jump. Plus I don't want to dig up that much of Freddie's land here," said Carson.

"How about a snare trap?" suggested Kareem. "We could have a loop on the ground, he steps in it, and it snatches him up in the air," he said.

"That could hold him because he wouldn't be able to run if he was hanging in the air. It could take away his power – but the challenge is getting him to step in that snare loop and pull it closed in time," said Carson.

Ty thought for a moment. "I think a big spring-loaded box trap would work best. Those doors come down quickly, they are steel so they are strong, and we could put some food instead to trap him. Once he walks in to get the food, he takes it, and the door closes behind him," suggested Ty. "They make traps here in Texas for catching feral hogs. I think one of those would work well for this guy," suggested Ty.

"I think that might work, but where can we get one?" asked Carson.

"I know some friends at the Texas A&M AgriLife Extension Service and the Cooperative Extension Program in Bexar County who use them. I could make a call. Or we could buy one from a local store. I think that Producer's Co-Op in Seguin and New Braunfels carries traps made by Texas Hog Traps. We could buy from there," suggested Ty.

"True...," said Carson, "but if we don't have to buy, that might be better. We are only going to use it once, plus we don't have a lot of money. Can you call your friends at Texas A&M and see if we can get one or two here tomorrow?" asked Carson.

"Definitely! I'm on it!" Ty said as he walked away and picked up his phone to make the call.

"This creature is about the size of a large feral hog, so a hog trap should hold him. Plus it's metal and spring-loaded. That may be the best option. We just have to get him inside," said Carson.

Ty returned to the group and confirmed the traps could be delivered by tomorrow. "They have two we can use," said Ty. "We should be set and ready to bring this creature in," he said.

Carson looked pleased and looked at the faces of his friends. All except Ty had an uncertain look on their face as to what was to come next. Yesterday's hunt was challenging. What would tomorrow's bring?

"Speaking of bringing it in…," said Carson. "How about we rejoin the others inside and finish off that beer?" asked Carson. "I can call for the pizzas and have them delivered," suggested Freddie. They walked back to the house as Carson checked the Astros pre-game on his phone. "The game is about to begin," Carson said. "In more ways than one," suggested Ty.

As they returned inside Freddie turned on the Astros vs. Angels game, Caitlin handed each person a Horchata Porter from Alamo Beer Commpany, and they sat on the leather furniture enjoying the game and conversation until the pizza arrived. Carson thought about the Old Bat Rastard and the new beginnings of a cheerful spring day he imagined while drinking it. Once again craft beer and meeting new people brightened his day and the pensive thoughts that three weeks ago were a regular part of his day were fading like a morning hangover after a big greasy breakfast.

15 TRACKING THE BEAST

Tuesday, June 23, 2015

Morning arrived and a white 2011 Ford F-350 Flatbed Truck pulled into the driveway of Freddie Marshall's house. Freddie walked out to greet the truck, and the group of Carson, Ty, Tegan, and Kareem walked down the road to join them. Freddie had offered to let the group stay in his house after the bottle shared the previous night, but they decided to return to the campsite to keep an eye on the equipment.

The driver was a large white man in his early thirties named Charlie Bennett, but everyone called him "Tater". He was what many classified as a "good ole boy". He worked on the farm, spent time hunting and fishing when he could, loved country music, and momma's home cooking. He had a big heart and was always willing to help his friends and neighbors. He meet Ty at another education conference in Abilene. Tater was a service staff with the Texas A&M AgriLife Extension in Bexar County where he worked to educate Texans in the areas of agriculture, environmental stewardship, youth and adult life skills, human capital and leadership, and community economic development.

Tater exited the truck wearing a camo print long sleeve crew shirt, baseball cap, and Vital pants. A couple of rifles were mounted on his inside gun rack and *40-Hour Week* by Alabama played louder as he closed the door behind him.

"Mornin' boys," Tater said, "...and ma'am," he acknowledged with a tip of his cap when he noticed Tegan.

"I almost didn't see you with all of that camo," joked Ty.

"I figured on dropping these cages off to you then headin' out and doin' a little elk hunting since I have the day off," Tater replied. He turned toward the bed of the truck, loosened the straps, and climbed up on the platform. "We generally use a 4' x 8' heavy duty cage box traps with spring-loaded lifting gate entries," he said as he removed the straps holding them in place. "What you wanna do is deploy these in an open area with scattered brush cover. You do have to pre-bait the trap. Trapping is a process, not an event, and pre-baiting serves to both attract the animals – generally for these its feral hogs, and it also gets them accustom to entering the trap. Before you set the trap, the bait should be placed near the gate and inside the trap," he guided.

"Are you trapping more than one hog?" Tater asked.

"Um...We're not actually looking for feral hogs," said Carson. "And we think there is only one."

"If there are more than one that could be difficult. One drawback to drop gate box traps is that they do not allow additional animals to enter once the trap has been sprung...so, you're not huntin' hogs...whatcha huntin'?" inquired Tater.

"We are going to trap the chupacabra," Tegan said. Tater looked at her for a few seconds before giving a jolly laugh, his large belly shaking.

"Woo. That's a good one, Missy....chupacabra. Now I done heard it all!" he said dismissively. "I mean, I used to hear stories, but I thought it was old men setting around tellin' their tales," he said.

"It's not tale!" said Kareem.

"That's right – we saw it night before last, right out here in these woods," said Carson. "This was not an animal that I have ever encounter in the woods, and I'm pretty sure I've 'bout come across everything you can come across in Texas," said Carson.

Tater slid the first cage toward the edge of the truck. Carson and Kareem reached up and carried it down to the driveway. Ty and Freddie took the second cage. With the truck unloaded Tater jumped down.

"I don't think you are going to find any chupacabras, but good luck with whatever is out there. I don't care what you catch as long as you don't beat 'em up too good. I can come pick up the cages this weekend if that's cool," said Tater.

Freddie said the group could just leave them beside the house when they were finished and Tater could get them anytime. Climbing back into the truck, he waved as he drove off.

The sun continued to climb in the mid-morning sun as the men picked up the cages and prepared to move them to the back. Unfortunately, the temperature and humidity also continued to climb and walking the cages to the back of the property proved to be a strenuous task. Two men on each cage slowly made their way through the backyard, occasionally putting it down to catch a rest. Tegan guided the way and provided encouragement as they again picked up the sides of the cage and moved closer to the goal. After three short breaks the group finally made it to the location they wanted to set the cages.

Looking around the property Ty and Carson searched for the best place to deploy the trap. "Remember we have to cover it with brush," said Ty.

Kareem, Tegan, and Freddie began walking around and collecting leaves and small brush to help camouflage the opening of the traps. Carson looked toward the wooded area the encountered the creature two nights before. He looked at the direction the animal ran and where they saw it on the drone. The spot it rested after the chase was right where they found the clawed tree yesterday, and close to the nest.

He speculated the trail was a regular route the animal knew well. One trap right near the trail would be a good location. The second trap they would place further along the running trail, just past the barn. The trap would not bother the horses, and even if they came up to inspect the cages they were too large to worry about getting caught. Another advantage of using a box trap instead of a snare trap. The later might catch the horses, and that could injure Freddie's animals as they would struggle to attempt to break free.

"After the other night, seeing those eyes, seeing the animal run, I know this thing's out here. There have been sightings around town, but it's right here. We have it on thermal video, we have it on photograph, and we found the nest and tracks. We are this close to proving the chupacabra exists. We need to finish setting up these traps ASAP. I'm a man on a mission to prove these things are real. Nothing's stopping me. We've dug too deep, invested too much time to not catch this thing. About the only thing you can trust in the world is your gut, and I know we are close," said Carson.

Ty helped place mud and leaves around the front of one of the traps. "I agree. You and I have hunted creatures for years and we haven't been this close. We know something is out in these woods and we are going to prove it to eat other, the community, and the rest of the world."

Kareem and Tegan looked on with a nervous agreement. They found the experience the other night to be a little scary, but there was something out there, and it was harming the animals in the community and causing people to live in fear. They knew they must overcome their fear to see that this animal is captured. But what then?

All of the sightings before have been people spotting it but not being confrontational. The other day they gave chase to it, but didn't threaten it. What happens when the try to aggressively pursue the beast tonight and capture it? And when the animal realizes it is being hunted and can sense a trap and it becomes a fight or flight situation? Will it flee, or will it turn and fight? They continued to work as the thoughts flooded their mind.

Carson looked around at the trap by the barn and decided it was adequately hidden by the brush. They walked back to the first and examined it with equal scrutiny.

"The traps are set. We're going to get him! We are going to show people this shit is real. And when we do it, everyone who is sitting around saying 'Oh, he's crazy' or 'He's a naysayer'... that's what they said about Nostradamus...until his predictions started coming true. Then it's like 'fuck! I wish we would have listened to him!'" scoffed Carson proving that this was more than just a job or an adventure to him.

It was about credibility and being taken seriously in the scientific community. "I do hope we see it again tonight," said Kareem. "But...normally it's active at night and sleeps during the day. This is its nest....So where is it now?" he wondered aloud.

"Just because it is day time doesn't mean they are sleeping. Many coyotes are killed during day light hours, and with feral hogs they don't have regular habits like deer," said Ty. "He could be maybe two miles away right now and have no intention of hitting this place till they just happen to wander over here again. It might have another nest somewhere and sleep here when it's in this area. If there is food around here then it will likely return," said Ty.

"We do need to bait the traps," said Carson.

"What are we going to use for bait?" asked Kareem.

"I've heard people catch boars with a bucket of mash or strawberries and sugar. Coyotes will go for canned dog food or scraps from the butcher shop...but this, we know he hasn't eaten meat so far. It seems to only feed on the blood of livestock...I heard a couple of years ago that a group in Brazil called the Association of Haunt Mariana offered money to people to serve as bait to attempt to catch a monster they called Caboclo D'Água. Papers reported it as their version of the chupacabra, but it lived underwater and came up on land only to attack humans. But our monster has not yet attacked humans," said Ty.

"How about a baby goat?" asked Tegan. "I mean, it's supposed to mean goat-sucker, right? So why not give it a goat?"

"Well damn," said Ty. "Maybe I can get Tater back on the phone. The Texas A&M AgriLife Extension Service does have a goat project," he said. He pulled out his phone and left a message for Tater. "Hopefully he will get that and come back before sundown. I'm sure he won't think too kindly of using the goats for bait, but we just have to be ready to protect it," said Ty.

"We've done all we can do right now," said Carson. "Until we get the goats later today and until this sun goes down I think we are in a holding pattern," he said.

Carson advised Freddie they would be out there later that night and to stay inside in case they angered the animal. Freddie returned to the house and the group to the campsite.

Settling back into camp Ty suggested they get some rest to prepare for the hunt tonight. Two nights ago they found they were well rested and once the hunt started adrenaline kept them alert, and all-in-all it had been a fairly successful night. They hoped for similar luck finding the animal tonight, but this time a better result. One that would hopefully lead to a caged animal that could validate credibility not only to them, but to all those who search for animals that until now had renamed off the radar.

As the group prepared for a nap, Carson stirred around the site going over the equipment. The headlamps were needed for all, the thermal camera, night vision goggles, the rifle and pistol, the stun baton, and the GoPro camera with chest strap. Feeling satisfied with the planning, he climbed into the sleeping blanket and closed his eyes.

When he awoke it was after sundown and the hot temperatures from the afternoon sun had begun to loosen their grip on the land. The group started to stir in the camp and get ready. Ty looked at his phone and saw a text message from Tater saying he dropped two goats off at Freddie's house.

"Looks like we're set," said Ty. Carson grabbed the rifle and a headlamp. "Let's go!" he said. Ty grabbed the pistol and a headlamp, then helped Carson attach the GoPro to the chest strap. Kareem took a headlamp and the camera, leaving Tegan with a headlamp and the baton. Carson put the night vision goggles in his cargo shorts pocket and they headed over to Freddie's to get the goats. They found two small kids tied to a roped stake in the side lawn. Kareem and Tegan each took the rope leash of a goat and led them into the woods.

"You're going to be okay tonight, little guy," said Tegan.

With only the light from their headlamps to shine the way, they made their way through the darkness to the cage nearest the barn. It was undisturbed and door down as they left it. Opening the door, Carson crawled inside, took the leash from Tegan, and used a nearby rock to hammer the post into the ground. With the goat tied to the post Carson crawled out and loaded the spring door. It was ready to catch its prey.

"Sucks for the goat," said Kareem.

"Yeah, but his sacrifice will help save others," said Carson.

"I think you spent too long talking to Emiliano yesterday," said Kareem.

They walked toward the chupacabra's nest where the other trap lay in waiting. Again Carson crawled into the cage, hammered the peg, and secured the second goat. Exiting the cage he loaded the door as he did on the first cage.

"Goats are ready, traps are ready…are we ready?" he asked as he searched the faces of his partners. The group members nodded in agreement and they set off to begin the hunt.

As they took a few steps Carson looked down and noticed a small hatchet that must have belonged to Freddie laying in the grass. He remembered how fast the animal was the other day.

"What if the animal avoids our trap?" asked Carson. "We know he is fast and big. If he goes on the run we are going to have a hard time keeping up with him. We have to slow him down," said Carson.

"How do you plan on doing that?" asked Tegan. Carson looked around at the trees, then at the hatchet.

"Punji sticks," he said.

"What the hell is a Punji stick?" asked Kareem.

"It something used by the Viet Cong in the Vietnam War," said Ty. "They would sharpen sticks and place upright in the ground, usually in large numbers. These could be used around a camouflaged pit into which a man might fall or they could hide them under cover where the surprised enemy might be expected to take cover, and in doing so the soldiers diving for cover would impale themselves," said Ty.

"We don't have time to dig a pit, but we can make several sticks and hide them along the trail before the cage. Then maybe he steps on the sticks and runs into the cage. But if he misses the cage, he will be slowed and we can capture him," said Carson.

He used the hatchet and chopped off several small sticks about eight to ten inches in length. He chopped the edges to a fine point and tossed them into a pile, making about thirty spikes overall before concluding that would be sufficient. They gathered the newly created spikes and found a location in the bend of a trail where they would likely be unseen once camouflaged with leaves.

"Just remember if we come chasing the animal through here…," said Ty, his voice trailing off. Everyone understood the message and the danger it may be for them if they forgot. Satisfied with their work, they set off in a group back toward the ponds near their campsite.

"The water is a good place to start. In case the animal is thirsty…there aren't too many places around here to get water – not like the pond at Fred's house, the lake, or the river on its way to the school. Chances are if he's here and he's thirsty, he will be around here tonight," said Carson.

Moving around the pond, there was no sign of the creature. Frogs were chirping, katydids and crickets were singing, and owls were hooting. A good sign that no danger was around. They slowly circled the three ponds looking in the thermal camera and the night vision goggles without seeing anything. Carson decided to lead the group into the woods, the route he and Kareem took the other night. The woods were quieter than near the pond, but an occasional owl was still heard. For more than an hour they journeyed slowly through the woods without sight nor sound of the creature they sought.

Deeper into the woods they walked, further than their first hunt. "We have to remember where Freddie's house and our traps are. We can't get too far out here, forget where we are, and chase the animal the wrong direction," warned Carson. Now more than a mile away from their campsite the group continued, turning to look in the direction of every noise they heard. The group slowing drifted toward the east and the far depths of Freddie Marshall's property.

"It's like looking for a needle in a haystack – a dark animal in the dark woods with lots of cover," said Kareem. They walked east for a while, then back south toward Freddie's house. The woods grew quieter as they moved through the night. They began to slowly spread apart as they came upon the trail they found in the woods earlier. "This looks like the trail that heads back toward the traps," said Kareem.

As they came around the corner looking for tracks or broken branches, Tegan's headlight shone on a tree right beside the trail. Just two feet from her the creature stood on its hind legs and let out a growl. She jumped in horror as she stared into its glowing red eyes, and saw its sharp fangs and extended claws.

Startled, it lunged toward her. Instinctively she reacted by jumping back and swinging the stun baton into the beast's midsection. It screamed in pain as its body flooded with 150,000 volts of electricity. It dropped and ran gingerly down the trail into the darkness, much slower than normal after receiving the intense jolt.

"Holy shit!" she exclaimed. "Oh my God! Are you alright?" reacted Carson. Kareem grabbed her as she shook from the initial shock.

"Yes-Yes, I'm fine...I'll be fine! We've got to go after it! It's slowed down now!" she said.

The woods filled with another loud scream and Ty speculated the creature found the spike pit set up along the path.

"Likely the stun baton weakened its vision and it didn't see camouflaged spikes. This might be our shot!" shouted Carson. He turned and ran into the darkness. Ty paused for a second, looked back at Kareem and Tegan, and then ran following Carson. Moments later, a loud metallic sound rang through the night. Carson stopped, turned toward Ty and said "That's the trap! Let's go! Get the gun!"

The two ran off quickly to investigate. "Are you planning on shooting it?" huffed Ty as he tried to keep pace.

"That thing almost had Tegan!" Carson said. "The time for preppin' is over. It's do or die tonight! That thing has seen its last day! Get up here!" yelled Carson.

"We can't just leave Kareem and Tegan alone in the woods!" replied Ty. Where are you going?" yelled Ty.

"We've got to check the trap!" Carson shot back.

As the two men reached the cage near the chupacabra nest they found the door closed but the cage was empty. No goat. No chupacabra. "Fuck! He got away!" yelled Carson. He turned quickly in each direction looked at the trail and the leaves. "He's been here, and he's injured. Tegan hit it with that baton, but look – there's blood all around here. It must have run into those spikes!" he said excitedly. "He got away, but he probably hasn't gotten far. Follow that blood trail!" he said.

Ty yelled to Carson, "We've got to stay together! You can't go running your ass off alone! He's injured, so he's pissed, and he's definitely in fight mode! If we split up it's easy pickin's for him!"

"Jesus. We hit it with 150,000 volts, we speared it with the spikes, and we put a cage right in its running trail, yet he still got away. How do you catch or kill this monster?" Ty questioned loudly.

Kareem and Tegan caught up to the two men and looked around at the cage and bloodied leaves.

"Isn't that a sign we should just get the hell out of here?" asked Kareem.

"We're in its territory now!" said Ty.

Carson kicked a rock that was on the trail. "Damn it!" exclaimed Carson. "It cannot get away! It is not going to end like this!" he yelled. Suddenly, he ran off again into the night down the trail.

"Carson! Damn it! Get back here!" yelled Ty. "This fucker's gone crazy!" Ty said to Kareem and Tegan just before he gave chase.

Kareem and Tegan soon followed to stay close to the others, but they were so nervous they were in little position to be helpful.

"There is safety in numbers," said Kareem. Carson put the night vision goggles on as he ran down the trail closing in on the second cage. "Look!" he yelled out to the others. "Glowing eyes up ahead!"

"I'm scared to death and I really want to get inside the house!" wavered Kareem.

"Ty! Get up here!" yelled Carson, "Can I get a little fucking backup?!"

Ty ran up with Carson. "I'm right here, man!" he said.

"I'm a like scared to death too right now!" admitted Carson. "All these years of hunting animals like this and we never found shit. I was beginning to doubt it myself, but here we are knee-deep in shit's creek and I'm not sure how we get out!" admitted Carson.

"First, you gotta calm your ass down, buddy. Now more runnin' off into the night like goddam Braveheart! That shit will get you killed…or me killed…or someone," said Ty.

"Damnit!" shouted Carson as he raised his rifle and fired shots into the night.

"What the hell are you doing?! Stop shooting!" reacted Ty.

"I definitely locked eyes with something up there in the bushes," Carson said.

"Shooting is only going to scare it off!" said Ty.

"Shhh! There's something over there…in the bushes," said Ty.

"What? Are you serious?" asked Tegan.

"Yes!" said Carson. "I see it too…"

"You're just kidding me right now, right? We scared that thing off and it's running away. Hasn't it?" asked Kareem.

Carson and Ty stood at the front of the pack and continued to stare off into the dark bushes ahead. Carson cocked his gun.

"What's the deal, Hoss?" asked Ty, "What is it?!"

"Something just ran right through here," Carson said in a hushed voice. "The trees are still moving." Ty looked into the darkness and saw the moving branches, but no sign of the creature. Carson turned toward his partner.

"You go that way and I will circle around this way," suggested Carson. "You guys stay back," Carson said to Kareem and Tegan. Carson yelled out "Ty, you see anything?"

"I think...," he turned quickly. "I just saw that son of a bitch go this way – to the right of me!" said Ty.

"Ty! Look out!" Carson yelled as the creature jumped from the shadows directly at Ty.

"Oh Shit!" exclaimed Ty. Gunshots rang through the night as Carson aimed the rifle. The creature lunged on top of Ty as he pointed the pistol right at the beast's face.

BANG! BANG!

A loud groan.

A thump.

Then silence.

Carson ran in the direction he shot. "Ty?!... Ty?!" He continued to run as Kareem and Tegan ran in shock as well. They all reached the scene as the bloodied gray creature laid on top of Ty.

Ty whimpered as the heavy animal knocked the wind out of him. He tried to sit up, but his ribs were sore - possibly bruised or cracked. His arm was bloody as the beast did manage to sink his teeth in just below the shoulder. The animal was dead and the trio standing above Ty struggled but managed to roll it off of their friend.

Ty collected his breath and his thoughts as he remained on his back looking up at the dark starry sky.

"You okay, brother?" asked Carson. He reached his hand down to his friend. Ty's eyes drifted down to lock into his friend's. He slowly reached his hand up to take Carson's. He was pulled to his feet and gingerly stood as best he could. He took inventory of his injuries – sore ribs, sore chest, and definitely sore arm with trails of blood. He exhaled deeply and wiped his brow.

"Yeah, man....I'm good," he said as he turned and looked at the body on the ground. "That's not how we drew up the plan, is it?" asked Ty. Carson looked down at the animal and up at his friend.

"Not exactly," he said.

The group stood around, a little worse for wear, looking down at the creature that had terrorized the local community. Even dead it was frightful. They got a good look at it under the lights of their four headlamps and they saw that the reports were accurate. It was about three and a half feet tall and over five feet long, its gray skin now covered with open wounds and blood. It had gunshots on the upper back, its rump, and two in the head that Ty had managed to get off. Those were the killing shots they speculated.

"Now what?" asked Tegan.

"I don't think we should leave it here," said Carson. "Something might come along and eat it...let's drag it back and put it in the cage," suggested Carson. Carson looked up at Ty. "Not you, big man," he said. "We've got this."

Tegan reached into her pockets and removed three sets of latex gloves. "Put these on first," she said. They reached down and grabbed the arms of the dead animal and started to drag its body toward the cage.

"This monster is heavy!" said Carson. Finally they reached the cage and managed to get the body instead. Carson used a long stick to hit the release and dropped the trap door. "That will hold him until morning," said Carson. "We can see if Fred can come out here with that 4x4 and load him up. We might need Tater's flatbed truck to haul it over to Sophie at the lab," he suggested.

"We probably need to get Ty to a doctor tonight too," said Carson.

"I'm good," Ty said.

"That's a nasty bite on your arm," said Tegan. "That fucker

might have rabies."

"Fine. I'll get it checked out tomorrow," he said. Carson checked his phone.

"Looks like urgent care closes at 10 p.m. The nearest doctor's office is closed too. We could go into town and take you to Baptist Health System at Southcross Boulevard," said Carson as he searched the options online.

"I am sure I will be fine until tomorrow morning," said Ty. A cry echoed through the night causing the group to stop. Carson looked at his friends then over toward the second trap by the barn.

"Someone get that goat!" he said.

16 EXPLORING THE EVIDENCE

Wednesday, June 24, 2015

Wednesday morning at 8 a.m., Sophie Thompson poured a cup of coffee from the Curtis Coffee Machine in the University of Texas (UT) Health Science Center at San Antonio Nucleic Acids Core Facility breakroom. She was sleepy from staying up late the night before attempting to finish the final chapters of *The Stranger Beside Me* by Ann Rule. With her profession as a lab assistant she loved true crime and frequently envisions herself being the one to solve the crime and save the day. She closed her eyes and sipped from the cup. Analyzing her senses to see if she attained the perfect combination of coffee, milk, and sugar in her mixture. A smile graced her face. It was good. She was brought back to her senses by the vibration of her cell phone in her lab coat pocket.

She sat the coffee on the counter and looked at the phone. It was Carson Quinn calling. "Hello?" she answered.

"Sophie – it's Carson. We met at the town hall meeting Saturday?" he said.

"Yes. Yes. I remember. How are you? Did you go searching for that animal?" she asked.

"Searched for it....and found it!" he said. "It didn't go quite like we had hoped. We had to shoot it...but we have the body. I wondered if you were still willing to help?" he asked.

"You got it?! What is it?" she wondered.

"Well, that's what we were hoping you could tell us. It is like nothing I've ever seen, that's for sure. Maybe you could run some tests on it and see if we can identify what it is. We could bring it over to the lab today. We have to swing Ty by the hospital also on account of the thing bite him pretty good in the shoulder. He's got some sore ribs and lungs too, but I imagine he will be fine in a few days," said Carson.

"Oh my gosh! Sounds like it was exciting and dangerous!" she said.

"Yep. But now it's over. We just have to figure out what it is and where it came from. That's where you come in to solve the mystery," he said.

"Solve the mystery?" She repeated. "Oh, I do like the sound of that. You can bring it by today. We are kind of slow right now so I can get started," she said.

"He's a big guy – over three feet tall, five feet long, and nearly a hundred pounds I expect," reported Carson.

"Yeah, bring him over. I can take a look at Ty too if you want. Save you an extra trip," she offered.

Carson's next call was to Fred Dalton. When Fred picked up the phone Carson filled him in on the night's events and asked if he could bring the 4x4 over to the Valero to pick up the carcass.

"How are you going to get it to the lab?" asked Fred. Tegan, sitting beside Carson, overheard Fred through the phone.

"It's not going in the Verano!" she yelled for Carson and Fred both to hear.

"Me and my buddy Eric were going to get some breakfast. We can load the 4x4 in the back of his old truck and then haul the animal in the bed," he suggested.

"Sounds like a winner winner chicken dinner!" said Carson.

Within an hour Eric's old '79 Scottsdale truck pulled up in the parking lot of the Valero where Carson, Tegan, Kareem, and Ty were standing. Eric and Fred walked toward the group, noticing Ty wearing jeans and sleeveless white undershirt t-shirt. His wounds visibly noticeable.

"What the hell happened to you?" inquired Fred.

"The damn thing tried to give me a kiss last night," he joked.

"Well you better get the shoulder looked at. Looks nasty," Fred replied.

"We are going to do that when we drop the big guy off at the lab," said Ty.

Tegan, Eric, and Ty stayed by the truck in the parking lot while Fred, Carson, and Kareem got on the 4x4. Fred had hitched a trailer to the back of the vehicle so they could put the animal on it. They drove down the road to Freddie's house, then through the side yard, and into the back where the creature remained laying in the cage.

"We thought best to drag him out here and leave it in the cage so coyotes or vultures wouldn't get to him before we had a chance to get him to the lab," said Carson.

"That's good thinking," said Fred. "Nature has a way of taking care of its own, and it moves quickly," he said.

They opened the door of the cage and grabbed the animal by its feet, then pulled. Slowly they drug it out of the pen, and between the three of them, were able to carry it to the trailer behind the 4x4.

"Well I'll be damned!" said Fred. "Ugly sombitch, isn't he?" Fred placed a hand on the animal's mouth and moved its lip up to reveal its large teeth. "Those will do some damage," he said.

"No shit?" responded Ty.

The trip back to the truck was much slower due to the extra weight of the animal on the back trailer. Once back to the parking lot the three of them, along with Eric and Kareem were able to lift the body into the bed of the truck. Everyone circled the truck to look and get their first real glimpse of the beast in the sunlight.

Carson suggested they take two cars since Fred and Eric were headed to breakfast. Then they could go from the lab and the others could drive back. Tegan looked at Ty.

"If that shoulder is still bleeding you're ridin' in the back with the chupacabra," she said. Tegan led the way and Eric followed with the animal in the back. Thirty-five minutes later they pulled into Floyd Curl Drive and called Sophie. She directed them to the back of the building where she opened a door and pushed a hospital gurney into the parking lot.

"We can put him on here," she said. Lowering the tailgate of the truck, the chupacabra was once again drug by its feet and a group of men lifted it onto the gurney. Sophie looked at the animal with a surprised look and slowly pushed her glasses back up the bridge of her nose with her index finger. "Oh…," she paused, not knowing exactly what to say. She gulped as she tried to find the words. "Let's get him inside before anyone out here sees him," she suggested.

With the help of Carson she wheeled the creature into an exam room. "We will just leave him here," she said. "Now, let's have a look at you," she said to Ty. He removed his shirt and jumped up on the exam room table. She pushed on his chest and stomach asking where it hurt, then focused on his shoulder. "Doesn't look infected, but I would put some peroxide on it and keep it clean. I suggest going back to the hotel tonight and no more camping outside while this is still open." She wiped up the blood and cleaned the wound. "It's mostly just those puncture marks from the fangs, but it looks like it tore a little bit in the struggle," she said. She grabbed a clean bandage from the drawer and wrapped it up. "You'll be fine if you keep it cleaned out and change the bandages…here. Take a couple more for later," she said as she handed him a handful. Ty scooted off of the table and put his shirt back on over the freshly covered bandaged shoulder.

"So what's next for this guy?" asked Ty.

"Well…," she said as she studied the creature, "I will look at its body and see if we can identify it from that. I will take some tissue samples and run them through some tests. We have a Beckman-

Coulter CEQ 8800 DNA sequencer here that I can run DNA sequencing and fragment analysis on the samples. Once I finish with the tests I can put that information into the database and search online to see what animal or animals it matches to," she said.

"How long will it take?" asked Carson.

"If we had to send it out it would take a few weeks. But we have the equipment here and I can start on it this morning, so we can begin making some at least preliminary findings probably tomorrow," she said.

"Thanks! Keep us posted if anything turns up," said Carson.

The investigators returned to their car. "Now what?" asked Tegan. Looking at the Google map on his phone

Carson said, "I think Ty needs a beer!" as he looked up into the mirror above his seat and saw Ty's reflection. "We're up on this side of town...Freetail Brewing isn't too far away," he said. "Which reminds me – we can't forget that bottle Freddie gave me when we head out of town."

Tegan was looking down at her phone. "Hey, I know what. Let's make a pit stop on the way to the brewery," she said. "We've got plenty of time."

"Where do you want to go?" asked Ty. "There's this place I saw on *Fact or Faked* a few years ago, and it's just nine miles from here," she said.

"I loved that show," said Carson.

"What place?"

"It's called Gravity Hill," she said.

"I remember that one!" replied Ty. "That's the one where you park below the train tracks and the ghost children supposedly push the car uphill," he responded.

"That's the one, and it's nearby. We have to try it out," she said excitedly. "GPS says it's at the southeastern edge of the city, at the junction of Shane and Villamain Roads, 410 exit 42. Turn south onto Southton Road, then take the second right onto Shane Road. Drive about three-quarters of a mile to the former railroad tracks. We just have to take Highway 181 down to 410 and we take the first exit," said Ty.

As they arrived at the scene of the former train tracks Carson suggested Tegan turn on the hazard lights.

"I was just checking it out online as we drove over here and the websites say the road is still in use and curves once attempting the roll, which could put you into oncoming traffic," alerted Ty.

"For full effect does anyone have any powder?" asked Tegan.

"There should be some Johnson's baby powder in my duffle bag if it's still in the back," replied Kareem.

"Why do you have baby powder?" asked Carson. "Dare I ask?"

"You know…for chaffing when I run. It's good for the nether regions."

With a stern smile Carson replied, "Good to know…"

The bag was still in the trunk and Kareem removed the white bottle. He shook it in the direction of Carson.

"With Aloe & Vitamin E," he teased. He sprinkled it across the back bumper of the car, giving it a generous coating. The guys stood around the back of the car while Tegan got inside, slowly drove to the upside of the hill, and put the car in neutral.

As the legend stated the car slowly rolled up the hill and over the would-be train tracks. Tegan turned the car into the curve and parked on the side of the road. As the guys ran up to the car they inspected the back bumper and also as stated in the legend, fingerprints appeared in the powder.

"That's so cool" said Carson.

"It is an amazing and thrilling effect," said Ty.

"What the Fact or Faked team discovered was the trees were causing an optical illusion in regards to the 'angle' or direction the driver is looking as they are sitting behind the wheel. At first glance it appears that you are going up hill, when actually you are downhill and your car rolls down the hill due to gravity and is able to catch enough momentum to push you over the tracks. After their tests came back, it was concluded and agreed upon that the story could be debunked. The handprints in the powder are real, but they are not ghost children. They are your own oily prints from all the times you opened your trunk or touched the back end of your car," said Tegan.

"But a pretty cool story none-the-less," said Kareem.

Back in the lab Sophie started preparing the creature's body for examination. It was laying on its back with its arms up drawn in like a burglar about to jump from the bushes. She put on a surgical mask and latex gloves, then adjusted a surgical headlight to her head. Prior to starting she paused and thought this could be her true-crime-novel moment, except it was an unknown animal rather than a person, and when it came to cause of death they already knew whodunit.

She knew people were calling it a chupacabra, but what does that mean? Nothing had ever been identified as a chupacabra before. Animals thought to be the mythical monster have always turned out to be coyotes, dogs, and or raccoons. But she knew this animal was different from those – primarily because of the ability to talk on its hind legs.

She would begin with a careful inspection of the body. In a true crime setting this could be important in the identification of the victim, locating hidden evidence, and finding the cause of death. In this case it would be for classification purposes. She walked to the desk and removed an audio recorder so she could report her findings as she worked, then later write up the paperwork. She would first weigh and measure the body and record physical characteristics such as eye color, hair color, and length. Measuring from the top of the head to the feet the creature measures sixty-two inches long – about the size of her. This would be the size of the creature standing on its hind legs. Measuring the size of the legs to the shoulder and adding the head she approximated the animal stood about forty inches tall walking on all fours like a coyote. Lengthwise it measured fifty-two inches. The scale showed the animals weight to be ninety-four pounds.

Looking over the body she searched for identifying marks such as scars and signs of injury. There were the two bullet wounds to the head – one in the forehead and one just above the orbital socket of the left eye. There were also wounds on the legs and stomach, most likely from running through the spikes planted by Carson along the trail. She rolled it over to the X-Ray machine where she planned to do a few scans to see if it would reveal bone abnormalities and the locations of bullets or other objects. She would get one of the skull as well to get images of the teeth.

One of the legendary attributes of the chupacabra has been the large fanged teeth, characteristics which caused it to appear different from a normal coyote. A coyote has forty-two teeth which are specially adapted for eating meat. It has large, round, pointed canines for grabbing and stabbing prey, and blade-like premolars and molars for both shearing and crushing bones. This animal had a large head that was thirty inches long and mostly made up of a large jaw with two wide jugals. These massive cheeks allowed for the attachment of powerful biting muscles.

The animal's mouth contained a mix of different tooth types, which seemed to match more closely to an omnivore capable of foraging for plants, ☐particularly certain parts like roots and tubers, ☐but also scavenging carrion, ☐just like warthogs have been seen to do in Africa today. Yet the long canine teeth on the top of the jaw gave it characteristics of a sabretooth cat. Surprisingly, a third smaller fang was located on the top jaw between the two much longer fangs. She found evidence for this omnivorous lifestyle comes from the animal's pointed incisors, recurved, pointed, serrated canines, serrated premolars, and an unusually mobile jaw joint.

She looked more closely at the mouth and jaws of the animal. The legend says the animal feeds by draining the blood of its victims. It certainly had the front teeth designed to pierce the skin of livestock. In the reported chupacabra cases that had been analyzed it was found those animals were physically incapable of sucking blood because the mouth and jaw structure prevented the animal's mouth from forming a seal that would allow it to suck the blood. The structure of this animal was different, and with the two wide cheekbones Sophie could not determine if it was capable. Certainly it appeared more likely than a wolf or coyote.

The skull also had unusually pronounced eye sockets that housed brown eyes that glowed red at night. At the top of the head and running down the length of the animal's back was a pronounced spinal ridge with scruffy black, coarse hair. Other than the spine, the beast was mostly hairless, with a leathery greenish-gray skin. Prior investigations revealed that the animal was some known animal with various stages of sarcoptic mange, but looking closely with a magnifying glass there were no signs this animal ever had hair.

She analyzed the claws of the animal. The claws on both the hands and feet were similar to a wolf or coyote, except the second and third toes being nearly conjoined. Long, sharp claws were located on each foot. The front legs of the animal were significantly smaller than the rear, causing the animal to lean forward when on all fours – like a hunkered down dog ready to pounce. The hind legs were thin, but muscular and strong. The hips allowed full rotation for the animal to not just raise up on its hind legs for short periods of time like a bear, but to be capable of full locomotion on two legs. Sophie recalled many reports of the chupacabra being similar to a dog or coyote, but the tail of this animal was much larger. The tail was thirty-eight inches long and was thick enough to provide some sense of balance to the animal while on its hind legs.

Sophie removed her gloves and looked for a few syringes to collect blood. She paused and thought about the creature's habitat. The animal that was thought to be a chupacabra just last year turned out to be a raccoon, and the characteristics of that animal, other that its appearance, matched those of a raccoon. It was living in a tree and it ate food with its hands. A true chupacabra, at least based on the urban legends, would not live in a tree or eat like that. The animal on the table was much too large to live in a tree, and Sophie knew from her conversation with Carson that this lived in a nest – similar to a coyote or a boar. From the past couple of weeks' reports she knew it was found to be attacking livestock, which also differed from the Ratcliff raccoon chupacabra that ate corn like a regular raccoon would. While it had not been seen in the process of attacking an animal, it did attack Ty by grabbing at him with its front arms then moving in with the large teeth.

Some say the chupacabra legend was created after a woman in Puerto Rico had seen the movie *Species* a few weeks prior. The description of what she saw that night attacking livestock, that of a bipedal creature with a spiked back and glowing red eyes, became the basis of the urban legend and as the internet spread in popularity, the legend of the chupacabra spread to other countries including the United States – especially in southern Texas. But this creature was definitely real and it was dead on her table. The physical makeup of this animal also appeared to answer the question of how the chupacabra transitioned from a Hollywood monster to a dog-like creature. What on the surface seemed like two distant descriptions made sense with this animal's ability to move equally efficiently on two legs or four. But she still didn't know what it was.

She put on a fresh pair of gloves and prepared to take blood samples. The animal would no longer be needing any blood it had, so she was able to take six vials that would be used for analysis. She used tweezers and sterile plastic bottles to gather hair samples that could be used in the DNA testing. Using the forceps she removed two of the animal's front claws and dropped them into a sterile bottle. She stood looking over the animal and paused to ensure she hadn't missed anything. Satisfied with the examination of the animal's external characteristics, and the blood, nail, and hair collection, it was time to look inside.

Before cutting, the animal was placed on a rubber block, to extend the body's arch and to provide greater access to the chest and abdomen. Sophie began the chest and abdomen autopsy by making a Y-shaped incision, the two arms of the Y running from each shoulder joint, to meet at mid-chest and the stem of the Y running down to the pubic region. Next she examined the organs in place by removing the rib cage using a rib cutting saw. This allowed her to begin an abdominal examination by freeing the intestines by cutting along the attachment tissue with a scalpel. Each organ was examined within the body, then removed individually by the Virchow technique, weighed and examined in further detail. Tissue samples were taken from the organs, the brain, and the stomach contents were tested.

Sophie decided the organs would remain out of the animal and tested. Whatever wasn't used for analysis would be cremated. The body would be sewn back up and either cremated or perhaps sent to a taxidermist for preservation. She would let Carson make that final determination. She was only there to analyze the body and determine what it was. She had everything she needed for the DNA testing, but the examination took the whole work day and the testing would have to wait for tomorrow. She removed her gloves and turned off the light in the exam room.

Following a quiet night at home watching *Law & Order: New Orleans* on NetFlix Sophie returned Thursday morning and began to prepare for the testing. Some of the tests set up the night before were ready for analysis today. She immediately jumped in eager to see if she could solve the puzzle. A complete blood count analyzed the red cell and white cell count of the animal. The tests general returns numbers that would appear to be normal for a wolf, but the lymphocytes were high, indicating a potential infection, stress, cancer, hormonal imbalance, or other conditions within the animal. Analysis of the blood samples revealed high levels of mercury.

Brain tissue analysis revealed no signs of rabies, which should make Ty feel more comfortable. The stomach contents analysis revealed the animal's stomach only contained large levels of blood, but also plant matter.

"Interesting" she said. "The animal is an omnivore that eats a large amount of roots and tubers, but also supplements itself on blood. For it to need that it must have a mutation causing it to be deficient in some vitamin or mineral," she thought. An analysis of the animal's claws reveals dirt between the nail and skin, indicating it pawed the ground to dig up food, but also it contained fibers that matched other animals. Hair and skin samples matching cows, goat, and a human -most likely to be Ty were found. To Sophie this indicated that the animal used its front legs to hold its victim prior to giving it the killing blow with the teeth.

To begin the DNA sequencing Sophie placed the collected DNA on the end of a slab of a gelatin-like substance. She placed electrodes at one end of the gel and applied an electrical current. This caused the DNA molecules to move through the gel, and smaller molecules move through the gel more rapidly, so she separated the DNA molecules into different bands according to their size. Electrophoresis can only separate about five hundred bases into clear bands—causing the need for chopping DNA up into small pieces in order to sequence it.

Following sequencing, she entered the results into the online database and awaiting a match. She let the system run and continue searching throughout the day as she carried on with other projects she needed to complete at work. She should have results by the end of the day and planned to check before going home.

Late that afternoon she returned to check the results of the test. The online database showed a high similarity to a known match. She stared at the findings with a surprised look and a crinkled brow, then sat down. She thought for a minute, then turned to the computer and searched online for further information.

"This doesn't make sense," she said under her breath. Thinking for a minute at potential answers, she picked up the phone and phoned a friend for assistance with the information. After providing some initial details, her friend said she would call her back a little later after looking into a few details that would potentially answer Sophie's questions. An hour later the phone rang with the information she was looking for. Satisfied with the information from her friend she ended the call and immediately called Carson.

"Hello?" answered Carson.

"Hello? Hello?" Sophie replied, having difficulty hearing Carson. "What's all that noise?" she asked.

"Oh, sorry. Let me step outside," he said.

"What?" asked Sophie. Carson walked to the nearest door and stepped outside Freeman Coliseum.

"Can you hear me now?" asked Carson.

"Yes, that's better. Where are you?"

"The others have never been to a WNBA game, so we decided to go before we wrap up and head back to Austin this weekend," Carson replied. "Tonight the San Antonio Stars play the Phoenix Mercury, so it should be a good game," he said. "Any news on the animal we dropped off?"

"Yeah. That's what I was calling about. I examined the body and dictated the physical characteristics of it, took bloodwork and tissue samples, and ran the DNA tests like we talked about," said Sophie.

"Sounds extremely thorough," replied Carson. "What'd ya find out?" he asked.

"The findings were surprisingly unusual. The bloodwork showed high levels of mercury, so there is a chance there was contamination from the lake water near the power plant. There were a lot of sightings in the area, so it probably spent a lot of time passing through there and drinking the water. That could have caused some slight mutation, but I am uncertain how much. I found that besides blood it also eats plants. The blood likely helps it fulfill some missing nutrients it didn't get enough of in its diet. But those aren't the strange things," she said.

"We got a match with the DNA in the database…but it doesn't make sense," she reported.

"What doesn't make sense? What does it match to?" asked Carson.

"It matched the DNA of a hyena," she said.

"Hyena? But there are no hyenas that live in Texas," said

Carson.

"Well, there's something else unusual with that too," she said. "Hyaena is the genus that includes two living species of hyenas. There's the striped hyena and brown hyena," she said. "They are mostly from Africa, but the striped hyena also inhabits western Asia. There is another genus called Crocuta that represents the laughing hyena, also of Africa. And there is genus Proteles which has the aardwolf hyena. It sometimes called a jackal and also lives in Africa," she added.

"Okay, but none of those are in Texas," injected Carson.

"Those animals are recognized by science as four species of modern-day hyena, and they have similar shaggy coats. But…there is visual evidence of a fifth hyena – one that has largely been unstudied and forgotten," she said.

"Okay…what is that hyena? And did it live in Texas?" asked Carson.

"Um…no, still from Africa. This was a creature depicted in three different illustrations from a 19th-century book Volume II of *The Natural History of Dogs…Including Also the Genera Hyaena and Proteles* that was published in 1840 illustrated by Charles Hamilton Smith and engraved by William Home Lizars. It showed an animal that was mostly hairless, except for a coarse dorsal mane and some tufts of fur on its tail. It was called the naked hyaena of the deserts of Nubia," she reported.

"And the DNA of this chupacabra matches the naked hyena from Nubia?" clarified Carson.

"Yes, but our guy is much thinner, likely from some level of malnourishment…oh, and our guy is not a guy. It's a girl….and she was pregnant," revealed Sophia.

"Holy crap! Really? So that means there are more of them out there?" asked Carson.

"Well, wolves and hyenas are separate species, so they cannot breed…so likely, yeah…it means there are probably more in existence," she said.

"But one thing is still not clear," began Carson. "How did this animal from Africa get to Texas?"

"Yeah, that was odd to me too so I called my friend Valerie. She works at the San Antonio Historical Society and I asked if she ever heard of hyenas being in Texas."

"Did she have any information?" asked Carson.

"She said just in the past month they received some items from an estate sale and finished cataloging them in the system. One of the things was an old journal from Ephraim Fontaine," she said.

"Who is Ephraim Fontaine?"

"In the late 1860's Swiss landscape designer John J. Duerler sought to open the first zoological exhibit in San Antonio. He thought it would be a huge attraction for people to see animals from around the world they would never see otherwise. It was initially going to be a private exhibit, but he petitioned San Antonio to allow it to be housed in San Pedro Park, near where the zoo is today. But Humphrey Whitman and Ephraim Fontaine were businessmen who recently moved to the area from Adams County, Ohio and they saw the opportunity to make money if they could open an exhibit of their own in Bexar County before Duerler received approval for his. They didn't seek the city's permission and tried to do it themselves. They were in a hurry and hired cheap labor to build the exhibit quickly. Whitman & Fontaine tried to find the rarest of animals to bring in so that after Duerler opened his, they would still be the better exhibit. Two of the animals they acquired were naked hyenas from Nubia. Fontaine acquired them from an expedition to Africa just months before and had them shipped to the United States," she added.

"Well that explains how those animals came to Texas." "What happened once they were here?" Carson inquired.

"According to the journal, because of the shortcuts in permits and the use of cheap labor, there were some issues. They did manage to get their exhibit up first, but a fire destroyed it before they had to chance to open to the public. Many animals died, but some escaped including two Nubian naked hyenas. Fontaine's journal said he and Whitman formed expedition parties to search for the missing animals. Some of the wild animals were caught and killed, but the hyenas and a couple of other animals were never found," she concluded.

"So likely the creature we found and called the chupacabra are descendants of those missing unknown species of hyenas that were never recaptured? Somehow they managed to survive in the wild, breed, and live largely undetected for the past one hundred years," said Carson.

"Yes, that's what it looks like," said Sophie. "The DNA matches up to the little-known records we have, and the journal explains how the animals got to San Antonio…and we have one here so it must mean they found a way to survive," she said.

"Well that certainly is a wild story," he said. "I will have to Google some images of this animal, but just a few questions come to mind. There have been hundreds of sightings, but everything that has been caught previously are other common animals. But these things are out there if ours is actually pregnant…so why hasn't anyone else caught one before?" wondered Carson.

"It could be there are more out there but you just happened to shoot one," Sophie responded.

"We will report it, present the evidence, and I guess the rest of the scientific community can come up with theories and further research," said Carson. "Thanks for all of your hard work on this. We couldn't have done it without you."

"What about the body?" asked Sophie. "What do you want to do with it?"

"I think we should send it to a local taxidermist and let the town keep it. I'm sure people would like to come and see this animal once word gets out. Might help out the local businesses with increased tourism," he suggested.

"There's Black Feather Taxidermy on US-181. We can send her there."

Still scratching his head from Sophie's findings, Carson went back inside the arena to join his friends. He sat down just as the horn blew to signal the game was about to start. Throughout the first half the team talked about what Sophie's findings meant and their experiences over the past week. They were also treated to an enjoyable first WNBA game as San Antonio took a 19-7 first quarter lead and 32-27 at the half. Carson was a little sad Dianna Taurasi, his favorite player on the Mercury, was not playing this season. Leilani Mitchell was filling in for her and put up fifteen points during the game. DeWanna Bonner had seventeen, Cayla Francis thirteen, and Candice Dupree twelve – but the home crowd got to go home happy as Sophia Young-Malcolm scored twenty-one, Danielle Robinson with fifteen, and Kayla McBride with eleven. Danielle Adams only had five points, but she made one three-pointer and six rebounds.

The Phoenix Mercury had a strong third quarter – a total of twenty-seven points, which marked their combined scoring in the first half, and took a 54-48 lead heading into the final period. But the Stars rallied and finished with an exciting 76-71 victory. Kareem, Tegan, and Ty were elated with the game and came away with respect for the play of both teams.

"Wow!" I didn't know the WNBA was this exciting. I will definitely come to more games," said Ty. "These ladies play hard and are exciting to watch!"

"Agreed!" said Carson as he tapped the edge of his plastic beer cup against his friend's cup.

"This will probably be our last night in town," said Kareem.

"Who's up for hitting a couple of downtown sites?" "The night is still young!" said Carson.

"We probably should at least visit the Alamo," suggested Tegan.

"You're right, and it's just about five miles away," Ty said as he consulted the mobile map on his phone. "Let just take Houston Street over...and guess what is close to the Alamo?" he asked with an inviting upbeat tone. The other three looked at each other uncertain of the correct response.

"Alamo Beer Company!" Ty said enthusiastically.

"Well, since we're this close...," said Carson.

Driving down E. Houston Tegan stopped at the light to turn right onto Chestnut Street. On the corner was a Red Roof Inn. "Why didn't we stay at this one?" she questioned Carson. "This would have been a better fit for tonight," he said, "but overall the other location worked better." She continued on Chestnut and four streets later a right turn onto Lamar. The brewery was on the right hand side and well-lit giant letters on the side of the building spelling out "ALAMO" provided an inviting entrance. The bar was crowded that evening as the events from Beer, Bacon & Bingo were continuing, but they managed to find a table.

Kareem's eyes widened and he turned toward Tegan as he noticed the offering of candy-coated, chocolate dipped bacon. The Box Street Social food truck was there and Myles Smith was playing guitar and singing *Ants on the Melon*. They each ordered a different beer: Tegan the Golden Ale, Kareem the Amber Lager, Carson the Pilsner, and Ty the German Ale. As they drank and enjoyed the beers Ty was particularly pleased with the German pale ale, noting the traditional style that isn't often found with the balance of hops balanced with the malty finish.

"We should probably just stick around for one since we want to hit up the Alamo," said Tegan. "I mean, it will be closed, but we can walk around the outside of the plaza."

"Plus, there is a haunted saloon right there near the plaza," mentioned Carson.

"How can you beat ghosts and beer?" asked Ty.

Kareem dropped $20 on the table, placing a salt shaker on top, and they headed back to the car.

Driving back down Chestnut Street, Carson noticed something out the car window. "What is that?" he asked. "Let's check it out!"

Tegan steered the car toward the strange object. "It's a giant buffalo nickel!" she said. Indeed it was.

Outside Old Time Wooden Nickel Company on 345 Austin Road stood what was described as the world's largest wooden nickel. Carson imagined that was an accurate description as it measured three feet four inches in diameter and five and a half inches thick. One thing was for certain, it was a photo op he was not about to pass up. He tossed Kareem his cell phone and bolted out of the car to stand beside the roadside attraction.

"Check!" he yelled as he returned to the car and Tegan continued the journey to Alamo Plaza.

"We can park here, walk over to the Alamo, then walk over to the Menger Hotel Bar across the street," suggested Tegan. As they walked the plaza they were surprised at how small it seemed. The image of the Alamo and status it has achieved in American history and lore caused them to picture a large facility, and once it was. What remains today are just two buildings: the Alamo Shrine (or church) and the Long Barracks. The plaza itself was once part of the original courtyard of the Alamo. The grounds were lovely and the ancient live oak was an awesome sight.

Carson could feel the history and passion of those who fought in the Texas Revolution of 1835. They observed the plaque and bronze line in the patio that marked the spot where in 1836 Col. William Travis used his sword to draw a line in the sand and asked his men to join him in the battle that would become the fall of the Alamo.

"It would be cool to do some EVPs and thermal imaging around here," said Carson. "Another time…"

Content with their time at the plaza, they continued walking, crossing over E. Crockett Street and coming to the Menger Hotel Bar. It was supposedly the most haunted hotel in San Antonio and the bar still contains bullet holes from the Old West days. The hotel contained an elaborate stained glass ceiling and lighted columns in the lobby, but the group was more interested in the bar. it was the bar that was modeled after the bar in the British House of Lords, and is also a spot where Teddy Roosevelt recruited Rough Riders, and is proclaimed to be the spot where more cattle deals went down in Texas, even today. It was San Antonio's oldest continually operated saloon and the first bar in Texas to have ice – which was great with the saloon's margarita on the rocks.

The history was very present in the air. Looking at the bar's decorations, the bullet holes in the wood, and knowing the pieces of American history that took place inside the walls added to the paranormal attraction of the building.

"I don't know if we will be seeing any spirits tonight, other than some tequila or whiskey, but this is a cool place," said Ty.

"Spirts sound good," said Carson, but I will stick to beer," he said as he ordered a Saint Arnold Elissa IPA. Kareem decided to stick with beer too and ordered the Pedernales Brewing Company LOBO Negro. Tegan continued the trend with a Real Ale Fireman #4, and Ty decided to make it unanimous and found a Jester King Biere de Syrah.

"Now this stuff right here, this is the shit – a little tart, subliminal funk, and lots of fruit. Plus it's a bomber, so score!" exulted Ty.

"Here's to a good and successful adventure," said Carson.

"And we all survived, at least mostly in one piece," said Ty.

"Let's wrap it up this Saturday with a town hall to let the community know what we found, then we can head back to Austin and maybe get some rest after this," he suggested.

17 LAST DROP

Saturday, June 27, 2015

News spread quickly through the small town of Elmendorf, and for the second Saturday in a row locals packed the City Hall building to hear about the creature that had been terrorizing the community. Except this time the creature was dead and there were several more reporters eager to learn more about the animal. Many wanted to see the animal and asked where it was. Carson reassured everyone they would be able to see the animal one day.

"It currently is with a local taxidermist and the work should be completed between eight to twelve months" he said. "When it is ready we will come back down here for the unveiling." Plans already were underway with the city about building a room on to the side of City Hall to house an exhibit for the animal once it was received.

They did show a presentation that included photos of the animal as well as information and artist rendering of what a naked hyena looked like. As the findings were unexpected and some tests were still awaited, they confirmed additional tissue and hair samples were being sent to three other independent labs for further analysis. Sophie sat up with the team during the press conference to address questions related to the DNA testing and analysis.

After the conclusion of the presentation most of the crowd

remained in hopes of getting a chance to talk with the men and women who had captured the creature and hopefully eliminated future threats to the livestock in the community. News reporters interviewing each member of the team were up first; the flash of lights from cameras filling the room. This would be a big story for the local print media and the TV news.

Once the word spread online it would likely bring people from far and wide to town, even more once the exhibit opened. Lily & Jonathan Shaw were in attendance, as was Jordan Phillips, Phillip Cooper, Ronaldo Amaya, and Sharon Chapman. Each thanked the team for meeting with them and working to solve the mystery. Dexter Allen was there to compare the photos of the animal captured to the one he photographed weeks ago. He was satisfied with the match.

As the crowd finally began to dwindle, Fred & Jess Dalton stepped forward to greet the crew.

"We can't thank you enough," said Fred. "I hope this takes care of your expenses," he said handing Carson a check for $10,000. "But it's more than just us. The whole community appreciates what you've done here. Yesterday we put together a car wash and we held a collection with some of the local businesses. People chipped in to say thank you," said Fred. He handed Carson a second check for another $3500.

"'Preciate it! I'm glad we could help out, and hopefully the community can get back to normal and not worrying about livestock or what's out there in the night," said Carson.

As Fred & Jess left Freddie Marshall, Caitlin, and Ellie came to say their goodbyes.

"Hey, Freddie. We'll stop by tonight and move those cages and the goat up to the side yard. Tater will come by in the morning to pick them up," said Carson.

"We really appreciate your hospitality" said Tegan.

Natalie Simmons stood ready to lock up. Carson, Kareem, Tegan, Ty, and Sophie walked out with her and stood at the front door thinking about their week-long adventure.

"We can clean up the campsite tomorrow then head back to Austin," suggested Carson. "But what about tonight?"

"Whatcha say we stop for one last San Antonio beer," suggested Kareem. "I am definitely in," said Ty.

"Join us?" Tegan asked to Sophie.

"Oh…I don't know," she said with a shy chuckle as she pushed her glasses up. "I don't really drink much beer," she said.

Carson put an arm around her shoulder. "Welp, it's time you learned!" he said.

"Where shall we go?" asked Kareem.

"Let's hit up the northwest side of town," said Ty. "I heard a new place just opened up last week. We might as well break them in while we are introducing Sophie to craft beer," suggested Ty.

"I'm game," said Carson.

"Mad Pecker Brewing it is!" said Ty. "They just opened July 18, so it is definitely a new hot spot."

Arriving at the pub, they walked in and luckily found an open table. Being a new location it was busy as locals wanted to check out the newest entrant in the craft beer scene on that side of town. A young, short-haired brunette server named Paige approached the table to take their order.

"Good evening, ya'll. Can I get ya started on something to drink?"

Looking over the menu Ty asked, "Do you have any house beers?"

"We do have a twenty-four-tap system that's filled with local, state, and national craft beers. Right now we don't have any of our own beers on tap yet, but they're coming soon," said Paige. "We have a one barrel, thirty-one-gallon system and will be using it to brew rye IPAs, English-style beers, and a cucumber wheat beer with orange and lime notes that have been winning local home brewing awards for a couple of years," she said.

Kareem noticed a flyer for Freetail Brewing Company night on

August 19 and pointed it out to Carson. Free glassware would be handed out to customers ordering one of three Freetail beers on tap.

"Hmm. Might have to drive back down for the glass," said Carson. "Something to drink that Old Bat Rastard in perhaps?" he said.

Ty replied "It is important to have the proper glassware."

"Yesterday was our Ranger Creek glass night featuring Purple Rhine, one of the newer beers from Ranger Creek," said Paige.

"I'll have one of those," said Tegan. Kareem ordered a Real Ale Brewing Company Full Moon Rye IPA, Ty an Oasis Texas Brewing Company Meta Modern IPA, leaving Sophie and Carson to still make a selection.

"Do you like sour things?" asked Carson.

"Yeah, I guess so," said Sophie.

"That Rogness Sophina might be a good choice then," suggested Ty. "It's a sour beer that's not too assertiveness, so it's a nice refreshing taste without being like a Warhead or Sour Patch," he said.

"And it's like my name, almost," Sophia said with a giggle.

"I guess that leaves just me," said Carson. "How about a Guadalupe IPA?" he selected.

"Sounds good," said Paige. "I will be right back to take your food order," she said. Five minutes later she returned with a tray of beer. "Are we ready to order?" she asked.

"Can we get two orders of the Potain steak fries, three orders of the citrus marinated chicken street tacos, one croquet monsieur, and a pepperoni pizza?" asked Carson.

"You got it!" Paige said as she returned behind the bar to place the order.

Looking at the people around the table, Carson reflected on the past three weeks. "Here's to new friends and new adventures," he said hoisting a glass. Everyone at the table raised their glass to meet his. "About three weeks ago I was alone, depressed, and uncertain of the future. Then one night I happened to run into Ty again. Even though we all have only known each other for a few weeks, we've been through a lot together – a lot more than most people who have been friends for years," he said.

"CHEERS!" everyone said as they clanked glasses and took a drink.

As they waited for their food to arrive, Carson's phone buzzed with an alert. He continued the conversation with the group, but picked up the phone to check the notification. It was an Expedia sale alert, which he usually would dismiss, but after this crazy week he decided to take a look. Maybe a trip would be nice to relax. He scrolled through the destinations listed as on sale in the email.

"Huh…maybe a trip would be nice," he said aloud.

"A trip?" questioned Ty.

"To where?"

"I don't know," pondered Carson as he continued to look at the list. "The trip can be booked throughout the end of the year….a fall trip sounds nice. Maybe to peep a leaf?" replied Carson.

"Peep a leaf? Where would you do that?" asked Kareem. He took a sip and contemplated new adventures

"New England sounds nice….what do you all say?" asked Carson.

To be continued.

Beer List

Alamo Beer Co. Amber Lager

Alamo Beer Co. German Pale Ale

Alamo Beer Co. Golden Ale

Alamo Beer Co. Horchata Porter

Alamo Beer Co. Pilsner

Anheuser-Bush Bud Light American Adjunct

Anheuser-Bush Budweiser North American Lager - Light

Austin Beerworks Peacemaker Pale Ale

Austin Beerworks Pearl Snap Pilsner

Black Star Co-Op Brimstone B.A. Crotchety Dockhand Porter

Black Star Co-Op Conceit Pale Ale

Black Star Co-Op El Vulcano Rye IPA Cask

Black Star Co-Op Epsilon Scotch Ale

Black Star Co-Op Moebius Russian Imperial Stout

Black Star Co-Op Waterloo Berliner Weisse

Branchline 5am To Midnight Dark Ale

Busted Sandal Brewing 210 Ale Blonde Ale

Busted Sandal Brewing Slippery Rock IPA

Freetail Brewing Co. #Whalezbro American Wild Ale

Freetail Brewing Co. Ananke (2013) Aged American Wild Ale

Freetail Brewing Co. Bat Outta Helles Lager

Freetail Brewing Co. Texicali Brown Ale

Freetail Brewing Co. Yo Soy Un Berliner Berliner Weisse

Guadalupe Brewing Co. Guadalupe IPA

Guns & Oil Maverick Lager

Independence Brewing Co. Austin Amber Red Ale

Jester King Black Metal Farmhouse Imperial Stout

Jester King Biere de Syrah Saison

Jester King Vernal Dichotomous Saison

Lakewood Brewing Company Mole Temptress Imperial Milk Stout

Lone Pint Yellow Rose

Naughty Brewing Bourbon Barrel-Aged Kentucky Streetwalker Imperial Vanilla Porter

Naughty Brewing I Think She Hung the Moon Saison

Oasis Texas Brewing Company Meta Modern IPA

Pabst Brewing Company Lone Star Beer North American Adjunct

Pedernales Brewing Company LOBO Negro Dunkel Munich Lager

Ranger Creek Brewing & Distilling Bourbon Barrel-Aged Imperial Brown Ale

Ranger Creek Brewing & Distilling Love Struck Hefeweizen

Ranger Creek Brewing & Distilling OPA (Oatmeal Pale Ale) Pale Ale

Ranger Creek Brewing & Distilling Purple Rhine Berliner Weisse

Ranger Creek Brewing & Distilling Red Headed Stranger IPA

Ranger Creek's Small Batch Series No. 4 Small Batch Series No. 4

Ranger Creek Brewing & Distilling Strawberry Milk Stout

Real Ale Brewing Company Fireman #4 Blonde Ale

Real Ale Brewing Company Full Moon Rye IPA

Red Horn Coffee House & Brewing Co. You Be Forty Red Ale

Rogness Sophina Sour/Wild Ale

Saint Arnold Brewing Company Elissa IPA

Saint Arnold Brewing Company Bishop's Barrel 8 Imperial Stout

Southerleigh Brewing Co. Darwinian IPA

Southerleigh Brewing Co. Dog At My Alarm Milk Stout

Southerleigh Brewing Co. Putin's Revenge Russian Imperial Stout

Southerleigh Brewing Co. Seawall Belgian White Blonde Ale

Southerleigh Brewing Co. Smoke on the Water Rauchbier

Southerleigh Brewing Co. Straight Outta Hopton Double IPA

Spoetzl Brewery Shiner Bock

ABOUT THE AUTHOR

Mark Trollinger is a fan of cryptozoology and craft beer. He grew up in Yellow Springs, OH and attended the University of Rio Grande in Rio Grande, OH, majoring in marketing. He completed a MBA in Global Management, a Master of Science in the Administration of Justice and Security, and all of the course work in a Ph.D. of Higher Education Administration (ABD). He currently is taking classes in screenwriting at Grand Canyon University in Phoenix, AZ.

He has authored articles for CDFL*Insider* and the author of the upcoming dissertation *A Quantitative Study of the Factors Considered During Undergraduate Program of Study Selection*.

The Chupacabra and the Bat Rastard is his first book.

Look for his upcoming book, *Champ and a Bit o' Sunshine*

Made in the USA
San Bernardino, CA
14 July 2018